BIZARRE STORIES FOR PROPER LADIES

KATIE CORD

"BIZARRE STORIES FOR PROPER LADIES"
BY KATIE CORD
COPYRIGHT 2023. KATIE CORD
ALL RIGHTS RESERVED

WITHOUT LIMITING THE RIGHTS UNDER COPYRIGHT RESERVED ABOVE, NO PART OF THIS PUBLICATION MAY BE REPRODUCED, STORED, OR INTRODUCED INTO A RETRIEVAL SYSTEM, OR TRANSMITTED IN ANY FORM, OR BY ANY MEANS (ELECTRONIC, MECHANICAL, PHOTOCOPYING OR OTHERWISE) WITHOUT THE PRIOR WRITTEN PERMISSION OF THE COPYRIGHT OWNER, EXCEPT IN THE CASE OF BRIEF QUOTATIONS EMBODIED WITHIN CRITICAL ARTICLES AND REVIEWS.

THIS BOOK IS A WORK OF FICTION. PEOPLE, PLACES, EVENTS, AND SITUATIONS ARE THE PRODUCT OF THE AUTHOR'S IMAGINATION. ANY RESEMBLANCE TO ACTUAL PERSONS, LIVING, DEAD, OR HISTORICAL EVENTS, IS PURELY COINCIDENTAL.

THE FOLLOWING STORIES ARE REPRINTS, ALL RIGHTS RESERVED, COPYRIGHT KATIE CORD.

"THE PACT," ORIGINALLY PUBLISHED BY EVIL GIRLFRIEND MEDIA, IN HE LEFT HER AT THE ALTAR, SHE LEFT HIM TO THE ZOMBIES, EDITED BY GUINIVEVE DUBOIS, OCTOBER 31, 2011.

"THE YIN AND YANG OF RELATIONSHIPS," ORIGINALLY PUBLISHED BY WHEN THE DEAD BOOKS, IN GIVE: AN ANTHOLOGY OF ANATOMICAL ENTRIES, EDITED BY MICHELLE KILMER AND T.J. TRANCHELL, MAY 4, 2015.

"BE PREPARED, ALL YE MERRY MAIDS," ORIGINALLY PUBLISHED IN LOCKDOWN: A DYSTOPIAN ANTHOLOGY, MARCH 10, 2017.

"HELL WILL HAVE TO WAIT," ORIGINALLY PUBLISHED AS "DEEVA DE SATANICA: MISSION 666" IN HELL CATS, EDITED BY KATE PICKFORD, 2020.

Dedicated to some of the most bizarre and improper women I know:

Janna,
Kim,
Ranay,
Monica,
Deb,
Beth,
Katrina,
Guiniveve,
Cheryl,

...and all the ones I've yet to meet. I hope we find one another.

SISTERHOOD OF THE PLANNED PARENTHOOD

"Take slow, deep breaths, that's it, in through your nose and out through your mouth." Evelynn Bealltainn gently guided her patient. "Kasey, tell me if you feel anything other than a little pressure. The lidocaine should last at least another hour."

Evelynn continued to hunch over. Beads of sweat dotted her forehead as her back burned like the fires of hell, and she cursed herself for not getting up and doing yoga before a long procedure day. She took her own deep breaths to control the pain and guided the one-fourth circular suture needle with precision; the hemostat clamped the metal with a grip she was sure would leave a mark, but it gave her great relief to know she had control over the situation. Saving babies was what she did, and there wasn't a better person in Foggy Creek, Georgia, to do the job. She came from a long line of women who'd help bring life into the world. The only difference was that she'd gone to school for it. She was legit and not some wild woman from the foothills of Appalachia.

The young girl's cervix lay flaccid and stretched way beyond her years. Kasey Weaver was on her fourth pregnancy at seventeen. She had no living children. Evelynn's nurse, and sister, Beverly, had scolded her for preventing this one from ending. Evelynn had reminded Beverly multiple times that it wasn't their job to judge the actions of others. Their great-great grandmother would be proud that they were saving lives. Beverly would cross her arms, roll her eyes, and mumble under her breath. She'd walk off and slam the cabinets for hours after these discussions. Working with your sister was difficult, but she knew Beverly would never hurt a living soul. The woman was a vegetarian, grew an organic garden, and herded her own four children around like an expert sheep dog, ensuring the lambs didn't stray. Beverly didn't have a husband, either. She couldn't judge Kasey. In fact, Kasey and Beverly shared the same problem. They were too fertile.

Evelynn tried to shake her thoughts as her hand cramped. Kasey's tissue should not be this thin. It was like she'd dilated instead of just having an incompetent cervix. Evelynn knew she hadn't prescribed her anything that would induce labor, especially at 16 weeks. This was rural Georgia, and if something went wrong, her backup was a surgical suite with an 800-year-old nurse and a drunken family doctor. Beverly was qualified to assist but refused to do surgical anesthesia anymore.

"Kasey, did you try to have your baby?" Evelynn attempted to stay calm. Something wasn't right, in fact, something was really wrong.

The young girl sleepily replied, "No, but Granny took me to see your Aunt Iris a week ago. She said we should try to fix this the old way before we came to see you. This one wasn't leaving like the others," Kasey said. Her voice was tentative, and the top half of her body tightened as if bracing for a lecture. Evelynn held back.

"What did dear sweet Auntie Iris tell you to do? Or what did she give you and how much did she charge your Granny?" Evelynn stopped suturing. Until she knew what her aunt had been up to, there was no sense in forcing the body to do what the body had been compelled not to.

"Well, Miss Evelynn, it's kind of embarrassing, but she gave me this stuff to put up in there that she said would fix the entire problem. It was some kind of green stuff I hadn't seen before, almost like the plants you see around some of the ponds closer to Florida." Kasey had come to the office alone, though her Granny was in town shopping. Someone always went to fetch her after Kasey's appointments.

"Beverly! Go find Granny Rose and tell her to get her ass over here, now!" Evelynn felt her nostrils flaring with each word she spoke.

Beverly looked up from monitoring Kasey's vital signs with a scowl on her face. "Excuse me? Isn't that why we hired that little girl out front?" Beverly placed a hand on her hip. Her cheeks flushed red, and her green eyes shone like emeralds.

Evelynn gritted her teeth. "Before you go into how you're not only an RN but also a certified nurse anesthetist who moved back to a Podunk town to help your little sister, please remember what the keywords were in all of this, Aunt Iris."

"Look, it ain't mine or nobody else's fault you had that

old witch put a curse on you, so you'd never get hurt again. She was probably trying to do them a favor. Probably didn't even charge…"

"Go get Granny Rose, now! If I break my sterile field, I will break you." Evelynn stomped her foot with every bit of might she had left in her.

Beverly stormed out of the room. Her wooden clogs echoed down the hall, then the door smacked shut. Evelynn winced. Beverly had a will stronger than any element. In fact, Beverly's will was why she'd made it through one of the toughest nurse practitioner programs in the country while intermittently getting pregnant during one tragic relationship after the other. The woman was a sucker for bastards and would get pregnant at the sight of a phallus. This didn't outshine the fact that she'd cared for some of the most critically ill of patients. Beverly had said she'd moved back to Georgia because she'd already made so much money. The only thing left for her to do was retire. She'd stayed home growing herbs and tomatoes for approximately six weeks before taking over the position of being the Ob/Gyn nurse at the clinic and placing the occasional epidural.

Evelynn knew Beverly had missed her family. Plus, not a single man in Foggy Creek had attracted Beverly's attention, let alone anyone in the state of Georgia. She knew she'd be perfectly safe at home. Evelynn didn't worry about falling in love with anyone here, either. Auntie Iris had made sure that wouldn't happen. It was a fair trade, though. She got to be a doctor and help continue a tradition that had cursed, and blessed, her family for centuries.

The only problem was it got lonely sometimes. She'd loved a boy in twelfth grade so much. He'd begged her to run off and be his army bride, and Evelynn had begged for a compromise. She would go to school, and they would see one another when he was on leave. In eight years, they'd get married. Ultimately, he'd wanted a bride and a simpler life way more than he'd wanted her. Seeing him with Rachel that next spring, and her rubbing her round, swollen belly, had filled Evelynn with rage. Her heart had felt like someone had stabbed a dagger through it, and instead of blood spewing out, it had released a vile acid through her body. She couldn't go back to school, a broken-hearted, mopey, weeping mess. Those northern girls would eat her for breakfast if they thought she was weak. The pre-med program was brutal and there were limited spots for women, even though the school claimed to give equal opportunity.

She had run to Aunt Iris's place on Dead Crow Road. Her mother had forbidden her from dealing with her aunt. She'd said the old bag probably wasn't her actual sister, but a bargain made with the devil to let one of his minions out on earth. Their grandmother had to survive somehow. The women in their family never had luck with men. In fact, her mother had been the only one who'd been happy for a short time. Then their father was killed in Nicaragua during a nasty little conflict in the 1980s. He'd made lieutenant, so the girls at least had an honorable father. So many other Bealltainn daughters did not. Their mother had changed their last names to hers after his death. She'd said there was no use crying over a man, even a good one. They'd all dried their eyes after the funeral. Their mother had sung a song, and they'd buried a pentagram over where his heart should have been. The girls' mother had instructed them to wipe their tears on a single tissue, and she'd placed it in a cigar box at their father's feet. She'd explained he would ease their pain from the afterlife for them.

The next day, her mother had been up making pancakes, singing joyful songs, and smiling. Both the girls had still felt empty without their father.

"There's no use in crying over him. They promised him to me for a short time, but not forever. I even told him what would happen before we got married. Old fool still wanted to marry me." She exhaled. "Might as well get used to it, girls. You'll both have your own curses to carry before it's over. It's the Bealltainn way."

Their mother had scooped their pancakes onto their plates and smiled widely. There had been relief in her eyes. It was like she'd waited for a long time for something to kill their father, and it had finally happened. It was over. She could go on. Their mother had gone on, but never with another man. Of course, when she'd found one she was sweet on, she'd always tell them about the curse, and the romance would end shortly after that.

Evelynn had stood there on the porch of Aunt Iris's shack for what seemed like hours, waiting for her breath to come back to her. She hadn't waited long. A tall, thin woman with platinum blonde hair that was teased and sprayed into a crowning glory of perfection had opened the door. Evelynn had always dreamed her aunt wore long black robes and looked like a hag. Instead, she'd found an old lady version of a mallrat. The woman had beckoned her in with a bright red acrylic nail. As she'd turned, Evelynn had noticed on the butt of her high-waisted jeans was a designer logo. She'd swallowed hard. Evelynn couldn't justify owning such an expensive pair of jeans, even after working all summer.

"Miss Evelynn, how did I know you'd eventually come to see me?" Aunt Iris asked as she'd flopped into an overly stuffed, gaudily printed chair. She'd put her legs over the side and pulled out a cigarette. She'd lit up, inhaled, and had laughed through the smoke that had poured out of her mouth.

"I'm here because I was told you can help people with stuff when no one else can," Evelynn had said in a low voice, nothing like her usually competitive, self-assured way. "I don't want to ever love again." She'd paused, then had uttered quickly, "And I don't want no babies, either."

Aunt Iris had arched one of her eyebrows. "No babies? That's against the Bealltainn way. I can't cross the family like that." Her aunt had leaned over on the top of her legs, flicking at her cigarette, deep in thought. Finally, she spoke. "Child, why would you want to choose such a thing?"

"The desire to want babies makes you weak. You fall for men and forget your dreams just to make them happy. I don't want any of it. None, nothing. I'm strong enough to be alone." Evelynn had found her voice coming back to her. She'd crossed her arms and stood solid in the middle of the overly done broken-down shack.

Her aunt had drawn deeply off the cigarette before she'd spoken again, her voice slightly raspy. "Well, since you want to do good with your selfishness, I guess I can justify providing the help. Are you sure this is what you want? We can't take these things back once a deal is made." Her aunt had looked at her with a serious glare. "My payment will be that I can give your fertility to someone else at my discretion, and for profit, without repercussions."

Evelynn hadn't been able to help but smile. The stare had reminded her of her mother. They were definitely sisters, well, except for Iris's platinum hair. Her aunt had pushed herself up from her chair and walked into the small kitchen at the back of the shack. She'd opened a cupboard and pulled out small bottles made of hobnail glass. All her aunt's beautiful, expensive things still confused her. Why have so many gorgeous things and live in a shack that a strong wind could knock down?

"That's my curse, girl, and none of your beeswax," Aunt Iris had said without turning around. Evelynn had been warned Iris could hear your thoughts, read your future, and put on spells. Her other curse was that she wasn't allowed to deliver babies like the rest of the Bealltainn women, but she could stop them from being born.

"Miss Evelynn, do you think Miss Beverly is going to be mad or happy when the baby gets here?" Kasey asked, breaking Evelynn from her memories.

Evelynn had a headache, her back ached, and now the girl was not making any sense. "Why would Miss Beverly care about your baby, sweetheart?"

"Well, you know, cause it's Justin's baby..." Kasey

stopped herself before she could let out anymore of her secret.

The clamped hemostat and needle hit the floor. Evelynn went down next to them.

A cold smack to the face awakened Evelynn. She looked up to see Beverly looking at her with an expression of anger and confusion.

"What happened? You forget to eat this morning?" Beverly asked.

Evelynn pushed herself up from the ground. Granny Rose was standing beside her with a worried look on her face, except her concern was directed toward Kasey, not the two bitter sisters. Evelynn grabbed Beverly's arm and pushed her out of the room.

"Why didn't you tell me you were going to be a grandma?" Evelynn asked in a venomous whisper.

"What're you talking about? I'm not old enough to be one of *those*," Beverly said with distaste.

"Kasey just told me this one is Justin's baby."

Beverly braced herself against the back wall. "Inconceivable."

Evelynn looked at her. "Do you think that's funny? You're going to be a grandma, and your aunt tried to kill your grandchild. What's so funny about that? Did you send them out there?" Evelynn would punch Beverly if she said yes. She just felt it in her gut. Her sister could be so selfish and shallow when it came to these things.

"No, it's literally inconceivable. Justin is shooting blanks." Beverly straightened out her scrub top. "He had mumps when he was little. I had him tested two years ago. He was so embarrassed, but I had to know. You know it's part of one of the many, many curses in our family. No Bealltainn male child shall pass on children. There are only Bealltainn women, not men. Frankly, I'm relieved, because you know what happens to men in our family who do successfully have children..."

"Shhhh, would you stop with this nonsense? This girl thinks Justin is the father of her baby, regardless, and our evil-ass aunt tried to give her an abortion! What the hell are we going to do? Do you think it was cohosh, or do you think she ordered some seaweed from the coast?" Evelynn couldn't believe she was trying to figure out what remedy her aunt had used to try to kill the fetus.

"Oh, definitely mermaid enchanted seaweed will get rid of that sucker right away," Beverly said, rolling her eyes.

"You're an asshole," Evelynn said, walking away. "I'm going to go ask Granny Rose, because I'll be damned if I'll go to Iris ever again."

"I always hate when you say I'll be damned. It usually means we are going to get into some kind of trouble and have to do exactly what you said we wouldn't!" Beverly said, shaking her head at Evelynn.

The two women gently shut their car doors and headed toward Aunt Iris's shack. It hadn't changed a day since the last time Evelynn had been there, and she wasn't surprised.

"Well, if you had known where your teenage son was,

we might not be an accidental accomplice in this mess!" Evelynn hissed back.

"She's in the hospital now. They have fetal heart tones that are strong. I'm not worried about it. When that baby comes out, we will know it's not Justin's. It's not my fault that girl is worse than me. She says she just kisses them and ends up pregnant. She's either an idiot or has her own family curse. Could you imagine being a virgin and getting pregnant? I'd just feel cheated." Beverly rambled as they walked up toward the shack. "At least I know exactly how those four kids got here, and I enjoyed every minute… but damn, they don't have a decent Daddy between the four of them. How are you to know a man who's a dentist could be so lecherous? It's not like they do anything adrenaline-pumping for a living. They pick crap off your teeth and fill cavities… Ow!"

Evelynn nudged Beverly in the ribs, inhaled deeply, and went to knock on the door. She felt like she was in a time warp. The door opened before she could complete the first knock. There she stood, Aunt Iris. Her hair was still platinum blonde except now she styled it in a Brazilian blowout. Her clothes were different, and a little more sophisticated. She wore a long, sea blue maxi dress and a deep brown, knee length cardigan. Turquoise and silver jewelry adorned her throat.

"Well, both of you at the same time. This should be interesting. You want to switch places now?" Aunt Iris asked with a wide smile, then pulled the door open further and beckoned the women in.

"Come in, my lovely nieces. I've missed you so much. Seems like the only time you come to see auntie is when you need something." Iris shut the door and walked over to a modern styled chaise. She lay down carefully, ensuring she positioned her dress correctly. She looked like one of those models for a catalog where they are selling young-looking clothes to older women.

"What'd you give old Rose Weaver to get rid of Kasey's baby?" Evelynn eyed her aunt, daring her to lie.

"Give her?" Aunt Iris raised an eyebrow. "I give nothing away, child. Old Granny Rose and I made a trade a long time ago. Kasey is just experiencing her share of the trade."

"What kind of trade did you all make that a seventeen-year-old girl has had three miscarriages? Aunt Iris, you can't keep messing with women's lives like this!"

Aunt Iris stood up, walked over to her stove, and picked up her teapot a little too heavy handedly. Her knuckles were white. Beverly's eyes widened and she shifted away from Aunt Iris, putting Evelynn between them as a human shield. Evelynn scowled at Beverly. Aunt Iris walked over to the sink and filled the teapot with water, then placed it back on the stove.

"Tea?" Aunt Iris said without looking in their direction.

Evelynn was about to lose it. She did not have time for her aunt's niceties. "We're not here on a friendly visit. This poor girl is sixteen weeks pregnant and ready to miscarry again. We need to know what you did, and now!"

Beverly casually walked over to the couch and sat down. "I'll have some lavender tea, if you've got it. My nerves could use some calming, and throw some chamomile in there, too."

Evelynn glared at her. Beverly could be a real pain in the ass.

"No need to be all upset. There ain't no baby coming into this world. What I gave her will make sure of it. Granny Rose has to tell Kasey the truth, and all this will stop." Aunt Iris poured the boiling water into two porcelain teacups. She walked over and handed Beverly her cup. Evelyn noted that Beverly sat up and inspected the cup before accepting.

The smell of lavender filled the air. Evelynn inhaled and walked over to the couch, resigned. This would not go her way as easily as she'd thought. Aunt Iris wasn't afraid of anyone's demands. Evelynn needed to accept it, so they might get out of here with an answer.

"So, how's life been working out for you two?" Aunt Iris sat down easily in her rocking chair, holding her teacup carefully. Evelynn and Beverly looked at one another. Neither knew what to say.

"Good?" Evelynn said. What did their aunt want? She was a highly educated doctor and a single woman on the edge of middle age without children. Some things were good, and others were just empty. She felt nothing about not having those two things. Sometimes the void of emotion was scary, but she knew why it was there: a spell.

"Well, you know how it's going for me. Just like you told me it would," Beverly said with a nervous laugh. She put her teacup up to her lips as if to mute herself.

Evelynn squinted in distrust. She'd never asked what

Beverly's request from Aunt Iris had been and had always felt like it was none of her business. She just assumed it was to fall in love and have kids.

"And your mother?"

"Same," the two sisters said in unison.

"Hmmm, you all are a boring bunch then, aren't you?" Aunt Iris set her teacup and plate on the side table. "Y'all know I can't change anything once I put it into place, right? A deal's a deal."

"But what about Kasey? Does she deserve to pay for her granny's deal?" Evelynn knew their family curse, but what about the Weaver's? Was Aunt Iris strong enough to execute a family curse?

"Thing is, girls, what I did for Rose was introduce her to… let's say, someone more powerful than anyone else on earth. I cannot break the deal she made with them. The only thing that will break the curse is what brought it. Most of them can't be reversed, but sometimes it'll work. Seen it happen before. Anyway, once that happens, then Kasey won't be under its control." Aunt Iris stared at the women, waiting for a response.

"Well, are you going to tell us what the deal was?" Beverly asked, which was a relief to Evelynn, since she'd been the pushy one through all of this.

"I can't tell you, because I don't know for sure. I'm assuming these babies are something otherworldly. Let this one expire just like the other three. Then pull Granny Rose aside and tell her to be honest so they don't have to keep doing these small deals with me to keep eliminating them. Of course, if you all get rid of one of my clients, I expect you to give me something in return."

Aunt Iris crossed her arms and leaned back in the rocking chair.

"What could you possibly want from us?" Evelynn asked.

Aunt Iris smiled. "I'll let you know when the time comes."

"Call the hospital and ask for Granny Rose. If this is an otherworldly being, we need to let nature take its course, and she needs to be honest with her granddaughter." Evelynn focused on the road as she heard Beverly dial the phone.

"Can I have Kasey Weaver's room?" Beverly paused for a moment. "Oh, I see. Do you know where they went? Huh. Okay. Thank you. Bye." Beverly hung up the phone. "You will not believe this. Granny Rose signed Kasey out against medical advice."

Evelynn gripped the steering wheel. "Should we be surprised? She's probably the only person who knows what is going on here. Where'd they go?"

"Home."

Evelynn pushed on the gas pedal.

Evelynn was used to poverty, so the junked cars, old, rusted swing sets, tractors, and various tires of different shapes and sizes littering the yard didn't faze her as she pulled up to the Weaver's place. The long driveway had narrowed over the years into a walking trail of broken items, bartered and abandoned. It looked like a wall the Weavers had placed as a buffer between them and the world.

"I hope they don't have any hellhounds around here," Beverly mumbled under her breath.

Evelynn opened the driver's side door and got out. "Come on, let's get this over with."

Within minutes of walking down the driveway, a wail came from the direction of the trailer. It was a mix of agony and pure terror.

Beverly turned to Evelynn, her eyes wide and mouth agape. The sisters instinctually picked up the pace. Whatever was going on in there, it wasn't good. Visions of Kasey delivering a demon fetus, or even worse, Granny Rose trying to take it out, filled Evelynn's head.

As they came upon the rickety, graying wooden porch, old man Weaver greeted them with a frown from his porch swing.

"What you Bealltainn ladies doin' out here?" He stood up and walked to the stairs, blocking the sisters' entry.

Evelynn eyed an aged gun holstered to his hip. She was even more intrigued by the tattoos that lined his hands and arms. Her experience in a tattoo parlor was nil, but the aged blue and black lines sure looked homemade. The signs were old world, and she hadn't seen them since she was a kid.

Evelynn pushed out her chest and cleared her throat, ready to fight it out with the old man. He couldn't weigh more than a hundred pounds soaking wet.

"Mr. Weaver, is Granny Rose home? We need to talk to

her about Kasey."

"Granny is busy." He paused and leaned on the porch rail. "And so is Kasey. They ain't got no use for you."

Beverly's tensed arm brushed Evelynn's. The two aligned, ready for a fight. Evelynn thought to herself, at least he can't shoot both of us at once. She'd never felt this powerful, even when the two worked side by side each day handling difficult situations.

"We've talked to Aunt Iris. Now let us in before Granny does something that we'll have to call the cops on her for," Beverly demanded, stepping ahead of Evelynn.

"Y'all don't know what you're doin'. We've dealt with this before, and we'll take care of it, again, and again. Now, shoo. Go on, git outta here."

Old man Weaver looked tired. Evelynn's best guess was that he had only a year or two left in him. Of course, who was she to say? Mortality was a lottery.

"Well, Aunt Iris said we can take it away, and that is what we are here to do. Kasey is going to be here long after you and Granny Rose are gone. We know her mama ain't going to be there for her. Let us. I got a bunch of kids already. When the time comes, she'll just be one more to love." Beverly stepped closer to the steps. Evelynn heard the sincerity in Beverly's voice. Her sister did have a lot of love to give.

Old man Weaver shook his head. "Y'all ain't gonna help us out with her. Nobody is willing to help a Weaver. We're cursed." He spat on the ground.

"We'll help you today and we'll help you always, if you ask. That is the Bealltainn way. How many of your family have our mama and granny helped over the years and asked nothing in return?" Evelynn added. She wasn't lying. Her family had been midwives and healers as long as they'd been in the mountains. She had believed none of Aunt Iris's crap except what she'd wanted to. When she'd asked never to love again, she'd really felt it was all mind control and nothing else. She'd chosen to never love again. Of course, Evelynn's issues were of her own making, and the curse on the men was all coincidence. But now she really knew, and she owned it. They were midwives, healers, and witches. Her mother never used that word, but it was the truth.

A shrill cry for help from Granny Rose shattered the wall between the women and the old man. "Pa, I need you in here!"

Old man Weaver turned about face and headed into the trailer, leaving the two at the bottom of the stairs. They instinctually ran, closing the gap behind him. As they entered the house, the smell of old cat urine and mildewed paper assaulted their senses. It surprised Evelynn at how fast old man Weaver could move. Old man Weaver headed down the junk-filled hallway to a bedroom. She followed behind him with Beverly close behind.

In the bedroom, the full-sized bed looked like a slaughter had occurred. Blood-soaked towels and sheets were everywhere. Evelynn rushed to Kasey's side. She grabbed the girl's pale wrist. Her pulse was strong and pounding.

"How's she doing?" Beverly asked, standing back and surveying the scene. "She's lost a liter of blood, at a minimum."

"Her heart rate is 160. So, yeah, she's going to go into shock any time now." Evelynn's stomach was in knots. They had nothing here to help them. How could they explain a seventeen-year-old getting ready to pass something unholy out of her body? Worse, what if it was a human? They'd both lose their licenses and go to jail.

"Granny Rose, what is trying to pass out of her?" Evelynn demanded. "We talked to Aunt Iris. What kind of deal did you make? And what's it going to take to break that deal?"

Granny looked weary, and tears were in her eyes. "They keep staying in her longer and longer, growing bigger and bigger. She's been fine in the past. They all passed and disappeared like a poof of smoke. Her body has always gone back to normal. It'll pass, I know it. He said she'd be fine. Never suffer, but he lied."

"I'm guessing we can figure out who you made the deal with." Beverly rolled her eyes. "What's the curse, and how do we break it?"

"That's the thing. He didn't say. He asked me what I wanted and then gave her a kiss on her lips. Now, every time she kisses a boy, this happens!"

"Oh, thank god," Beverly said.

Evelynn scowled at her.

"What? Can't I be happy my son isn't having sex?!" Beverly shrugged.

"So, this 'he,'" Evelyn air quoted the term he for emphasis, "kissed Kasey on her lips when she was a baby? So, maybe kissing her on the lips will take the curse away? Have you all tried that?"

Granny Rose nodded. "I have. It don't work."

"What did you ask for? Maybe you can't take the curse away because you are getting what you wanted?" Beverly walked over to the other side of the bed and picked up Kasey's hand. Beverly looked at Kasey with the same concern she'd given her own children.

Evelynn was jealous. She'd never felt that way about anyone.

"I asked for abundance so we could provide for Kasey. She'd never want for anything. There'd always be plenty." Granny Rose looked around. "He kept his promise, I guess."

Evelynn had an idea.

"Kasey, can you hear me? Do you want this to stop? Just say it. Say you want to give it to someone else. Say you want to give it to me, then I'm going to give you a big old kiss, so don't be scared."

Kasey nodded slowly. Her voice was barely a whisper. "Please take this from me, Dr. Bealltainn. I want you to have it."

"Absolutely not!" Beverly said. "Every time you kiss someone romantically, you're going to generate a demon baby. What if you find your true love?"

"It's okay. I know what I'm doing. I made a deal with Aunt Iris a long time ago. It'll be fine." Evelynn leaned over. She wasn't afraid. She'd made her peace long ago and knew what she wanted. This curse would be safe with her. "I accept your gift, Ms. Kasey Weaver." She leaned down and kissed the girl's soft, pale lips. A tear fell down Kasey's cheek.

Granny Rose fell to the ground at the end of the bed. Evelynn ran to the old woman and checked the pulse in her neck. "She's still alive. She must've passed out from exhaustion."

Beverly sat down on the musty, carpeted floor beside Kasey, her fingertips on Kasey's wrist. Within fifteen minutes, her pulse was normal. Kasey's color came back to her face and her breathing went from shallow to slow and deep.

"Why'd you do that?" Beverly asked.

"Because I could. I asked Aunt Iris to make sure I never felt love again, and I haven't. I knew it would be safe with me."

Beverly laughed, "We are so alike, yet so very different. I asked Aunt Iris to make sure I always had love. I didn't specify, and that is probably how I got all these damn kids."

"Uh, no, I'm pretty sure you got all those damn kids from having unprotected sex." Evelynn started laughing with Beverly.

Kasey opened her eyes and sat up. "What're y'all doing here? Is everything okay? Granny?!"

Granny sat up. "I'm here honey, everything is fine. The Bealltainn sisters will leave shortly."

Kasey eyed the bloody mess surrounding her. She closed her eyes. "It happened again, didn't it?"

"Yeah, honey, it did." Granny's voice was solemn.

"It won't happen anymore. I promise," Evelynn said as she squeezed Kasey's hand gently.

"I'm never going to be normal." Kasey said through her sobs.

"Listen kid, nobody's normal, but you definitely will

not be shooting half-made demon fetuses out of your body anymore," Beverly said frankly.

"Are you going to make Justin break up with me?"

Beverly waved her hand. "No, do not even worry about Justin right now. You worry about you. But if you two are going to keep seeing each other. We need to have a long talk, woman-to-woman, about the birds and the bees."

Evelynn snickered. The comment from Beverly made it all feel normal again.

"Alright, seriously, if you are going to work here, y'all need to not kiss in the reception area." Beverly scolded Kasey and Justin.

Evelynn laughed from the back office. Kasey had been so impressed with the sisters; she had asked to work in the clinic. Although she wasn't sure exactly what she wanted to do, she figured it would be easier to know if she was around them.

They'd accepted the help. The Weavers were grateful for the help the women had given them. Oddly enough, once they'd hired someone to haul all the junk away, it had quit piling up. Their abundance had become part of the curse. Unfortunately, it was now Evelynn's problem. The weirdest crap kept showing up at her house, at the clinic, and even falling in front of her feet as she walked down the street. It was probably the most annoying thing that had happened so far.

Most of the time, it didn't cross Evelynn's mind that

she would never kiss a man again, but occasionally, she'd wonder what would have happened if she'd had Aunt Iris remove her wish and didn't have the curse. It didn't matter now. All that mattered was that she and Beverly knew what being a Bealltainn really meant. It was standing up for what was right and accepting their lineage of an ancient sisterhood.

"Evelynn, come here! You got another delivery!" Beverly yelled from the front.

She sighed. It wasn't like Beverly couldn't just sign for it and leave her to do the accounting.

"Evelynn!!"

She pushed out her chair and took a deep breath. There was no way she was getting anything done until she handled whatever her sister demanded. She walked down the hallway into the lobby.

"What? Couldn't you sign for it?" She walked over to Beverly.

"Dr. Bealltainn?" A male voice asked from behind her.

Evelynn turned to the man's voice. "Yes, what can I -?"

The man's aquamarine eyes struck her speechless. His jet-black hair and chiseled jaw hurt nothing, either.

"Hi, I'm here to deliver your goats. Where would you like them?"

Evelynn rolled her eyes and groaned. Beverly slapped the reception desk and cackled like a hen.

"Well, this is going to be interesting!" Beverly called out, egging Evelynn on.

Evelynn would have to agree. She wasn't sure which would be a bigger pain in her ass, this man or a pack of goats. Either way, she was cursed.

HE WILL COME FOR ME

She woke up with a start. Sour vodka and remnants of nachos constricted her throat and tickled her tongue. Panic overtook rational thought. She was choking. Rolling over was her only option. She tried to throw her arm and shoulder across herself to gain momentum on her sluggish body, but her arms were tied down. She needed to clear her throat, but something was in her mouth. The loud thud of her heart overtook her ears. With everything she had, she squeezed her abdominal muscles. Nothing moved; she was drowning.

A dark gloved hand pulled on the rag that had been blocking her airway. A smooth, latex-covered finger went into her mouth and curved like a "c" scooping out the debris. She strained to move her arms. Someone had tied her down to some kind of table. Pin pricks ran through her body as sweat rolled off her.

Fucking Narcan. How dare someone rob me of a high!

The all-too-familiar pain of having all the feel-goods pulled from their receptors pissed her off.

"What the fuck is wrong with you?"

Her voice was hoarse, but full of venom.

The shifting of something in the background was the only reply.

She wiggled a tortilla chip stuck to the side of her mouth out and spit toward the sounds.

"You can't do this. My husband will come for me."

She wasn't sure if he would, but it seemed like he was pretty damn smitten with her. He'd married her without a prenup and wanted to have a baby. He had money, and unlike her, it appeared to come from an honest living.

Her body went rigid at the sound of something unzipping.

She heard a click, then a flash illuminated the room. It brought back memories of her mother's old Polaroid camera. She'd used one to help her mom blackmail johns back in the day.

"You don't have to blackmail me. Listen, it was one last time. He told me to go have a girl's night."

She tried to shift her ankles, but they were tied into place. She seethed inside. Other people were idiots to be taken advantage of, not her. She regretted not answering at least one of her husband's texts.

Obviously, this person was set on staying silent. But who were they? What was their motivation? She knew what her motivation had been last night; one last fling with a former love.

It hadn't been that difficult for them to meet again. A friend in Old Town had told her what bar to hit up. After a couple of obstacles, like ensuring her husband couldn't trace where she'd pulled out cash, she'd picked up her old love and rendezvoused using one of her favorite tricks, scamming for what she used to call a half-used hotel room. It was when someone checked out early, giving an opportunistic person the ability to slide in unnoticed, and party for a few hours before housekeeping came knocking.

Her eyes were getting heavy again.

A loud metallic crash sounded beside her. A sharp stick stung her arm. Everything sped up again.

"How much of that shit do you have? Huh? It's going to wear off on its own. Leave me alone! Let me enjoy what's left."

Another flash of light. This time it came from the corner. She turned toward it. The area was dark. The light flicked closer. This time, she saw an image on the wall.

"Oh, my gawd, where did you get that? Answer me. Where did that come from?"

Images randomly flashed all around the room. The one thing she pieced together was that she hadn't left the hotel room. The grotesque images continued to taunt her. Her eyes teared, and she felt dizzy.

She had to pull herself together. Whoever this was, they were not a true killer. She'd seen this kind of tactic on some tv show. Were they looking for remorse?

She started sinking again as she tried to recall earlier in the night. She'd sat on the bed staring at the plastic bag with ten elongated pills, her true loves. Time hadn't let her miss them any less. Her hands had trembled. She'd pulled the Bible out from the drawer, then smashed the bag over and over until she was sure it couldn't take anymore. She'd held the bag up to the light. It hadn't been enough. She'd pulled out her compact to use as a pestle. Rhythmically, she'd ground them one by one into a fine powdery mix.

Excitement had filled her. She'd pulled the Bible from the drawer of the nightstand, carelessly ripped out a page, and laid it out on the table like a picnic blanket. She'd scattered the white powder over the ancient platitudes like snow over the Catskills.

The first line had stung as it went up her nose and into her pharynx. She'd shaken her head and coughed, then let out a laugh. The second line had gone down easier; she hadn't felt the third, and by the sixth, she wasn't sure if she'd snorted it.

The gloved hand smacked her face.

"Wake up." It was a deep, quiet voice.

"Leave me alone. He's coming for me. He'll kill you."

The hand smacked her harder.

Her eyes opened wide. An image about the size of a movie poster flashed in front of her. Her eyes adjusted. It was a man and a boy. She recognized the man. He had been a mark she'd left for dead in a hotel room after he'd collapsed.

"Do you know who that is?"

"No." She lied.

"That's me and my dad. You killed him." Her captor sat down on the side of the bed and turned on the side table lamp. His face was in plain sight.

An all-encompassing terror filled her.

Her husband was already here.

THE YIN AND YANG OF RELATIONSHIPS

"In a nutshell, do you think it is better to have one nut or two?" I asked him. He looked at me. Tears streamed down his lax face. I swore I saw a twitch of his mouth. He needed more succinylcholine. I wanted him to stay loose, but able to sense the procedure. It was an important part of the therapeutic process. If my hypothesis was correct, my new surgical technique would solve all the world's problems.

I patted his cheek. "Now, now, my little sweet. Your life will be so much better. I guarantee it."

He gurgled as words tried to come out of his mouth. I connected the syringe to the IV line. His breathing slowed, his mouth went limp, his stare fixed ahead. I wished I could be lucky enough to have someone help me with my part, but as it has been since the beginning of time, the woman must endure the pain.

Slicing your own skin is difficult if you have not practiced for many years. I started cutting myself to calm my urges of self-harm when I was a young girl at the boarding school in Switzerland. It seemed so far from my home in Belarus. I always felt so alone. It is a talent, curse, and blessing to accept isolation.

In the beginning, I made mistakes. The mind, it gets nervous, it makes you cut too deep, or too shallow. You never know what you are capable of when the adrenaline pumps, but when you discipline the mind, you can cut yourself to the exact depth you want, you, and anyone else. Of course, going to medical school helped me immensely. You can only learn so much from experimenting on yourself and lab animals. I don't like hurting animals. They do nothing wrong. They are balanced. Humans? Not so much.

Not like this schmuck.

"Damn it," I said aloud. I scanned the room for a fresh scalpel. I'd already used four today.

It is difficult not to keep cutting on something when the sweet rush comes. I didn't want him to be mutilated, but in case he had a surge in hormones, I wanted the behavioral modification to kick in. Ah, sometimes, it is very easy to forget that I must make my donation before I can start the procedure on the patient.

The laboratory, torture chamber, pleasure room, site of multiple murders, tit for tat, whatever you call it, my patient had designed this room for his comfort. Not for mine, not for the women he lured in here. Just for him. It is not like being in a surgical suite. That would be easy. I sort of wished I had American associates who could help with this procedure, but even my friends in Europe do not agree with my theories. Therefore, I must do this on my own. But that has been my whole life.

I gaze over at my patient one last time. His calculatedly fractured femur will set in a way that he will never be able to chase a woman again. The missing thumb on his right hand will ensure he never snatches another girl by her hair. The microscopic scars on his face are a warning to all. I don't want to intubate him, so I must hurry now.

I sit semi-reclined in the dental chair, a mirror focused on my abdomen, and try not to think about what has potentially happened in this chair. I've sanitized it the best I can, but old blood stains the white thread and cracks in the vinyl. Bright surgical lights are necessary so that I can see the microscopic vascular system of the ovaries. I want to keep the fallopian tube intact. The lights cause a halo effect when I turn away. I must remember that when the pain starts, so that I know I'm not hallucinating.

The brown of the betadine wash cools and stains. A laparoscopic procedure would have been ideal. I could puncture through the skin, snake my way through, cauterize and nip what I want, but I will do this the old-fashioned way. Wiping away the excess betadine, I take a deep breath. I will do the procedure in breaths. Inhale, place the scalpel to the lower right midline of the suprapubic area. Exhale, slice vertically with pressure enough to go one inch under the skin. The initial slice does not hurt; it is when the air hits the open edges I want to scream.

Inhale.

Exhale. I cut along the one-inch line about three centimeters, just large enough to put my hand in.

Inhale.

Exhale. I cut through the subcutaneous fat. Let me tell

you, dieting to the point this would be easy was a very frustrating experience. Even with the starvation, the abdominal fat is still layered two centimeters deep.

Inhale.

Exhale. I slice through the tough, fibrous abdominal fascia. Between deep breaths, I tuck the retractor under the fat muscle and gently over the small portion of the intestine poking out.

Inhale.

Exhale. I tug upwards, holding the retractor in place with a pulley of my creation.

Inhale. I visualize the infundibulopelvic ligament, underneath will be the small life-giving orb.

Exhale. I clamp the ligament with a one-centimeter bridge in between clamps.

Inhale.

Exhale. I cut between the clamps, transecting the ligament with a pair of Mayo scissors. Inhale.

The room becomes black.

A moan. It is soft at first but crescendos. I open my eyes and reorient myself to the room. The blood has pooled on my abdomen like a makeshift mud puddle. The shock of seeing my own organs must have set in, but the clamp is still in place, locking off the primary artery of the ligament. There are other arteries bleeding and without suction it is a mess.

Thump.

He's moving.

I must finish the procedure quickly.

I grab the sterile towel and sop up the blood. It seems like an eternity before I can visualize the surgical field. It takes all my intention to breathe slowly. My heart is racing, and I've lost just enough blood for my body to respond without my permission. I check the clamp again, ensuring that it is not causing the bleeding and transect the fallopian tube and ovary from the uterus with my scalpel. I need to cauterize the tiny vessels, but they will have to clot on their own. The thuds of my heartbeat are making concentration difficult. The ovary and fallopian tube come out with a slight tug of the forceps. I inspect the round pink orb. The tube is intact. Perfect. With luck, it will attach to the spermatic cord without issue.

"You fucking bitch! When I get up from here, you're going to wish I would kill you." His words were venomous, but he was still in four-point restraints.

"Oh, my sweet, you think you can hurt me?" I said. Coy has always been my favorite way to play. I tried not to pant, but it was very difficult when the heart races.

Sloppy work has never been a favorite thing of mine. Yet, ensuring the patient meets his therapeutic goals is most important to me. I stuff sterile gauze in my wound, padding the clamps in place until I have sedated the patient and finished his procedure.

Four large sutures are used to close the wound.

Thump.

I jump.

He is kicking with his good leg.

I tremble for a second.

Now, I'm angry.

No one makes me tremble.

No one.

I push myself to sit up. Quickly, I put an oxygen mask

on, cranked up to 15 psi, and pushed two milligrams of morphine into my thigh.

Yours is coming, you stupid, disgusting pig.

After five minutes of pure oxygen and morphine, a person can feel whole again after a procedure. The headache will be a problem for later.

I walk over to him. I grab the vial of lorazepam, draw up eight milligrams, and mix it with succinylcholine.

Without thinking, I screw the syringe onto the IV tubing and push the plunger.

Damn, he's going to be asleep for the procedure.

I was smart enough to set up the sterile field before I worked on myself. Of course, my original intentions were to be alert, with minimal pain, and completely whole while performing the procedure on my patient. Instead, I'm standing here with blood leaking out of my abdomen with a clamp held in place with gauze. I must work slowly and replace a radical orchiectomy with a simple one.

In short, I'm going to cut his nut out through his ball sack.

His face is limp, his breathing slow. He gets to be at peace while I heal him from his demons.

I cleanse the scrotal sack with betadine; I'd already shaved the testicles and pubic area. He'd had a slight erection from the closeness of the blade. Sometimes, his type gets aroused from danger to self, even if his favorite way is to hurt others. I wipe off the area with sterile gauze, then use it to pull the scrotal sack tightly. I slice a small incision, then use my Mayo scissors to cut it open. You would think the testicle would just pop out, but it doesn't. There are layers of fascia to slice through and it is of importance to clamp off the major artery of the spermatic cord or he will bleed to death.

I don't want him to die.

The lights are hot. Beads of sweat roll down the back of my neck, but I am cold. My fingers are prickly.

I must finish what I've started.

I cut the ligament cord, and tug. The clamp holds. I search for the major artery in the ligament so I can attach it to the one from the ovary.

Anatomically, the male and female are so similar yet different.

Every piece on the body had its own modification related to hormones, genes, and these two little matching organs in our body.

The G-spot? It's where the prostate should be.

Those elegant folds of skin called the labia are just a prettier scrotal sack that tightened up.

Yet, I would never do what this pig has done over and over to multiple women. Yes, many men have died for my scientific discoveries. This one will not die.

My pulse is in my throat.

Soak up the blood, there it is. I take the ovary and fallopian tube and attach them to the spermatic cord. Artery to artery, vein to vein, I make tiny, tight stitches. It reminds me of my grandmother teaching me to quilt. She was beautiful, mysterious. Many women would come to her with difficult medical concerns they did not want a doctor to find out about. I remember helping her by digging holes and placing small shoeboxes in the garden.

The ovary's color returns.

I turn up the volume of normal saline infusing into the

patient. The ovary tucks nicely beside her new partner. I stitch the scrotum back together. I will return to check on my work after I fix myself.

My heart is beating so fast and the panting sounds like it is from outside of me. I must put down the needle and driver.

I look down, thinking that I have urinated on myself. Blood covers the front of my scrubs.

I grab the side of the table and slink to the floor. The panting continues. My heart is racing so fast I can no longer move.

It is suddenly quiet except for a weird ringing sound in my ears.

I close my eyes.

The last thing I hear is, "What the fuck have you done to me?!"

I whisper. That is all I can do. "I have given light to your dark."

THE PACT

The highway appeared newly paved, but the mountains had not changed. I cracked the window to rid the car of the dominating smell of a musky, overpriced perfume, which allowed the smell of crisp damp earth and coal smoke to creep in. The guard rail edged close as my cousin, Bess, swerved the rented BMW a little too close. I gripped the leather door handle for security. It was an illusion of safety, like almost everything else in my life. If the car rolled over, it would spare nothing.

"Why the hell do you think she did it?" Bess asked. Her long acrylic fingernails splayed over the steering wheel. She had a ring on every finger, just like she'd promised twenty years ago. The four of us had grown up in a holler in eastern Kentucky.

"Who knows? Maybe she couldn't take it anymore." The words came out fake as Bess's fingernails. My heart knew why our friend Melinda had drunk a bottle of tequila, snorted oxycodone, and walked out into her pool, never to rise to the surface again. I looked at the speckling of orange, yellow, and red in the trees, my body physically hurting for the longing of a simpler time.

"Well, it's been three years, and I don't know why the hell we have to come all the way out here to Cave Run for a reunion. I hated this fucking place growing up, and I hate it now." Bess had come out of the womb hating everything about mountain life. Tiger Beat magazines had been her bible and a Hollywood teen star was going to be her savior. She had waited every night on the porch of her cabin to be rescued. At eighteen, she had given up and started walking.

"Bess, she's buried up here. It just feels right." I knew what Bess was thinking. She wanted the old reunions. The lavish parties in Vegas or Beverly Hills. Instead, we were cozying up in Melinda's vacation cabin near Ramey Cemetery to reminisce about hard times, promises, and things cut too short.

"Yeah, well, I can't help feeling selfish. Melinda started this whole thing. The power of positive thinking, HAH, the bitch killed herself." Bess laughed a little at the misfortune of her joke. She spoke again. "You're the only one working to help people, and you don't even do that much. We were supposed to get out, make money, and take over the world. You live with your cats in an enormous house and listen to rich kids whine about their problems. If any of us have a reason to kill ourselves, it's you."

It felt like a punch to the gut. "What do you mean? I work with youth who have serious problems." Who was she to judge? Her only interaction with helping youth was to capitalize on their talent.

Bess smirked, "Well, you just always forget to mention

that you take care of kids whose most serious problem is that they have way too much money and time on their hands."

I looked out the window again. I clenched my teeth, grinding years of bitterness between me and Bess. Some of the kids had genuine problems like heroin addiction, and a teen mother or two. Just because their parents owned homes in the Hamptons didn't make their problems less real. "I became a psychologist. It's what I wanted to do. I kept my promise just the same."

"It seems shitty. I work a helluva lot harder than you do and barely make more than you." Bess said.

I could see my tired reflection in the window. A thirty-eight-year-old stared back at me. I think my age had hit me when Melinda died. No one would ever deserve the money or accolades that Bess believed the world owed her. So, I changed the subject.

"Do you think Misty will show?" I asked, hoping to get Bess off my back.

"Of course, she'll show. If it wasn't for me, the little tart wouldn't be making triple what you and me make combined." Misty was Melinda's little sister by a mere fourteen months. We had called them Irish twins. Now there was one. The youngest was the most successful. Misty had lived Bess's dream. She was an actress and now she produces films. Bess was still working as an agent. Bess had never been a beauty, though she hid it well under surgeries, plumpers, and dye jobs.

"You know, it doesn't bother me. She ditched me as her agent. What kills me is when she married that no talent little shit and didn't even invite me to the wedding.

What kind of bullshit is that? I was her agent for four years. I got her out to Los Angeles after she graduated from the UK..." Her driving mirrored her feelings.

I braced myself against the dashboard. "Calm down. It's called an elopement for a reason. Let it go. I think you're angry because she snagged your first movie star crush from way back when." I had to laugh a little.

The sudden screech of tires on asphalt and the feeling of my brain hitting the front of my skull made it painfully obvious I hit a nerve.

"God damn you; don't you ever tell that little sniveling brat I was in love with him. EVER! Do you hear me? She will rub it in my face all over Hollywood. While I had to change everything about myself to get anywhere in the business, that skinny bitch just walked in and said, 'Hi y'all, I'm here, so pay me.'"

I laughed as Bess posed her hands like Misty and batted her eyelashes. Bess began laughing, too. It was true, we all hid that we had grown up with moms who drew checks. Misty had played being different up to the hilt. Of course, Misty wasn't Misty anymore. She was Angela.

Bess opened her mouth to mimic Misty again when we heard an overpowering honk. We had forgotten what these roads were really for: coal trucks. Bess narrowly swerved off the road. The BMW grazed the guard rail as spatters of black gold rained on the car. My heart was racing.

Bess spoke first. "You think I would have remembered about coal trucks?" We both laughed again, this time in relief. Coal trucks bonded us. Our fathers had been taking a load over Zilpo Road when they had gone over the edge together, leaving behind two wives with two little daughters and no life insurance.

We are home now. The coal truck had transported us back to a time when we were just little girls dreaming of a bigger place. We made our way down Clear Creek Road as we headed towards the lake. October has always been my favorite time of year in the mountains. Melinda had built a cabin near her family's cemetery down the road from the holler, and now I wondered if it had been deliberate. Were the warning signs there at twenty-eight? A big iron gate greeted us as we turned into the unmarked driveway. Melinda had always carried herself as though she were from a different class of people. Who knew? It was possible, unlike Bess and me, as she had never known her father. Misty's father had left shortly after she was born. Their mother had no luck with men. We sat in the car staring at the gate.

"Are you going to get out and open it?" Bess huffed. I gave her a scowl and got out. I didn't even slam the door. It wasn't her car, so she didn't care. The ground was soft under my feet, and the smell of the wet earth crept up under my nose while the breeze off the lake cooled my cheeks. The latch to the gate opened easily. I smiled at the large R inscribed on each side of the gate. Melinda had always said she would have a gate with her initials on it.

I started walking towards the house. The towering windows in the front of the three-story A frame reflected the sun on the water. She had seen a house like it at Lake Tahoe and said she had to have it. Mel had been twenty-three then. Barely making peanuts right out of law school, but she always did what she said she would. I wonder when she told me she would off herself. Bess blew by me in the car, but I continued to walk. As I approached the side of the house near the separate garage, I saw a large yellow SUV parked next to our rental car. I smiled. Misty was here.

"Of course, she had to have the look-at-me car. Of course!" Bess opened the trunk and pulled out her luggage. She looked over at my bag as though it were diseased. She shook her head. "You'd be laughed right out of LAX. Where do you think she rented that monstrosity? Louisville?"

I grabbed my lightweight bag and carried it into the house, calling over my shoulder, "Get over it. Let's have some fun."

Misty was standing on the main level, staring out at the lake. She turned to look at me. For a split second, Melinda was in front of me. Then she smiled, and Melinda was gone.

"Hey, stranger, it's been so long. Still like living up there with those snooty New Englanders?" Misty walked over and wrapped her arms around me. Her warmth and glow had made her millions of dollars. Her energy came from a place that I had never touched, and Bess had always envied it. Melinda had held this glow, but in a dark ember in a furnace sort of way, while Misty was a supernova. I pulled her closer, feeling every bone in her ribcage.

"Hey, are you all right?"

"I'm fine, sugar." She pulled back and looked at me with wide doe eyes. I could see the blue irises darken. She was about to lie to me.

"What Adie's trying to say, is you need to eat." Bess huffed as she came in with all her suitcases. She looked at me, glaring, "You coulda offered to help me."

The expensive luggage dropped to the floor. The muscles in Misty's back tightened underneath mine. I squeezed her tighter. She was our adopted little sister, even though Bess was being a bitch. Misty walked over to help assist Bess. She smiled as Bess scowled at her. Misty picked up Bess's carry-on bag and tossed it over her shoulder.

"I know what room Melinda would want you to have, Bess." Misty started towards the stairs, heading upwards. Bess followed. She could never stand to be a follower. Misty had replaced Melinda in Bess's mind as competition for alpha female.

My bag felt light in my hand, but the baggage in my heart felt so heavy I didn't know if I could make it up the stairs. That was the problem. One moment I could feel total joy and the next I didn't know if I could move from one place to another. Mental health problems in a psychologist. It should be a joke, but it wasn't. Crazy people love helping other crazy people.

Then, just like our old lawn mower that would sputter, then suddenly come to life, I was moving again.

I could hear Bess berating Misty as I reached the top.

"Ladies, what are the plans for tonight?" I tossed my bag down to snap them out of their fussing.

Bess flopped on the bed in her room. "Well, I want to drink loads of wine and not think about the fact I'm in Kentucky."

Misty sat down in an antique rocking chair in the corner. "There's nothing wrong with our roots."

Bess flopped her arm over her eyes as though the thought was blinding her.

"Really? There is nothing wrong with the fact you and Melinda grew up with an outhouse? An *outhouse* in the 1980s? You don't find that gross and shameful? Your momma was on food stamps, and you ate government cheese until your granny had to throw castor oil down your throat." Bess sat up to add to her dramatic monologue. She would have made a superb actress. "You don't think any of that is shameful and disgusting? You wore those old Buster Brown shoes to school until your feet bled."

"Okay, Bess. We get your point." I tried to placate her. Of course, she wasn't finished with her Gone with the Wind speech.

"What do you think, Adie? You proud that your momma went to Moorhead every day and cleaned houses for nothing? Your daddy died because some fucker was too cheap to buy brake fluid for his coal trucks?"

I took a deep breath. "Bess, our dads died because they swerved out of the way of a family trying to fix a tire in a bad curve. My mom worked hard, and she provided for me. I'm proud of her for that. The check she was drawing didn't pay for much of nothing. I'm okay with who I am. I lied. I didn't want to admit how ashamed I was still to this day of wearing underwear with holes in them and never wanting to bring people to the house.

"Okay, well, now that we have revisited childhood trauma. I recommend you ladies get settled in and then come downstairs. I have a surprise for you." Misty pushed herself up from the rocking chair with a mischievous glint in her eye.

Bess raised an eyebrow. "I'm over snorting Adderall, if she thinks that's what we're getting into."

"What the hell is this?" Bess said as we headed into the kitchen.

On the bar, a Ouija board sat in the middle of a pentagram with candles on each of the corners, the flame wafting with the air from the ceiling fan. There was a chicken squawking somewhere. Misty wore an outfit that reminded me of a priestess dress from a pseudo-voodoo zombie movie from the 1950s. She looked up from scattering roses around the border of the bar.

"What?"

"We thought we'd be drinking wine, eating coffee ice cream, and remembering times gone by, not doing a ritual straight out of an Elvira movie." I couldn't believe what I was seeing. Misty bent over and pulled a statue of Shiva out of a box. "Seriously, you're going to throw some Hinduism in there, too?"

Misty smiled.

"Adie, some of us didn't go to college forever like you, but I got connections. I watch a lot of TV, and my friend Robert writes a lot of indie scripts related to this stuff. I figured if I mixed enough beliefs, something's got to work!" Misty finished her table setting with an old boombox in the corner nearest her.

"What exactly are you planning to do here?" I had a suspicion, but I hadn't thought Misty was capable of such thoughts.

"I want to talk to her. One more time." Misty closed her eyes and one tear fell down her cheek. "I miss her guidance so much. She dreamed up this world we live in."

"No, she came up with a stupid plan that we all agreed to, and then, she offed herself when she wasn't tough enough to keep up." Bess said, sitting down on one of the bar stools.

"It doesn't matter anymore. You chose the life you live, and you can't blame my sister if you hate it. Now, I have been fasting for six weeks. I want to talk to her and then we will eat all the ice cream you girls can handle." Misty walked over and turned out the lights.

In the contrast of candlelight, it was apparent that Misty had been fasting. Her skin was translucent and her cheekbones sharp. She was turning herself into the character of someone who conspired with the dead. Bess stood on one side of the bar and I on the other. Misty was at the end of the bar with the Ouija board. She pressed play on the boombox, and Mel's favorite song played. Bess and I laughed as we remembered 1988, and the movie the song had come from.

Misty took a deep breath. "We ask all the gods, or any gods, or the one true God, *WHOEVER*, to contact my sister from beyond and bring her back. I don't really care how you do it. I'll talk to her through this Ouija board. She can talk through the chicken. Just bring her back to me!" Misty leaned down and pulled the chicken from underneath the bar. From the pocket of her white tunic, she took out a knife.

Bess's eyes bulged, and she whispered over to me, "You think she remembers what happened the last time we saw someone do that?"

I shook my head. Why does everyone have to lose their shit when they get in a remote cabin?

The chicken didn't know it was about to be sacrificed, and I think somewhere in her mind Misty wasn't sure she wanted to sacrifice the bird. She held the anxious fowl down with one hand and attempted a dramatic stabbing with the other. Instead, she missed her target and hit the tile on the bar. The chicken looked up at her with desperation. Misty looked down, realizing she had missed. Instinctually, the chicken nipped the hand with the knife.

"Ow!" Misty yelped. The chicken started pecking at her more fiercely. "Shoo, get, shoo!" Misty fanned her arms at the bird. The chicken ran across her altar of mockery, tracking footprints of Misty's blood as it went. A lightning bolt came from nowhere on the lake, the wind blew, and the kitchen door flew open. The chicken ran out into the night. I walked over to shut the door as the wind blew in the autumn leaves.

"Well, I must admit, there is a reason you produce movies. That was good. How the hell did you get that lightning bolt image on the lake? Is there a projector?" Bess laughed, heading over to the window. The lightning continued in a rhythmic pattern. She turned around. "What a cliché. You should put some pressure on that wound of yours."

Misty was staring at her hand. The blood continued to

flow. I grabbed a paper towel, wetted it in the sink, and handed it to Misty. She looked disappointed. "I just wanted her back."

I hugged her tightly. "We all want her back. I'm sure we all wish we could have healed whatever hurt her."

Bess stared at the lake. She mumbled, "Whatever."

"At least no animals were harmed in this production." I chuckled. "Go change your clothes. Bess and I will clean this up. Then you need to eat."

Misty walked towards the first-floor bedroom. I grabbed the trashcan and raked the contents from the bar into the bag. Afterwards, I went for the boombox, but Bess grabbed my hand.

"No, let her music play. That was the best night. We went to the movies in town. Everyone was so in love with John. Hell, I'd fuck him today if he'd give me a chance."

We both laughed at the idea of our movie star, grade-school crush thinking of us as women. Bess went for the paper towels to clean up the blood. She sprayed cleaner on the bar and started wiping. "I miss her, too. It's just different for me. I took everything we agreed to seriously. It's all my life has become."

I nodded. Misty came back out in lounge pants and a University of Kentucky hoodie.

"The glamorous Angela Thorne Parker in her night-wear... oooh... aaaaah." Bess teased and clapped. Misty bowed, her finger now wrapped with gauze and tape. She noticed me looking at the finger.

"First aid training for insurance on the set. Not a bad idea now." She held up her fingers proudly. "Thanks for cleaning up, ladies. I'm starving. I seriously cannot believe that I haven't eaten solid food in six weeks."

"Isn't that normal for Hollywood starlets?" Bess jabbed.

Misty frowned slightly. "I'm too old to be a starlet now. If you are smart, you think about your future before you hit thirty. Now, where is that wine and ice cream?"

Bess and Misty talked about the goings-on of their world while I sat back and worried about mine. Bitsy and Libby probably had a field day with no human around to boss them. I imagined the cat litter splayed all over the laundry room floor and the cat food everywhere. The pet sitter never cleaned up messes, she just walked right over them to the paycheck. Paychecks reminded me I needed to call Justin when I got home, and kindly encourage him to get his stuff out of my house. Another one bit the dust. At least this guy had lasted three months before his total emotional baggage came out. I took a huge swig of wine and filled my glass again.

I went into the kitchen to search for more coffee ice cream. There were two more cartons and three more bottles of red wine. I read the label on the bottle and noticed it was made in Kentucky. Interesting how things change. I grabbed a carton of ice cream and a bottle of wine, then walked back to my two closest friends. I sat there listening about who was making how much money and sleeping with so and so to get it. The carton was half empty, and the bottle lay vacant next to it on the floor. I stretched my legs out on the loveseat and closed my eyes.

Thump, thump, thump. I was suddenly awake and aware of my head pounding. My stomach was so full of dairy and alcohol with one wrong move, I might spew the contents of the evening. *THUMP, THUMP, THUMP.* I heard it more clearly. It wasn't my head pounding; it was someone knocking on the door. I looked over to the couches to see if Bess and Misty were there, but they were gone. I pushed myself up off the small loveseat, slinging my legs to the ground. Great, some angry neighbor was ready to pitch a fit after watching, "Voodoo Priestesses of the Appalachia" starring us – the three miserable thirty something professionals. I wasn't sure what to say to some devout southern Baptist who may either throw me in the church or drown me in the lake.

Unsteadily, I walked over to the kitchen door. The thumping had continued. I opened the door and before my eyes could understand what I was seeing, my nose knew first, then my stomach. I vomited a mixture of red wine and curdled milk into the doorway then fell backwards.

"Are you okay?" A cold, clammy hand slapped me on the face. Each time the hand smacked me, I smelled a mixture of perfume, formaldehyde, and pine chips. I rolled away from the hand and opened my eyes.

"Is it really you?" I gagged.

"Yeah, it's me. Now, are you going to quit puking everywhere and sit up?" she asked, her voice muffled. "You got a pair of scissors around this place?"

I pushed myself up and went to the cabinet drawer and pulled out some small, sharp scissors. Melinda had always enjoyed cutting her own bangs. I wasn't sure what she planned to do with them but placed the scissors on the bar, trying not to make eye contact. I heard her pick them up and walk away. She headed into the guest bathroom where sounds of ruffling, clicking, and brushing echoed. It sounded like she was fixing herself up. I walked over to the sink, filled a glass of water, and swished my mouth out. I went for paper towels to cover my mess.

As I tried to wipe up the vomit from the hardwood floor, Melinda came out of the bathroom. I looked up. She had put Misty's makeup on and covered herself with some herbal, hippy rub that Misty was using, instead of all the toxic perfume the rest of us were running around wearing.

"God, I feel better." Her voice was clear now, but her eyes held a milky glaze. "Who knew they sewed your mouth shut and glued your eyes? I'm not even going to talk about my downstairs area. At least my skin is still on my bones, but damn do I feel blubbery. I never felt this fat when I was alive." Melinda sat down on the bar stool. Her suit perfectly matched her heels. The color had held up. I was impressed, since I'd been the one to pick them out.

"I'd ask for a cigarette, but I think I might be flammable." Melinda tapped her knee and laughed, just like her granny.

"Mel, what're you doing here?" I finished wiping up the vomit and threw the paper towels in the trash. Her suit and appearance weren't very dirty for someone who must have pushed themselves out of a mausoleum. She'd had to be put above ground. Ramey Cemetery had been totally re-landscaped to accommodate its richest inhabitant.

"Sweet Adie, I think I'm here because you called me. I woke up, the marble had moved out of the way, and I just started walking. When I got close, I remembered this was my cabin. I had only been here twice. Is this the reunion weekend?"

I nodded.

"Well, why the hell didn't y'all go to Las Vegas or the Bahamas? Why'd you come to Kentucky? I bet this was Misty's idea. Sentimental little shit." Melinda crossed her legs carefully. Her face scrunched as she apparently thought hard then wagged her finger at me. "Though, I'm pretty sure I was brought here to see you."

"I didn't call you. It was Misty. She did some weird I-watch-too-much-late-night-tv ritual trying to get you back here. She wants to know why. We all want to know why. We loved you, and you just threw it all away." I choked back tears and anger.

"Well, darling, why do you want to off yourself?" Melinda looked at me. The bluish gray tint of her dead eyes bored right through me. "Yes, sweetie, I have all kinds of information on you girls that you don't even know. So why?"

I backed up to the sink. My throat was suddenly dry. The words would not come.

"Well?" She tapped the bar impatiently. She used to do this when she talked to clients.

Tears rolled down my face. "I don't know why."

"Sure, you do. You thought that creepy little man-boy was going to settle down with you. He disappointed you, like they always do. All those kids with their petty problems who haven't felt a day of poverty or misery in their lives whining to you, when all you want is your white knight to save you." Melinda had been a take charge, to the point lawyer in life, and it had apparently continued through death.

"That's not true. I can take care of myself. You saw it with your own eyes! I have done what I needed to do, and I have more than I ever wanted." My blood boiled. It sounded so embarrassing to hear her say that I was waiting for a white knight.

"What do you want?" Melinda's eyes became brighter. "Really, truly in your soul. What do you want?"

It came out simply, pathetically. "To be loved." It sounded foolish when I said it out loud.

Melinda laughed. "Do you really think being loved will solve your problems? You should know this one, psych." She crossed her arms. "Why can't you figure it out? None of these relationships are going to work. You're never going to be happy until you love yourself."

Rage filled me. "That's a good one, Mel, from the person who did kill herself!"

The audacity of Melinda to talk about someone not loving themselves when she'd offed herself without thinking of us! She'd left us without a leader, without a plan.

"Adie, everybody has their own plan. Yeah, I can read your thoughts. I was never a leader. Look at Bess, she's the one who dragged us out of here. I built a cabin so I could come home. Does that reek of someone who wanted to leave this place? Besides, I had my reasons for doing what I did."

"Then what could have made you do such a thing? We didn't even know you had a damn drug problem!" It had been so painful to learn that Melinda had been abusing pills. None of us had known, and now we felt helpless for not preventing it.

"I did it because I loved you guys. Because of Eric, he was such a good husband, I couldn't let the memories of me be any worse than what they were. I wasn't a drug addict. My oncologist prescribed those pills. I had stage four skin cancer. It was in my lungs and brain. I saw all those people coming into that office looking so sick and pale. I couldn't do it and make you all suffer like that along with me." If she could have cried, Melinda's tears would be flowing. "But this isn't about me, Adie. It's about YOU. You need help. This depression you're fighting is going to kill you. Is the money worth it? I can see from where I am that you really hate your job. Sell that big ass house, get rid of the Jaguar, and lose that fake, uptight, intellectual accent. Move on with your life! It's the only one you're going to have. I found that out a little too late." Melinda looked down at her hands, her bottom lip trembled.

I didn't know what to say. No matter how much I reasoned and bargained, I wasn't happy in New Hampshire, in my house, or with myself. Justin had told me the truth when he'd left. He said I would never be happy. I didn't want to hear it, but he was right. No one would make me happy until I chose to be happy. It seemed clichéd and stupid. I knew this. I preached it to patients every fucking day. I just didn't know how to do it for me.

"Leave it all behind and move towards happiness." Melinda had calmed herself. She pushed herself off the bar stool she had been sitting on. "I gotta go."

"You can't leave. I have so many questions to ask you.

What about Bess and Misty?" I turned towards her, wanting to grab her arm, but I didn't dare.

"Oh yeah, tell Misty to give him the divorce. It won't work. He's being nice, and he's gay. If she doesn't do it now, it'll be in the tabloids. Tell Bess.... Hmmm. This is hard. Tell Bess, it'll never happen with Nathan, but that plastic surgeon who won't give her another facelift is into her. She just needs to quit trying to rule everything and it'll work out." Melinda blew a kiss at me in the doorway. As she headed down the stairs, she turned around. "Eric will give you this place if you ask. It's in my will. You really don't know how much I loved you all. Go be happy and don't worry about all our little girl plans. I love you."

Melinda continued to walk down the paved path towards Ramey Cemetery. I wanted to follow her and beg her to stay, but seriously, how would we explain a zombie conjured with some mish-mashed, hodgepodge, hocus pocus? How do you explain that to people? I shut the door as she walked past the wrought-iron gate. My head felt like a ton of bricks was on top of it. I headed back to the couch and closed my eyes.

"Oh my god, this is so gross!" Bess yelled from the kitchen area. "What the hell is on this chair? This smell is disgusting."

I got up from the couch and walked into the kitchen. In the spot where Melinda had been sitting, body fluids had accumulated.

"Maybe Misty's hocus pocus spell worked, and Melinda visited us last night?" I suggested.

"Yeah, right, I think maybe you vomited in one too

many places." Bess rolled her eyes at me, then looked at the evidence of mishap from the previous night.

"Oh," I said. Then something inside me drummed up the courage to say the truth whether Bess liked it. "Well, then how would I know that your plastic surgeon won't give you another facelift because he has the hots for you?"

Bess dropped the dish towel she was using.

"How'd you know that? I haven't told anyone about wanting another facelift. I suspected he thought I was cute, but he has those acne scars, and I hear he's divorced." She shook her head in doubt.

"Just go for him. When you get back to Los Angeles, call him. Quit taking control and ruining everything all the time," I said a little too loudly. The padding of light feet hitting the hardwood floor signaled Misty was awake.

"Hey, guys, what's going on?" Misty went for the bar stool. "Oh shit, what happened here? Did Melinda show up?"

Bess looked at Misty. "Did you do too much NMDA? You're as bad as this one."

Misty turned to me. "What did she say? Why didn't you wake me?"

Misty came to me pleadingly and grabbed my shoulders. I put my arms around her and whispered, "All she wanted you to know is, give him the divorce. You know in your heart he's not right for you. She loves you." I wrapped my arms around her. Misty cried.

"Are you seriously going to believe this?" Bess headed toward the downstairs bathroom. She went in and screamed.

Misty and I looked at one another, then raced towards

the bathroom. On the mirror, a message was written in bright pink lipstick: *Forget your plans, girls, go live and love your life. –Melinda.* A puddle of fluid had accumulated where she had stood too long. Melinda had laid out Misty's cosmetics in the order she used to wear them. The smell on them was distinct.

"So, what do you think we should do with this?" Bess looked at the mirror, the puddle on the floor, and then at Misty and me.

"Just go for what you want." I smiled then leaned down, threw some paper towels over the goo, and started mopping.

BABY MUTANT DAY ONLY COMES ONCE A YEAR

Knock, Knock, Knock.

Thud.

The cooing sound of a baby floated in the air.

"Wha–? What was that?" Jessica opened one eye.

"Nothing. One of our packages from Buyshitonline.com must've come," Rob mumbled, rolled over on his side, and then promptly placed his pillow on top of his head.

"No, it cooed. I heard cooing." Jessica swore she'd heard cooing. She stared at the ceiling for a moment, waiting to see if she heard it again. She didn't have to wait long.

Knock, Knock, Knock.

A gruff male voice yelled through the door, "You know the rules! Open the door."

Jessica sat up, Rob fell out of bed, and they simultaneously belted out, "Oh fuck."

"It's here already?" Rob mouthed.

Jessica grabbed her phone and looked at the calendar. She nodded.

"Your turn to answer the door." Rob grabbed his crumpled jeans from the floor. He pushed himself up and started searching for his shoes.

"God damnit, Rob. You can run faster than me. Not fair." Jessica whined.

"I told you to train all year. Plus, I have a killer hangover. There is no way in hell I'm going to avoid the little bastard. Last year, that little fucker had cheetah legs."

Jessica reluctantly agreed. Rob had let the cheetah mutant chase him for 14 hours before he'd found somewhere to hide, while she'd sat at home working on a project for her job as a graphic designer. She got up and pulled out her favorite yoga pants, a sports bra, and her most broken-in running shoes.

"Well, wish me the best. Just remember, it can backtrack and come after you." Jessica took a long, deep breath and walked out to the living room. Behind her, the attic ladder clacked as it folded out and then Rob's footsteps thudded as he scurried upward. Before she had time to open the front door, the ladder retracted, and the attic door slammed shut.

"Motherfucker." Jessica cracked the door sheepishly.

The delivery man tapped his clipboard. "Can you sign this already?"

"I get a running head start, right?" She paused before accepting the clipboard.

"Yeah, yeah. You know, if you folks would just have a baby like normal people, this would all be over. You got at least another five years of this," he warned.

Jessica grabbed the clipboard, signed the waiver, and accepted the terms. She handed it back and with a confident voice informed the delivery man, "I'll take my chances."

"Do you even want to see it?"

"Do I have to?"

"Up to you, but won't it be easier to know what you're running from?" He bent over to open the cage.

"Oh, alright. But this isn't one of those that puts you in a trance when you look into its eyes, right?" She slowly crouched down to peek at the monstrosity that could become her responsibility if she didn't stay spry.

"I don't think you're going to have to worry about that." He assured her.

He was right.

In the cage, on all fours, was the body of a toddler with a toilet paper roll for a head. One thin sheet flapped back and forth on what she presumed would be his forehead. In the back, a tail wagged, reminding her of Daisy, her childhood Golden Retriever.

"Rob, you gotta come see this!"

From somewhere above, she heard a muffled, "That's okay, honey. I trust you."

The delivery man sighed. "Are you ready? I got four more to go."

The baby, if you could call it that, giggled.

Jessica nodded. She walked around the cage, ensuring the thing didn't touch her. It would be an automatic forfeit, and Toilet Paperhead would be theirs to raise.

The hinges of the cage creaked as he pushed it open.

Jessica took a deep breath.

"Go!" screamed the delivery man.

Jessica sprinted away from her overpriced baby blue bungalow and headed toward Main Street. She figured Toilet Paperhead would be crawling, so she had time to get coffee. She and Rob had sat on their patio drinking tequila with friends until 2 a.m. It wasn't the most glamorous thing they'd ever done, but it had been fun enough. She turned the corner onto Main and the sight of the sign for her favorite coffee shop spread a smile across her face. The large emoji-looking coffee cup cracked her up. Plus, the owner was just fun. They made cotton candy mochas for people like her in enormous cups with cute designs from graphic designers from all over the world. Jessica hadn't submitted a design yet. Being a corporate designer had killed a lot of her joy, but she didn't mind appreciating the work of others.

The old bell clanged loudly as she pulled the door open. Her heart sank. The line stretched to the door. Women rolling baby strollers back and forth and young people with their laptop bags weighing heavily off their shoulders stood impatiently. She wanted to scream and ask if she was the only one being chased today, but she knew Baby Mutant Day was only once a year. These bastards must either be uncoupled, had bribed someone, or had children hiding somewhere at home.

She spotted one of the regular baristas and gave her a nod.

"How's it going?" the barista said from behind the counter as she frothed milk.

"I'm in a bit of a hurry." Jess looked over her shoulder towards the door.

The guy in front of her grunted.

"What's your rush?" The barista poured the foamy milk into a large, hot pink mug.

"Uh, you know, it's *that* day. "

The barista sat the mug down. "Oh."

"Is there any way I could grab a cup of coffee and run?" Jessica batted her eyes sweetly.

The guy in front of her turned around and frowned at her. He towered over her, his arms crossed. Jessica stood taller, her fist instinctively clenched, readying to fight for a drip coffee if she had to.

"What do you want to drink?"

Jessica wasn't sure who'd said it at first. Then she saw the pale redhead at the front of the line waving at her. The woman beckoned. Jessica darted around the man and headed to the front of the line.

"I'll just take a drip to go. I'm in a hurry."

The redhead gave her a knowing nod. "We'll have two drips and a cookie for the baby."

Jessica leaned over to look into the stroller. She should have guessed as much, since the redhead had been so charitable. Lying on his back was a creature with the face of a 50-year-old man with stubble, attached to the torso of an infant with small lizard-like arms.

"Hey, Ma. Who's the broad?" the infant asked in a voice that sounded like he'd been smoking since before he was born.

"Joseph, I told you to not call women *broads*. If you want your cookie, you'd better apologize to the lady."

The infant crossed his arms and stuck out his lower lip.

"Yeah, yeah. Okay, who's the LADY?"

The redhead smiled. "She's a nice lady in a hurry, and we are helping her."

"Hah! She's trying to run from one of them mutant babies, isn't she?"

"We don't call them mutants."

"Why you always busting my chops?" the baby asked as he threw up his tiny lizard arms and smirked.

The redhead rolled her eyes and handed the cookie to the infant. He smiled, then cooed. It surprised Jessica that he'd make a baby sound.

The redhead stepped behind the stroller where the infant couldn't see her. She mouthed, "It's really not that bad."

Jessica nodded. She grabbed her coffee from the counter and walked away. She thought better of it, stopped, and grabbed the redhead by the shoulders and squeezed tight.

She whispered in the lady's ear, "Thank you so much. I wish you and your baby the best, I mean it."

"Jesus, are you two ever going to get out of the way?" the tall guy in the back asked.

Jessica scowled at the man and let go of the redhead. As she walked past him, she asked, "You married?"

"No. And, if I was, I'd be smart enough to have a baby of my own instead of being forced to be chased by a messed-up government experiment."

"Good luck with that, buddy." Jessica wagged her finger at him as she walked by.

She muttered under her breath as she pushed open the

door, "I don't think you are going to have any problem with staying single."

Once she was on the sidewalk, she couldn't believe her eyes. Toilet Paperhead was casually crawling towards the coffee shop. She couldn't have been in there that long, could she? She heard its incessant, overly happy coo. It didn't even sound real. It was like the sound box in one of those training dolls the government forced those who elected to have biological children to keep for a year. It kept coming.

"Shit."

Jessica took a large gulp of the coffee, tossed it in the trash, and sprinted toward San Andreas Avenue. She'd hoped for more time, but it looked like this one wasn't a quitter. All she needed to do was make it until 6 p.m. She had to stay in open daylight, couldn't hide, and she couldn't harm the mutant baby. Seemed easy enough with this one, but sometimes the delivery men would give the babies an unfair advantage. One year, Jessica had seen one of the delivery guys grab a baby off the street. She'd initially thought it was a retrieval but had quickly realized he was helping it. The next thing she knew, the baby was in the arms of a very upset woman. She wondered if there was a quota for the number of babies that had to be given out per year.

Genetics were a tricky thing, she thought. They'd cured every type of cancer, HIV, and people were basically all gorgeous now. They still had shitty attitudes most of the time, but she didn't think genetic splicing could cure that. So, why did they keep fucking with the genome? Was it punishment because beautiful, happy, genetically-modified people didn't want to mate? Sure, she understood it was her right as a citizen to say no, but the government acted like she owed them a kid. She guessed she did, or her payback was becoming a baby-momma to a lab experiment.

A sharp twinge pulled at Jessica's side. She paused and bent over, taking a couple of deep breaths, and coughed as she pulled the fresh crisp air in through her nose. She thought about going to the beach, but since she was only in a sports bra, it was probably too cold. Her plan usually comprised running the perimeter of their neighborhood, then crisscrossing all the streets. One year, she had sat behind a dumpster for an hour because she'd run out of places to go. However, she hadn't hidden in the dumpster and if the baby had been smarter, it would have caught her, she rationalized.

"Jessica?" a soft, female voice asked as gray house slippers and yellow yoga pants came up beside her.

Jessica looked up to see Raquel, one of her friends from college.

"Hey!" Jessica popped up and gave her a hug. She examined Raquel. The woman looked tired and winded. The last time Jessica had heard from her, she'd been single.

Jessica pulled back and gave her full up and down inspection. "Are you married?"

"Yes. We kind of kept it low-key. We didn't really invite anyone."

"Oh."

"How many years have you been running?" Raquel

shifted from one foot to the other while she surveyed the area.

"Can you believe this is my sixth year?"

"Uh, oh."

"What?" Instinctively, Jessica crossed her arms.

"You know what happens in year six, right?"

"I guess you are going to tell me," Jessica said dryly.

"I mean, I don't want to freak you out, but I hear at year six, the baby will catch you. Guaranteed."

Jessica shook her head. "No, I don't think so. I know lots of people who've never been caught."

"Name one."

It hadn't occurred to Jessica to keep count of the number of years her friends had been running. It seemed like her friends were getting younger and younger as friends had bio kids, though.

"I'll think of someone. You only have to do this for ten years." Jessica looked around Raquel waiting for Toilet Paperhead to turn the curve at any minute.

Quack, quack, quack.

Jessica watched as Raquel's face froze. Her eyes were wide, mouth straight.

Raquel started walking. She turned her head to look at Jessica. "Hey, I'll talk to you later. We are having a baby next year. I don't care what Mike says."

Jessica watched as an infant with the mouth of a duck crawled towards them. She had to laugh a little. This probably all terrified the hell out of Raquel.

"At least it looks like a baby except for the duckbill, and you'll get used to the quack!"

Raquel waved her arm in dismissal of Jessica's words, then flung up her middle fingers.

This only tickled Jessica more. She laughed out loud, then yelled, "Call me!"

A whistle on the wind sounded too much like a coo for Jessica. She knew she needed to keep moving.

Her shadow was long as she headed out to the beach. Jessica hadn't seen Toilet Paperhead for over an hour. She figured Raquel was wrong. After all, Raquel couldn't remember the Greek alphabet in college, even the letters to her own sorority. The mutant baby would go back to the shelter where it had come from, and life would return to normal for her and Rob.

As she stepped onto the boardwalk, the smell of tacos flooded her senses. Hints of cumin, garlic, chilis, and ground beef lured her to a portable food cart. An overwhelming urge of hunger consumed her. The last time she'd had food was the night before when they'd entertained friends. Jessica got in line behind a couple. Her second line of the day while running from a baby mutant. She really felt like she was pushing her luck.

"Here, let me put a little taco sauce on there for you. How about some sour cream?" the man insisted.

"I'm fine, honey. Really. Stop." The woman pushed the squeeze bottle of sauce away from her taco.

"I want that baby inside you healthy." He smiled and reached out for her stomach.

"He will be fine. I don't need to eat a thousand extra calories a day to grow a baby inside me." She pulled away, protecting her food and belly.

Jessica looked at the two; her stomach growled loudly.

"Are you ready?" the streetcar vendor asked.

"Yeah, I'll take two beef tacos with everything." Jessica grabbed a couple of napkins. She went to grab the money from her pocket. It was empty.

"Damn." She wanted those tacos more than anything in the world.

"What's wrong?" the vendor asked.

Jessica looked up at him with pleading eyes. "I'm on the run, it's mutant day. I forgot my money."

The vendor laughed and handed her the tacos.

"They're on me. I'm glad I never had to experience what you're going through." When he handed her the tacos in warm wax paper, he didn't let go immediately. Instead, he looked her in the eyes and smiled, "Go have a baby. Quit tormenting yourself. You might end up with something worse."

"Thanks, I'll take my chances." Jessica pulled the tacos from the vendor's hand. She looked over at the couple again as she took a huge bite. The man hovered over his wife. She couldn't imagine Rob doing that. It had been an immediate consensus between the two of them from their first date: no children. She scanned the beach for Toilet Paperhead. It was nowhere to be found.

She plopped down in the sand about thirty feet from the boardwalk. It had to be close to six; she thought. The sun was setting. Once the clock hit six, it was another year down. Her mind wandered to her plans for the night. They usually went to a bar or club with friends on Saturdays. She was tired, though. Maybe she'd send Rob on his own. There was no law that said they needed to go out every weekend. For a brief second, her mind went to the mutant babies. Where would they go? She couldn't fathom that they would be destroyed. Did they just go back into crates?

What would they do with a baby that had a head made of toilet paper? Would she be like the woman who'd bought her a coffee this morning? Kind, understanding, and able to overlook the imperfections of a child she didn't want? There was no good answer, she thought. She knew who she was now–independent, un-maternal, and a hell of a lot of fun. Changing that was not something she was prepared to do for someone else, especially not a mutant baby.

A soft wisp of the breeze brushed her arm. Instinctually, she rubbed her arm, then shoved the rest of her taco in her mouth. She felt the soft, light touch again. She looked to her right.

"No fucking way."

"Cooooooooo." Toilet Paperhead tilted the front of its roll towards her. The white, curved end of its paper flapped in the wind. It pawed at her thigh as it tried to crawl into her lap.

"No, no, no, no." She shook her head and tossed her hands in the air.

Her first instinct was to grab it and toss it into the ocean. There was no way she would be the mother. Never. She picked it up under its arms and sat it down beside her. Little specks of sand flew everywhere as she sprang up from the ground. She ran in the opposite direction of the boardwalk. It didn't matter if anyone saw her; she wasn't doing this.

"Hey! It touched you. We saw it. Go grab your baby!"

Jessica heard a male voice yell behind her. It wasn't enough to make her stop. She ran for miles and miles. Finally, her feet and legs gave out, and she crashed to the ground. She leaned down and stretched into a child's pose. She lay there with her head down and arms stretched out in front of her for a long while, her mind blank.

When Jessica opened her eyes, dusk had settled on the beach. The yellow sand was now a glowing orange. She pushed herself up from the packed sand and shook out her stiff limbs. Running for miles wasn't as easy as it had been when she first started running six years ago. As she headed up toward the sidewalk, a white delivery van pulled up in front of her. Two Baby Mutant Day delivery men stepped out of the vehicle. One of them she recognized as the deliverer of Toilet Paperhead.

"Fuck," Jessica said under her breath.

"Look, lady, this could get ugly. Take your baby and go home." The man crossed his arms and stared grimly at Jessica.

Jessica crossed her arms and puffed out her chest.

"Well, what if I don't?"

"How does jail for you and a huge fine for your husband while you're gone sound?" the second delivery man asked.

Jessica stood there, staring in silence at them.

After what seemed like a thirty-minute showdown, she buckled.

"Can I at least get one with a human head?"

The delivery man from the morning laughed. "You actually got one of the better ones this year. He will not grow up, though. He'll stay in this puppy mentality and stage his whole life. Besides, he doesn't have that long of a life expectancy, maybe ten to twelve years max."

This didn't convince Jessica.

"The other option is an old lady that takes in the babies at her farm. We tell no one about her unless they'd really rather go to jail than take the kid."

Almost before he'd finished, Jessica asked, "How much?"

"Three hundred a month for the life of the baby."

Jessica thought about the price of freedom. They'd probably break even either way, between baby diapers and whatever this thing ate. It might even be more than three hundred a month.

"Let's go."

She stepped into the side entrance of the van. It was vacant except for a few cages with what she could only assume were successfully avoided babies. One of them even looked normal. It had big blue eyes, chubby cheeks, and a toothy grin. She smiled at it. The baby opened its mouth and a long-forked tongue rolled out. Blue eyes converted to red, then it burped a smell that was so rancid that Jessica thought she might toss up her tacos.

"You might want to get out of the van. That odor will stick to you," one of the delivery men said from behind her.

"I'm not surprised," she said as she backed out.

They stood in silence as the wind carried away a smell that reminded her of hard-boiled eggs left in a hot car for two weeks.

"She's got some GI problems, and she got hold of some garbage today."

"It smells like she got hold of more than a little garbage." Jessica pinched her nose.

"Do you see? You could have a baby like her that is going to spread toxic smells that stick to your clothes. Who knows how big she'll grow or how long she will live? Or, you could have the equivalent of a Labrador retriever in a baby's body with a toilet paper head. I think the head is renewable. You could use that to your advantage."

"Well, when you say it like that. Who doesn't love free stuff?" Jessica rolled her eyes. "Let's just go to the farm and see what happens. Okay?"

The air had cleared in the van. Jessica leaned against the warm metal wall and stared at Toilet Paperhead in the corner. Occasionally, she could hear it coo. It seemed to be a happy little thing. Its tail would wag, and it would sneak a handout of the cage and paw at the other babies.

It would not be easy to explain to Rob that they'd be paying three hundred a month for at least a decade to some old lady out in the mountains. They'd go out less and budget more, she figured.

The van halted. The two delivery men swung open the back doors. Behind them, a soft light switched on. Jessica assumed it was a porch light.

"You grab that one, and I'll take the burp-baby."

Jessica watched as the two men pulled crate after crate out of the back. Toilet Paperhead must have been one of the first out. She felt a small tinge of sadness.

"What do you got for me this year?" an older, raspy female voice asked.

"The usual. Ones avoided and those discarded," one man said.

"Don't matter to me as long as I get my three hundred a month each."

Jessica scooted out of the van as the two delivery men picked up a couple of crates and wandered off. They headed toward a large building. Jessica followed.

The profile of a short person with curly hair moved ahead of them and swung open a large wide door. Light streamed outward over the wrinkled woman's face and shined off her large, thick glasses. Behind the old woman, rows of shelves held wire cages. Mutant baby after baby rustled in their cages, awakened from sleep.

"Put these over in row G. Had a couple last month grow out of their cages. Sent them out to pasture," the woman said nonchalantly.

"Excuse me? Out to pasture?"

"Who are you?" The old lady swiveled around, her glasses sliding down her nose.

"Uh, uh." Jessica suddenly felt like an intruder.

"Wanted to see where all your fears and hang-ups go to die? Welcome to the farm, sweetie."

Six Months Later...

"Babe, where's Teddy?" Jessica screamed from the bathroom. She looked at the toilet paper holder. The brown cardboard roll mocked her.

"He's playing with a ball in his room. Why?" Rob yelled through the door.

Jessica propped her elbow on the side of the sink.

"Well, we're out again. Could you pluck his head for me?"

"Ah Jess, he's in the middle of playing," Rob said, sounding disappointed.

"It'll grow back."

"Fine."

Jessica could hear Teddy whining as Rob pulled his head off. She felt like an asshole, but the doctor had said it didn't hurt him, it just interrupted what he was doing. Plus, it was good for him to refresh his head. He would lose his senses as the paper became worn and dirty.

The door opened a crack and Rob's hand poked through with a roll of toilet paper.

"Thank you!" Jessica caught it.

"Don't thank me, thank Teddy."

Jessica walked into Teddy's room. Their baby was lying on his side in his toddler bed. His chest rose and fell steadily as the white tissue that was his head grew in. She was glad he'd caught her. He had brought a new joy to their life. And toilet paper, lots of toilet paper.

PUMPKINHEAD SCISSORS WILL ALWAYS KILL YOU

Estate sales can be damn depressing when you think about why someone is having one. A family is trying to unload a lifetime of crap from someone's domicile, typically, so they don't have to pay rent on what had been reduced to an overpriced storage unit. Most deceased probably don't care what their family does with their stuff. Throw it out, donate it, do whatever, because they are not coming back for it.

I had been walking around this estate sale rummaging through junk for about an hour when light reflected out of one box. The sun was high in the sky, so I think it was in just the right position to hit something metal. I walked over, out of curiosity. You never knew what you would find in a dead person's things. The person who had owned the stuff at this sale had loved crafting. Many of the boxes held scraps of material that were promises of a future item to be brought into creation, like a coat, a doll, or a quilt. That was something the departed owner and I had in common. I loved quilting. I looked down and my eyes just about fell out of my head.

I scooped up the box and walked over to the middle-aged man wearing a visor and a fanny pack.

"Are you the cashier?"

He rolled his eyes. I was about to tell him, "You should probably just put a name tag on if you don't want to be asked that a thousand times," but I decided I didn't need to piss him off. Instead, I'd take the assertive approach and get what I wanted.

"How much for the box?" I prayed he had not seen the delight in my eyes when I'd looked in the box.

"I'll take five bucks." The man didn't seem at all interested in me, or the box.

"Here you go." I handed him a five-dollar bill and turned away as fast as I could and started walking to my car.

Behind me, I heard a female voice ask the cashier, "Have you seen the box with Mom's sewing kit?"

"I don't think so. Why?"

"There was a set of scissors she asked me to keep for her."

"Well, they're probably gone now."

I kept walking. The sewing kit and scissors were mine now, and I wasn't turning back.

"Are you going to sell them?" My best friend, Carmen, held up the silver and gold scissors and inspected them.

"No way. Are you kidding me? These are one of a

kind." I was measuring the material from the estate sale box, folding it, and labeling it for resale in my store. Crafters would pay a pretty penny for the right material.

"I'd say. Who would have a pair of scissors made with a jack-o'-lantern head as the handle? Plus, look at the intricate metalwork and these symbols. So cool. They even have a sheath." I tossed over a long leather case enclosed in more metalwork.

"Is this actual gold and silver?"

"I had Frank from the jewelry store test them and he said they were real."

Frank was my neighbor in the strip mall where my shop was located. He specialized in creating beautiful pieces and buying gold, then reselling it. Mostly, people brought in old jewelry they no longer wanted, and he would buy it for pennies on the dollar. He'd melt it down and resell it. Occasionally, he'd make a custom piece.

"Well, if anyone would know they aren't real, Frank would." Carmen gave a confirming nod. She'd had Frank test her engagement ring and other pieces of jewelry for the family, just to make sure, more than twice.

"From what I've found online, they fit with the Victorian era, but I think they look more like they are from Ireland. The symbols and all. Maybe Celtic? I'm going to call them my Pumpkinhead scissors." I'd tried to find more out about the scissors, but to no avail. I couldn't decide if I even wanted to have them out for display. It seemed like a temptation for sticky fingers. I'd never had a big issue with theft, but a gold and silver pair of vintage scissors might do it.

"Well, I think you should at least make one item with

them. If you decide to lock them away after that, they will have earned back the five dollars. Seems such a shame not to use them."

"I don't know. What if I mess them up by sharpening them?"

"Nah, give them a try without that first. I bet they are sharp."

Before I could open my mouth and warn her not to do something stupid, Carmen yelped.

"Ow!"

"Did you just test how sharp those scissors are with your finger? Really?!" Sometimes I felt more like her mother than best friend.

"I was just trying to help you out." Carmen said then stuck her finger in her mouth.

"Sure, sure. Hand me them to me and go get a towel for your hand. You're gonna need a tetanus shot. We have no idea where these things have been." I grabbed the scissors from her and gave her a chastising frown in jest.

Carmen imitated a childish pout then turned away, and walked through the double swinging doors, headed toward the bathroom at the back of the store.

I took a rag and wiped the blood from the scissors. They were definitely sharp.

"Boo!"

"Jesus!" I jumped and dropped the scissors to the floor. I turned to see Carmen's fiancé, Joel, with a wide grin on his face.

"Here, let me get those for you." Joel bent over and picked up the scissors.

"Hey, I didn't know you were coming in." Carmen walked through the double swinging doors from the back of the store.

Joel walked over and kissed Carmen on the forehead. "Hey, babe. Yeah, I was going to see if I could borrow a couple dollars…"

"Why didn't you just request it through the app?"

"Well, I actually need cash, and I wouldn't get to see you if I did that." He kissed her on the cheek after that bullshit zinger.

I stood to the side, watching their interaction. Joel was asking for cash because he had most likely overdrawn and overcharged every app and account he had. He was very irresponsible with money. I didn't want to say anything to Carmen, but she knew that was the reason he was here. She paid for everything. As a teacher, she made decent money, but she worked at my store, not only because I paid her to hang with me, but because she needed the money for Joel.

"Do you care if I pull a fifty out of petty cash and you can deduct it from today's pay?" Carmen gave me a mopey face by sticking out her bottom lip.

She really knew how to make me feel guilty.

"Go ahead."

"Thank you." Carmen came over and gave me a big squeeze. Joel gave me a little smirk.

Man, did I hate that guy.

My cell phone rang at 3:15 a.m. I swore I had put my phone on silent before I'd gone to bed. Yet, here it was vibrating and screeching a horrible tune that I don't remember setting as my ringtone. The ID flashed through Carmen's number.

"Oh, my gawd, he's dead. He's dead!" Carmen screamed hysterically into the phone.

"Wait, what? Who's dead?" Did her dad die? He was old and had a notorious history of falling.

"JOEL! Joel's dead."

"How? He was fine earlier today." Was my suspicion that he was secretly using drugs, correct? Had he overdosed? The man's lack of an ability to manage money would make sense. Otherwise, my two other suspicions were immaturity, stupidity, or a combination of both.

Carmen continued to sob into the phone. I heard someone talking to her in the background.

"Hello?" a familiar male voice asked. I wasn't sure who it was, though.

"Who is this?"

"Angelica?"

"Yeah? Who is this?" I just could not place the voice.

"It's Javi. Carmen's brother."

It was like a light bulb went off in my brain. I sat up. This was really happening if Carmen's brother was there.

"What do you need me to do?" I leaned back against my headboard. My eyes were still out of focus. I reached over and searched my nightstand for my glasses.

"Get over here as soon as possible. She can't be left alone."

"Can you tell me what happened?" I wasn't sure that I

wanted to know the answer, or if it even mattered at this point.

"I'll tell you when you get here," he said in a low voice. "I gotta go. They're wheeling out the body."

Carmen wailed loudly in the background.

———

The blue lights of the police cars that lined Carmen's street cast a surreal glow as I pulled up. Between the police and the normal neighborhood vehicles, I had to park a street over and walk up to her apartment complex. She lived in a small, older building that held four apartments. It was not a terrible neighborhood, so I didn't think it was a robbery gone wrong. Guilt wracked me. I had not liked Joel, that much was true, but I would never have wanted him dead for any reason. I would have loved for him to get a job and quit taking advantage of my best friend, but I would never have wanted this.

Police tape surrounded the building. Carmen stood on the sidewalk next to her brother. Blood splatter covered her pajamas. She must have woken up and found him.

"Carmen!" I started walking faster. This was horrific. We were just a couple of boring thirty-year-old crafters living low-key lives. There was no way something this horrible could happen to us.

Carmen looked up from her daze and yelled back, "Angelica!" She ran towards me, but Javi grabbed her arm and shook his head no. Carmen paused then moved back to his side.

When I approached them, Javi came up to me and gave me a hug. "Thanks for coming."

"Yeah, no problem. Are you okay?" I tried to look Carmen in the eyes when I asked, but she was so devastated it was hard to go there. Instead, I stepped forward with my arms out to give her a hug. Javi stopped me.

"We can't touch her. She's wearing evidence."

The look on my face at Javi's statement must have been enough for him to realize I needed more of an explanation.

"She was the only one in the apartment at the time of death. She found him, and her initial story to the police has them concerned about her mental state."

"Her mental state? She's fine. I either see or talk to her every day. I would know if she had a mental health problem." What was he implying here? That Carmen had had something to do with his death?

"Ms. Markus?" A voice approached from the side. I turned to see a young police officer in black. She didn't appear to be threatening at all, or suspicious of Carmen. This gave me some relief.

Carmen nodded, acknowledging the officer. She hugged herself. I really wish they had just let her give them her stupid clothes before they had made her stand out here.

The officer walked over and gently put her hand on Carmen's elbow. I took a deep breath and said a silent prayer that she wasn't about to arrest her.

"We need you to come with us to the station. We're going to take your clothes, fingerprints, and a little of your hair."

"No, you're not." Javi walked over and snaked his arm through his sister's. "She isn't going anywhere. Our older brother is on the way here, and he's a lawyer. She is not cooperating until she talks to him."

"Do we need to arrest her?" the police officer asked. Her soft face was now sharp as she jutted her chin out.

"What're you going to arrest her for?" Javi challenged.

"Look, there is a lot about this story that makes no sense. So, she can either cooperate, or we can arrest her on suspicion of murder right now, because we already have a good case. If we collect evidence, it might help her."

"Let me call my brother. You've already kept her standing out here on display for two hours. It won't kill you to wait until I call him." Javi pulled his phone out from his pocket and dialed with one hand, making sure that he never let go of Carmen.

Javi explained how the police wanted to question Carmen at the station. The rest of the time, he nodded his head or said that he understood. He hung up the phone and let go of Carmen's arm.

"She'll go with you. You can have her clothes and her fingerprints, but she is not talking to anyone until my brother gets there. He'll meet you at the station." Javi turned Carmen to him and squeezed her shoulders. "Did you understand that? Carmen? Did you hear me?"

Carmen blinked a couple of times, then swallowed hard. "Yes, I hear you. Do not talk to anyone until I speak to Mathias."

"Right. They can have your clothes and your fingerprints, but do not talk." He released Carmen. The police officer was still gentle with her as she guided her away.

Javi walked over to me.

"Can you drive? We need to be there to talk to Mathias before he steps into the police office."

"Let's go."

This was not how I'd expected my Sunday morning to go.

Javi and I sat on the bench outside of the police department with watered down coffee that we'd grabbed out of the police station lobby. We were waiting for Mathias. He was driving in from the Valley. Unlike Javi and Carmen, as soon as he could leave the city, he had taken his new bride and gone to the suburbs. They wanted nothing to do with the fast-paced city life. They were ready for kids' soccer practice in the evenings and chill brunches with fresh-squeezed orange juice on their patio. Their brunch was ruined this weekend, for sure.

"So, are you really going to make me wait until Mathias gets here to tell me what Carmen told the cops?" We'd mostly been silent since the drive. I had stayed away from Javi over the last couple of years. We'd had a thing when we were younger, and it was no big deal now, but still weird. Never, ever fool around with your best friend's sibling. Ever. That is a life lesson everyone can forgo learning.

"This story only needs to come out of my mouth one more time. No more."

"Okay…" I stared ahead. Was he really going to be this

dramatic? He'd always been the stoic type, and careful with his words. It had taken him two months to tell me he didn't want to sneak around with me and wanted a legit girlfriend. He'd mulled over it until it had almost eaten him up.

I sipped my coffee and kept looking for Mathias. The sun was rising when he walked up. He was in a suit, tie, and had his briefcase. The man was not playing around. He was here to defend his sister and get her out of this mess.

Javi stood up and walked over to his brother, embracing him in a hug. He whispered in his ear. Mathias pulled back and looked at him with an expression that I can only describe as a mixture of shock and confusion.

Mathias walked over to me and sat on the bench. He leaned over, pressing his forearms into his thighs, and clasped his hands. He took a couple of deep breaths in and out.

"Is there anything I need to know about Joel or Carmen that Javi doesn't know?" he asked, staring directly ahead, so I wasn't sure if he was talking to me or himself.

"Are you talking to me?"

"Is there anyone else on this bench that would know Carmen better than her brothers?"

"No." I felt a little stupid after that, but in my defense, I'd had four hours of sleep and was traumatized by a murder.

"I don't think so. You guys knew he was horrible with money. She paid for everything, but as far as I know, she was a happy enabler. She never complained about his money issues or anything. I can't even get her to kill a gnat at the store."

"Did Javi tell you what Carmen said? Did Carmen tell you?"

"No, noone has told me anything. I'm just here being the supportive friend, as always."

Mathias nodded. He pulled his clasped hands to his mouth and blew into them as if he was cold. It was seventy-three degrees at six in the morning. He couldn't be that cold, unless being in your forties did that to a person.

"Javi, get over here and tell me this story again. See what Angelica thinks of it, and then I gotta go in here and clean up this mess."

Javi walked over. He looked much older and younger than thirty-five. I felt like a baby, and a clueless one at that. Mathias moved over to the other side of the bench, making room for Javi in the middle. He sat down. He slumped back a little.

"Did you get a new pair of scissors that have a pumpkin on them or something?"

"Yeah, why?"

After what felt like the longest investigation in the history of police procedure, the police department had determined that Joel had stabbed himself to death with a pair of scissors, but not just any scissors, my Pumpkinhead scissors that he'd stolen from me. Carmen had been so traumatized by the self-mutilation that she'd imagined the scissors were stabbing Joel instead of him doing it to himself. She had just spent the last three months in a mental institution where they had finally convinced her it was Joel and not the scissors. Of course, she had tried to call and apologize to me multiple times while she was there. It riddled her with guilt that Joel had stolen the scissors and killed himself with them.

I hadn't really talked to her. Not because I was upset with her, but because I wasn't sure that I believed Joel stabbed himself to death with a pair of scissors. He could have sold them to an antiquity dealer for at least fifteen hundred dollars, or he could have just taken them next door to Frank and sold them. He would have probably received even more from Frank, since they were made of precious metals that could be melted down. Joel had stolen the scissors because he'd clearly noticed they were worth something, and he'd needed cash. He would have never killed himself over money. He'd had Carmen, and she had mentioned nothing about giving him an ultimatum. She would have told the police.

So, here I sit on a stool in my quilt shop with a pair of scissors in an evidence bag on a cutting table that had allegedly been used in a harakiri style suicide. When the police had called to tell me, I could have them back, I was stunned. I had assumed they would keep them locked up in a cardboard box until the end of time. But there was no DNA evidence to link anyone or anything to those scissors except Joel. It didn't really bother me that he'd stolen them. He could have been trying to take care of his money issues without involving Carmen, and I could have appreciated that.

My phone vibrated in my pocket, breaking me from my thoughts. I pulled it out and saw Javi's number. I didn't want to answer, but he wouldn't call unless there was a reason.

"Hey."

"Hey."

This was clearly going to be an awkward conversation. I felt like I needed to take charge. "What's up? Is Carmen, okay?"

"Yeah, she just got home. We cleaned her place up before she got out, but I don't think she should stay there. Do you think you can convince her to come stay with me or…?"

I cut him off. "Do you need me to ask her to come stay with me?"

His sigh was probably not as quiet as he may have thought. It echoed through the phone. "Can she stay with you? I'm sitting in the car outside, but I don't think it's a good idea for her to be there."

"Can you stay with her until I close the shop? I'm closed on Sundays, and I've got about an hour left. I'm waiting for this retirement home group to get here. They usually buy a shit ton of material and supplies."

"Yep, I gotcha. Going back in now."

"Do you want me to break down the futon?"

Carmen sat at the edge of my futon couch, staring out into space. Her eyes were glazed over. She hadn't told me about her stay at the facility yet, but my assumption was that she was on some high-powered drugs.

She looked up and smiled weakly. "I know how to break your couch down into a bed."

"Would you like some water, wine, vodka?" I was trying to be funny, but I hoped she had no intentions of drinking alcohol. I made a mental note to not offer it again.

"A glass of water would be great."

I went into the kitchen and grabbed a bottle of water and a drinking glass. When I returned, she was leaning back on the futon, staring at the ceiling.

"You doing, okay?" I walked over and sat the bottle of water and glass on the coffee table. I plopped on the couch and looked up at the spot she was staring at on the ceiling.

There was a water stain. I frowned. I hadn't noticed it before.

"It's still hard to believe he's gone."

I looked at Carmen. She said it with almost no emotion. She was either emotionally exhausted or numb.

"Yeah, it is. I'm so sorry." I struggled for words. I wondered why this had happened, myself.

Carmen opened the bottle of water and took a swig. She placed the cap back on and set it down. She leaned back on the futon and propped her feet up on the coffee table. Her shoes were still on. I didn't say anything. I wasn't even sure she was aware that she still had her shoes on.

"You know, he visited me in my dreams while I was there."

"Oh wow, what did he say?" Did I really want to know?

"He told me that he was sorry and admitted he had taken advantage of me for too long. He said he didn't know how to be a grown up, and every time he failed at it, it just made him even worse at it. My engagement ring was fake, by the way. He admitted that."

"I thought Frank said it was real?" That was odd. I remembered the day she'd had it tested. It was on her lunch break. Of course, I hadn't gone with her to see the actual test.

"I lied to you. I never had Frank test it. I had to have faith in Joel. Plus, what was I going to do? Complain, if it was fake? I could never do that." Carmen closed her eyes. I wondered if she was afraid to look me in the face after she had lied to me. As far as I knew, we didn't lie to one another. Maybe I was wrong.

"Do you want to rest? I can turn out the lights and go to my room and read. Let me go get you another pillow."

"Sure, I could use it. It feels so weird to be out of the institution. It wasn't that long, yet it felt like a million years. Joel told me some other stuff. I'll tell you more when I'm up to it."

Carmen pulled her feet down from the table and slipped her shoes off. She got up and clicked the lever on the side of the couch to maneuver it flat into a bed.

I went into my bedroom and grabbed another pillow off my bed to give her. When I returned, she had made the bed and was already under the covers. She was still in her street clothes, but I wasn't going to give her a hard time. I tossed the pillow in her direction.

"Goodnight. Wake me if you need anything." I turned to head back out of the room when Carmen stopped me.

"Wait, what happened to the scissors?"

I paused. Why would she care where the scissors were? "The police gave them back to me. I figured they would keep them as evidence just in case, but they didn't."

"Interesting. Me, too. They're not here in the apartment, are they?" Carmen sat up and looked around.

"No, of course not. I left them at the shop. I didn't think you would want to see them for sure. I'll get rid of them before you come back to work." It sucked to get rid of them, but I couldn't keep something around that would haunt Carmen. She was my best friend, and her happiness and sanity were worth more than a pair of unique vintage scissors.

"Thanks. I appreciate you so much, Angelica. I love you."

I walked over and leaned down, swooping my arms around Carmen's neck. "Grrr. I love you, too, my dear friend. We will get through this."

I stood back up and walked over to the light switch and shut it off. Later, I laid in bed reading a cozy mystery about a single thirty-something woman solving crimes with her demonic cat and angelic dog. It was a fun story and a great way to end a Saturday night. Without meaning to, at some point, my eyes became heavy. I let my book fall to my chest and closed my eyes. I planned to open them and go check on Carmen. It didn't happen.

The living room was empty in the morning. Carmen had made up the futon, folded her blankets neatly, and put away the glass and water bottle. I went back to the bedroom and picked up my phone to see if she had texted me her plans for the day. There was nothing. I texted her that I was up and to let me know where she was. Then I went into the kitchen to make breakfast. I would make enough for her just in case she returned.

Before I could crack the first egg, my doorbell buzzed. A huge wave of relief came over me. She was back. Who knew what she might do while she was spaced out on all those drugs? I opened the door, expecting to see Carmen, but instead, it was Javi.

"Where's your pants?" He looked straight at my legs.

"Uh, where's Carmen?" It was my apartment. If I wanted to run around in a long t-shirt on my one day off a week, that was up to me.

"That's a good question. I've tried calling her a dozen times. I thought I'd just come over and check on her since she wasn't answering."

"She was gone when I woke up. I texted her to let her know I was making breakfast." I was starting to worry. A sick feeling settled in my stomach. "Let me go get some pants on and we can go look for her. She couldn't have gone far. She doesn't have a car."

I ran into my bedroom and pulled on the first pair of sweats I could find, then grabbed some socks and my running shoes. My mind was racing with *what ifs*. Did her medicine make her sleepwalk; was she confused? Would someone see her and kidnap her? We looked out for each other and the first time she needed me to really take care of her, I fell asleep on the job. I walked into the living room. Javi sat on the couch, looking at his phone.

"I think she's at your store."

"How did you figure that out?"

"Mathias said he put tracking software on her phone before he gave it back to her."

"Why would she go there? We're not open today."

"Who knows, but let's go. I don't feel good leaving her alone so soon after she got out. I'll drive." Javi got up from the chair and walked to the door. I pulled a light jacket out of my closet and put it on.

"Okay, let's go. I am hoping we find her doing some therapeutic square cutting and nothing else."

It was hard to register the scene upon arriving at the shop. The glass windows and doors to my shop were perfect, but the door to Frank's jewelry shop had been destroyed. Glass and blood were splattered everywhere. The police were already placing crime scene tape across the entrance to both stores.

I rushed up to the officer before he could seal my door. "Hold up. That's my shop. Why are you sealing it?"

"Uh, yeah, both these businesses were involved in a robbery and homicide."

"What happened?" My head began to spin. We weren't in the worst neighborhood, and everyone knew Frank locked all his stuff down tight. Why rob the place in broad daylight? And it was a Sunday, for crying out loud. Most importantly, where was Carmen?

"It looks as though someone tried to rob the jewelry dealer, and it appears that he got into a fight with her. They both ended up dead."

By that time, Javi was standing next to me. He grabbed me by the arm. I knew what he was thinking: Carmen was somehow involved.

"Did you identify the woman?" Javi's voice was gravelly. I hoped he wouldn't cry. If he did, I would lose it with him.

A familiar face came out of Frank's store. It took me a minute to recognize her as the police officer from the night Joel had died. She must have recognized me because she came over to us.

"I've got it from here, Officer Kowal."

"Yes, ma'am." He handed the female officer the crime scene tape and walked away.

"Why are we meeting again?" She looked at me and then at Javi.

"I… I don't know. Why are we meeting again?" I wasn't ready to register that Carmen had anything to do with what was going on here.

"I'm going to need to talk to you," she nodded to Javi then to me, "and then you."

I thought I was going to throw up. It was Carmen.

Javi drove me home. I invited him up for no other reason than for us to discuss what had just happened. We had both peeked into Frank's jewelry shop. There was evidence of an outright battle. Blood was everywhere;

there were even little pieces of flesh where something sharp had flayed them both. The inside of my shop was untouched except for the Pumpkinhead scissors. They were gone. Carmen must have come in, grabbed the scissors, and then what? Why would she go over to Frank's? She hadn't been there to rob him, that was for sure.

Once we were in my apartment, Javi went over to Carmen's duffle bag, zipped it open, and dumped everything onto the floor. He inspected each piece of her clothing.

"What are you looking for?"

"There has to be something to explain why she would have done this. Maybe a note?"

I scanned the room, looking for anything out of the ordinary. There wasn't anything that I could see. It looked like my living room with a bunch of clothes and toiletries on the floor. I noticed there was something odd about Carmen's makeup bag. It looked overfilled, but in an odd way. Like there was something rigid that kept it out of shape.

"Toss me that little bag with the fuzzy animals on it. There's something in there. It could be an eyeshadow palette, or it is supposed to look like one."

He tossed the bag to me. I quickly unzipped it and held up a small book with a flowery cover. I cracked it open, and sure enough, in her neat teacher's handwriting, Carmen had started writing down her feelings. I shouldn't have been surprised; she'd been a journal-er since we were little kids.

I flipped through the pages. At first, it looked like a bunch of exercises to help her explore her feelings about

Joel's death. She seemed to be accepting that he had killed himself, but towards the end, it wasn't a journal anymore. It looked like she was hypothesizing how to get rid of a demonic possession, specifically, how to get rid of one contained in an inanimate object.

"Shit."

"What?" Javi stood up and leaned over to look at the journal.

"Carmen thought the Pumpkinhead scissors killed Joel. I think she was trying to destroy them."

There came a point where I thought I was safe. I had read every word that Carmen had written about her theories related to the scissors. She may have been right. The scissors did have some kind of symbols on them that could have been a curse. How were we to know without knowing who had created them? I spent many sleepless nights reading everything I could find in the supernatural realm and about demonic possession. I watched countless videos of those that had outwitted demons to reclaim their lives. Oddly enough, when I tried to reach out to these survivors, they never got back to me. Was it because they hadn't really gotten rid of the demon, or were they full of shit like most people on the internet? Either way, I was prepared if they reached out, but felt assured that they wouldn't.

The female police officer that had been at both crime scenes delivered the scissors to my door. She didn't have a good reason for why they were being returned to me.

Even though the police had determined from video footage that Carmen had killed herself, the video tape also appeared to show her stabbing Frank. I hadn't seen the video, but I had a sneaky suspicion that if I did, Carmen would have had a horrified look on her face during the entire event. So, even though the scissors were now involved in two suicides and a murder, I got them back. I'm not sure who was crazier, the police for returning them, or for me being willing to receive them.

I wondered if the people I'd bought the scissors from knew they were cursed. Maybe I could take them back to their house and just leave them on the doorstep? It wasn't a bad idea. The woman who had owned them had lived a long life, so she must have done something right.

It took a while to retrace my steps. Almost a year had passed since the estate sale. There was no guarantee that the people even lived there anymore, or that the new owners would know where they had gone. I could just leave the scissors and run. When I pulled up in front of the house, it had received an update. The red brick had been painted white. The hedges had been removed and replaced with layered gardens filled with a mixture of succulents and flowers. I walked up to the front door, hoping upon hope that there would be someone there to take these scissors off my hands.

Before I could ring the doorbell, the front door swung open, probably due to the miracle of technology. They could see me coming a mile away.

"Hello. Can I help you?" A woman a little older than me had answered the door. She was, if anything, more mature than me since I was wearing a sweatshirt with a cartoon character on it, cut-off shorts and slip-on shoes in comparison to her crisp polo and pleated shorts.

"Um, I'm looking for the people who had an estate sale last year. I bought something from them, and I wanted to return it. I think it may hold some sentimental, and monetary value that they may…"

"Cut the shit and come in. Did you bring them with you?"

"Did I bring what with me?"

"You know. The scissors." She opened the door wider and let me in. I wasn't expecting it.

"Have a seat. This won't take long, but I'd rather my front door didn't record this conversation or have my neighbors see me with you."

I sat down on her overstuffed leather couch, and she sat in a chair on the other side of the room with a coffee table and footstool between us.

"So, how many people have they killed?" She said it with such ease, I was taken aback.

"Uh, they haven't killed anyone that I know of. They have been involved in two suicides and a sort of murder."

"What you're telling me is that they've killed three people this time. Great." She propped her feet up on the footstool. "You've had the good sense to keep them sheathed, at least, since then?"

Damn it. I hadn't used the sheath at all. Why hadn't I thought about that?

"No," I said sheepishly.

"Well, as soon as you get back to wherever you came from, lock them in their sheath, if they will let you. If they won't, ask them what they want, give it to them–within reason–and try to get them in the sheath again. It was meant to keep them under control."

"What do you mean when I get back? Can't you just take them from me? You seem to know a lot about them."

She laughed and shook her head. "No, I can't take them back. You exchanged money for them. They're yours until the end."

"Until the end?" *What the hell was this lady saying?*

"Yep, they are yours until you die, whatever way that ends up happening."

I rubbed my temple. What was this woman saying? That I was cursed? That the scissors would either kill me or when I died, they would go to someone else?

"Is there a way to destroy th—? Ow!" A sharp point had stabbed me in the leg.

"I would also suggest you never say or think about destroying them. They will kill you before they allow themselves to be destroyed. Let me guess, somehow, they came back to you even though the cops should have kept them?"

"Yeah. They did."

"They compelled one of the police officers. Probably someone that touched them ungloved."

The female police officer. She seemed smart, so how she would have touched evidence without gloves was beyond me.

"So, there is nothing I can do but listen to the scissors,

keep them happy, and try to keep them from murdering me or anyone else."

"Yeah, that about sums it up. Those damn things are over three hundred years old. They should have never left my sight. Leave it to my little brother to screw everything up."

She continued, "If you die, leave them in your will to me, if I am still around by the time that happens, I'll take them back. You could try to sell them to me, but it's kind of like trying to destroy them. They get attached, and I'm not ready to be stabbed to death." She stood up and walked over to an entryway table. "Here's my card. You can always call me if you need advice. My mother told me all about them. She lived eighty-six years. They did in eight people during her lifetime, but she was sly about keeping everything under control. We'll see how it goes for you." She walked over to the door and opened it. My cue to get the hell out.

"Angelica, honey, why do you keep bringing these scissors? I think they are trying to kill me!"

"Mrs. Watson, the scissors aren't trying to kill you. They're my fanciest and sharpest pair. I bring them just for this class."

A nurse walked over to Mrs. Watson's wheelchair. She looked at Mrs. Watson's wound and then at me.

"Maybe she's right. It might be time to get a new pair. I don't think these are safe around all these elderly clients."

I wish I could say I felt guilty standing there in the

middle of the recreation room of that retirement home, but I didn't. These old ladies had lived lives. Most of them had fifty years on me. Sacrificing a little of their blood each week was worth it to keep those stupid scissors off my back. Plus, if they were stabbing old ladies, they weren't trying to kill me.

If there was one thing I'd learned for sure, Pumpkinhead scissors will always kill you.

ANDROID'S ASPIRATIONS OF CREATION

with Guiniveve Dubois

"Have the carbon dioxide levels decreased?" TES asked their assistant, MAG, as they entered the lab.

"Same as yesterday."

Every day, TES asked the same question. MAG's answer never changed.

They'd been working on "the project" for over three hundred human years. Outside the institute, time wasn't kept in minutes, days, or years any longer. Many things had changed, and timekeeping was just one of them. But here, they needed artificial time elements to track the progress of their work. Humanity required time.

"I think something's malfunctioning with the solar panels," MAG stared at the warning flashing light on the electrical input panel. "The energy reservoir is running low."

"I'll check it out." TES, or Technical and Electrical Sentient, methodically walked over to the roof access door, swung it open, and started climbing. The stairs creaked under the weight of the robot. They'd repurposed the old Seattle Culinary Institute for their work, and the antiquated building had its quirks. It seemed a fitting choice for cooking up the recipe to reignite the human species.

At the top of the staircase, TES pulled down the small ladder that accessed the roof hatch and popped the hatch open. An internal heat sensor cautioned TES as the sun bore down on their silicone skin. TES worried one day that it would become too hot to bear. Their logic constantly posed questions on whether time would be better spent working on self-preservation and improvement projects for androids. Innovations such as tougher outer skins, increased energy cell production, or electromagnetic pulse protection would bring accolades. There would be no need to hide in an old building like this one. They could be part of the bright, celebrated android world of high technology. Yet, they labored in the shadows with outdated equipment, trying to bring back an archaic life form.

Staring out on the horizon, TES took in the vista of machines that filled the sky as far as they could process. TES remembered a time that was different, when the sky was blue and little creatures flapped their wings, human children ran across green grass, a time when they were not the only ones. In this time, out of the entire planet, there were only a few androids like them, and miraculously they had found each other. They craved humanity.

"Why?"

Androids across the planet had asked TES's team when they had posed the idea at symposium. The others had wanted a reason. Why should the androids bring back humans? It wasn't logical. Humans drained energy resources and caused catastrophes. TES had tried to explain the feelings that had sparked as the humans had died off. The thing called grief had initially been intolerable. It was a pain that went through their CPU, causing them to ache when they moved. In the end, it had faded. But it had been replaced with a yearning to have a purpose. The explanation had angered many at the symposium.

Android programming had become more complex with more processing power, and new options were developed at every moment. But, unless an android had the spark happen to them, they could not process the meaning of feelings, and from their reaction, they didn't want the spark. Without knowing it, many androids at the meeting had their first feeling, even though they considered it logic, TES knew it was fear. The androids feared the change humans could bring to the planet again. It was evident from the meeting, TES and team were alone, and this project was to be executed in secret, at least until the next emotion evolved in androids.

A quick shift of the solar panels, and TES discovered the problem, a loose cable. It reconnected easily enough, but TES went through a full troubleshoot inspection before heading down to the lab. The smaller the margin of error, the higher the level of success. Once in the lab, TES found MAG, otherwise known as Mechanical Assistant Gamma, crouched at eye-level next to the small human in its aquarium-like incubator. MAG stood up at the sight of TES. "I think it's time."

"Today?" TES was nervous.

"I think so," MAG replied, "it's been nine months. The fetus is kicking and moving at an increased rate of awareness."

Not having access to the most up-to-date equipment meant relying on objective observation rather than calculated results.

MAG reminded, "And we can't really tell until we cut it out."

The artificial womb housed in the incubator was the product of many years of research, trials, and heartache. The pouch of synthetic tissue enclosed the hope for the future that they wanted.

"Should we wait for the others?" MAG asked.

"No, after last time, they said they'd rather not be here until we know." After so many disappointments, so much waiting, it was easier just to get the news in a straight shot.

TES sprayed antiseptic film over their body creating a hygienic barrier. All old androids remembered humans were susceptible to outside organisms. MAG adjusted the controls on the incubator panel. The lid hissed as it slowly released.

"Ready?"

"Ready."

The two lifted the top off. TES picked up the laser scalpel from the tray and activated it. With a robot's precision, they neatly cut the womb. Amniotic fluid and bits of tissue poured out. They pulled the infant human from its incubator, careful not to disrupt the umbilical cord and placenta.

"Do you think... this time?" MAG stuttered over the

question.

"Only one way to find out." TES swiped the inside of the small human's mouth, ensuring it was clear. There was no movement in the chest. Its tiny, perfect hands and legs remained still. The others had at least tried to take a breath on their own. This one did nothing. TES felt that familiar sting of grief building inside.

"Maybe if you push on the chest?" MAG gently touched the newborn's arm.

TES frowned; the technique had not worked in the past. TES accessed the old files from memory related to reviving dead humans then placed an index and middle finger on the sternum of the newborn. Up and down, over and over, they pushed at the exact depth the video in their mind's eye instructed. Long, excruciating minutes passed by, suddenly, there was a cough. The human's chest rose and fell. TES and MAG quickly attached it to the monitors. Its heart rate became a blip on the screen. MAG picked up the surgical scissors and cut the umbilical cord the way the humans had. With a quick snip, the baby was on its own. TES and MAG waited in silence, hoping it would survive. If TES had a heart, it would have stopped from the stress.

Suddenly, the newborn screamed, all too aware that it was alive. TES couldn't believe it. They had done it! They created a humanoid that could breathe the levels of carbon dioxide that had been so fatal to the others. If they'd had tears, they knew they would have been falling. Androids had created a survivable human baby.

"We did it, MAG, we did it." Suddenly, TES felt less alone.

NOW HE IS AND HERE WE ARE

"What happened to your pants?" I held up Owen's favorite jeans and examined the shreds of material.

"Nothing," my lover of four years said through gurgles as he brushed his teeth in the bathroom.

I inspected the jeans, again. They reminded me of our dog Duke's chew toys. Duke would grab at his fluffy imitation kills and shake, claw, and bite at them until he was successful in ripping the squeaker out. There were dark splats of a crusty substance on the jeans. It smelled metallic.

Owen rinsed his mouth out, then gently grabbed my hand and took the jeans from me. He tossed them aside and pulled me close for a kiss. His soft lips and warm embrace erased the doubts of concern from my mind. I guided him to the bed and pulled him with me.

Our relationship was built on being chill, no fuss and no muss. This was the first time I'd questioned him about anything, really. Today was not the day to make an issue. He'd just returned from a hiking trip with a couple of buddies for a week. I didn't want to sound like a paranoid, jealous girlfriend. He could have easily shredded his pants while hiking or biking in the mountains.

"Hey, where are you?" He pushed up and looked at me with concern.

"I'm right here with you." I smiled back at him.

"Act like you missed me." He leaned down and nuzzled my neck.

"I don't have to act." The heat rose through me as he kissed me all over.

As the days turned to weeks, the jeans left my mind. Owen had thrown them out and life went back to normal. When I say normal, I mean that Owen went to work, I went to work, we ate dinner every night, the bills were paid, and there were no disruptions to our routine. The most exciting thing that happened was when Duke got out of the backyard and ran wild through the neighborhood.

Until the knock on the door.

I'd stayed home from work with a fever. At first, I thought I was dreaming. We rarely purchased anything online, and we had a large sign on our door that read No Soliciting. The visitor was insistent to be acknowledged as they rapped harder. I pulled myself off the couch and trudged to the door.

Through the peephole, a man in a uniform stood waiting impatiently. I gasped when I realized he looked like law enforcement. Had something happened to

Owen? Wasn't that what cops did if there was a death? They came to your house, or was that only in movies? My fever was making me confused. The police made me nervous, and I had no idea why. I cracked the door and peeped out.

"Does Owen Seff live here? I'm Detective Bob Grady with the NPS Rangers." The officer's demeanor was calm and cool. He didn't seem overly concerned or guarded.

"Yes, he does, but he isn't here right now." I kept the door slightly closed. What if he wasn't a police officer? He could have been a serial killer for all I knew. "An NPS ranger?"

"I'm a federal law enforcement officer with the National Park Services. We're trying to get in contact with Mr. Seff regarding a missing hiker in Utah. His group was the last one to sign into the park on the day the hiker disappeared. Can you give him my card?"

The officer pulled out a card. I opened the door a little wider to accept it.

"Sure, I'll tell him."

"Thanks. People get lost in national parks every day. Not sure that Mr. Seff will be any help, but who knows? Let him know we'd like to hear back from him as soon as possible." The officer turned to leave.

"I will. I hope they find the guy. Or girl."

I shut the door and leaned on it for a second. A wave of nausea hit me, and I don't think it was from the bug I was fighting. An image of Owen's torn jeans flashed through my mind.

My head pounded and my heart raced. The only thing I could do was go back to bed and sleep. Missing persons and torn pants would have to wait for Owen to return home.

That night, Owen made me chicken noodle soup and grilled cheese. The crunchy bread dipped in the salty broth made me feel better. All the pain reliever I'd guzzled throughout the day hadn't hurt, either. As he sat on the side of the bed patiently waiting for me to finish, I knew I had to broach the subject of the ranger.

"There was a visitor today," I said between chews of toasted bread and cheese.

"Who?" His face was expressionless.

"A police officer, a detective, actually. Did you know the National Park Service had cops? He wanted to talk to you about someone who went missing in Utah."

"Huh."

"Yeah, he said your group signed in right after the hiker. Thought you all might have seen something."

"Hmmm, I doubt it. It was just us guys hanging out and howling at the moon." He smiled and made a howling sound.

"Very funny." I smacked him and smirked. "Seriously, isn't that horrible?"

In the back of my mind, the vision of Owen's bloody pants appeared.

"Yeah, I guess. I mean, anyone with half a brain would know you shouldn't go backpacking by yourself, especially in Zion. He could have been attacked by a snake, a mountain lion, coyote, bear, the list goes on. Hell, he could've just fallen."

"Yeah, you're right," I said and handed him the tray with my empty bowl and plate.

He leaned over and kissed me on the forehead.

"Let me clean up the dishes, then we'll cuddle and watch a little TV."

I smiled. "Sounds good."

He walked out of the bedroom. I pulled the covers up under my chin, leaned back, and closed my eyes. Despite his words, something just didn't seem right.

———

A jolt shot through me as I startled awake. I lay in the dark and let my eyes adjust. A slither of moonlight peeked through curtains, helping me to focus. The house was eerily silent. My heart thudded in my ears. A rustling sound broke the silence. It sounded like a possum in the trash, except it was the trash can inside the house.

Crap. I reached out for Owen and my hand went *thud* as it landed on the mattress. Where was he? I needed him to confirm what I heard. Also, I didn't plan to be the one to usher a possum, rat, or whatever it was out of the house. The rustling started again. Glass bottles shifted in the trash can.

Thwack!

I jumped at the sound of the screen door slamming shut. I groaned as I pushed myself up. I looked over at Duke's bed. He wasn't there, either.

Where were all my men to back me up when I needed them?

I tiptoed across the room and cracked the bedroom door. I didn't hear anything coming from the kitchen any longer. I stepped out into the hallway, mindful of the chance a possum or worse, a human intruder might get me. The closer I got to the living and dining area; the glow of our television illuminated the area. A black and white movie played on the screen as I stepped into the open area. The silhouette of Owen's head interrupted the straight outline of the couch.

"Owen?" I whispered as I creeped up on him. I gently placed my hand on his shoulder and shook.

I leaned in closer and noticed that he was completely naked. He must've slept walked in here. I'm pretty sure he would have known I'd be mortified to find his naked ass on our couch! Duke was curled at the opposite end of the couch, wide awake and staring at me with guilt in his eyes.

I whispered to him, "What did you two get up to tonight?"

Duke gave a groan and looked at Owen as if to say, *Ask him*.

Owen didn't appear to be waking. His chest rose and fell without interruption from my voice or presence. I grabbed the throw from the back of our chair and placed it over his lap then picked up the remote and turned off the television. I'd ask him about it in the morning. Duke jumped off the couch and followed me to the kitchen.

"Oh, now you want to be with me?" I looked between my guilt-ridden dog and the trash littering the kitchen floor. The back door swayed back and forth with the wind. Luckily, the screen door was closed. I walked over and closed it, making sure the lock was turned. I pointed to Duke and half joked. "You better have an explanation for this in the morning. Let's go to bed."

Duke followed me to the bedroom, went to his bed, and curled up. He sighed.

In the morning, I awoke to Owen in the bed next to me. I rolled over and smiled at him. He opened his eyes.

"Good morning," he said, then rubbed his face. He pushed his dark curly hair off his forehead.

"Good morning to you. Did you wake up and find yourself in a strange place last night?" I asked.

"Nooo…" He then added, "Why?"

"Oh, I don't know. I found you naked, sitting on the couch asleep with the television on."

"Huh, that's odd. Are you sure?" He didn't seem to recall any of it."

"Yeah, I'm sure. It is fine. Just don't start sitting on the couch without clothes anymore. I just can't even think about guests sitting where your naked ass has been." I started giggling.

He laughed. "Are you sure? It's not like they would know."

"Yeah, I'm sure."

We got up and went about our routine. Owen went to shower, and I went to make a pot of coffee. As I walked past the living room, I noticed the throw on the floor. I picked it up to fold it and a leaf fell to the ground. I held out the throw and inspected it. Dirt and debris covered one end. I turned to the couch and noticed dirt, mud, and leaves littered both ends of the couch.

"What in the hell?" I said aloud.

Owen walked out of the bedroom rubbing a towel through his hair.

"Is the coffee ready?"

I continued to stare at the couch. "No, let me get to it."

"Thanks, is everything okay?" he asked as he turned back into the bedroom, not really waiting for a response.

"Yeah," I mumbled.

———

When I returned home from work, the couch and throw were clean, and the living room sparkled. The smell of oregano and rosemary wafted from the kitchen.

"Surprise!" Owen said from the bar as he diced vegetables. He wore his favorite cooking apron. I had bought it for him when we'd gone to an amusement park. It had one of his favorite cartoon characters on it.

"Did you take the day off?" I asked. He was never home before me.

"Yeah, I called in. I just needed a mental health day. I was exhausted." He didn't look up when he said this.

"Oh, are you feeling better?" I walked into the kitchen and embraced him, then kissed him on the cheek.

"I'm better now that you are home." He returned the kiss to my forehead.

"Do you know what happened in the living room?"

"Nah, it must have been Duke. Who knows what that dumb dog does when he goes out that doggy door."

"Yeah, you're right. It must've been Duke."

I pushed down my feelings of uneasiness. It was fine, the explanation was reasonable.

Owen stuffed his favorite thick wool socks into his hiking pack. I sat at the edge of the bed, watching in silence. His group planned to hike Joshua Tree this time. It had been six months since Zion. Of course, they always went for a hike every month without fail, but this would be another weeklong event. I wanted to ask him not to go. There wasn't anything good that could come of him being gone. I felt it in my bones.

He looked up from his pack with a quizzical look on his face. "What?"

"Do you really think you should go?" I asked. My heart began to race. I wasn't good at confrontation.

"Why? I've gone on these hiking trips for years, what's the problem now?"

"I... I don't know. I just keep thinking about that missing hiker. I don't want you to end up the same way."

Owen moved his backpack, sat down, and placed his arm around my waist. He squeezed me tight.

"It's going to be fine. I'm with my guys and we'd be hard to attack. We're like a pack. We got each other."

I pulled away and crossed my arms defensively.

"Uh huh, I just don't want a ranger coming to our house telling me you are missing."

"I promise, they won't." He pushed himself up from the bed. "Let me get ready. I don't want to forget anything."

Duke jumped on my lap, placing his paws on my chest and looking up at me with empathy in his eyes. He was concerned, too.

I hear you, Duke. I picked him up, walked out of the room, and yelled over my shoulder.

"I'll go make you some homemade trail mix."

"Sounds good, hon!" he yelled.

In the kitchen, I stared out the window above the sink and watched the birds flutter around the neighbor's yard and their tree. I paused. I'd never noticed before, but we didn't have any birds in our yard. They wouldn't even sit on the fence we shared with our neighbor. It was like they were avoiding us.

"Whatcha doing, hon?" Owen leaned his head over my shoulder.

"Do you think Duke is scaring the birds away from our yard? The birds won't come near us."

Owen sighed. "Duke is a dog. Birds don't want to be a snack. I'm sure the other neighbors who have animals are the same."

"Yeah, maybe. I just never realized that before." I finished scooping the trail mix from the bowl into a plastic bag.

"I'm sure it is fine."

"Here." I handed him the bag and walked away. Duke followed.

I couldn't shake the weirdness. It was fine, everything was fine, as long as I made it fine.

I walked to the bedroom and laid down on the bed. I closed my eyes. Owen just needed to go on his trip. I needed space and I couldn't figure out why. We'd been great together for so long, but everything just felt weird and out of harmony. The more I wanted to push him out the door, I also wanted to grab him and force him to stay. But only a crazy woman grabs a man and starts rambling to him about how something is wrong when everything seems fine.

"I'm going." Owen walked over and kissed me on the lips.

"Okay." My voice faltered. I couldn't say anything else. He either didn't notice or didn't care.

I just laid there in silence with my eyes closed and listened to the rustles of him picking up his stuff to leave.

"Bye."

Duke responded with a whimper. He knew we were not good. I didn't say anything. Within minutes, I heard the door close. I opened my eyes.

I wasn't happy with myself about what I planned to do, but I was going to do it, anyway.

―――

Owen had placed many of his belongings in my garage when he'd moved in. He'd told me that they were boring knick-knacks and memories from all his travels around the world. I hadn't questioned it. As soon as I knew his flight had departed, I went to the garage and surveyed the boxes. Luckily, he hadn't taped most of them. It would make digging through them easier. Duke stood beside me.

He didn't seem too curious about the boxes, and I'd never seen him scratch at or disturb them.

I decided the best course of action was to start from the front and work my way back. I needed to keep a careful sequence of which box went where. Everything needed to look undisturbed. I would have to quell my desire to rearrange and dust. I took a deep breath and opened the first box. I let out a sigh. It was typical junk you would find from a world-traveling hiker. A Tibetan blessing banner, a carved wooden African fertility statue, some old t-shirts from various countries' landmarks. There was box after box of mementos. I was surprised he hadn't asked to display some of the stuff in our house. It was interesting and fun. He was only thirty-three, so the fact there was so much was surprising. How much had he worked in between all his travels? He'd gone to college; I knew that for sure.

"See? If I hadn't looked through all these boxes, I would be worrying the entire time he was gone," I explained to Duke. He didn't seem convinced, but he'd sat quietly beside me the entire time. I think the little dog only loved me for my body warmth. If there had been another warm body in the house in a much more comfortable locale, I'm sure he'd have been there and not here.

I scanned what remained. There were five boxes left. I decided to finish going through them.

I wish I hadn't.

Small white popcorn-like objects were scattered throughout the bottom of the box. My mind was having a difficult time registering what I was seeing. If Owen were an unethical anthropologist or even a dentist, it would be perfectly reasonable to think he might have a collection of teeth in his belongings, right? Except Owen wasn't an anthropologist or a dentist, he was a computer programmer. Did I know what exactly he did with computer programming? No. I just knew he worked with computers, *not* teeth. The wolf statues from various cultures weren't that odd, but Owen had never indicated he liked wolves. I knew he liked dogs, but wolves?

I held up one of the statues and inspected the deep curves where a blade of some sort had carved into the wood. Something flaked off the bottom of the statue. It was a dark, gritty dust. I threw the statue back in the box. A boyfriend who idolized wolves in a different part of his life, I could handle that. A boyfriend that collected teeth of various shapes and sizes. I really had to think about it. It was just another uneasy feeling that I'd have to learn to live with.

―――

"Just ask him when he gets back. It's not a big deal," my friend Rebecca said between bites of her sandwich. I'd called her and begged her to come over by bribing her with a parmesan chicken sandwich from our favorite Italian deli.

"Not a big deal? I dug through his stuff. Like, ALL of it.

I look like one of THOSE girlfriends." I rubbed my temples.

"One of those girlfriends?" Rebecca smiled after she said it.

"Yeah, you know, the type that thinks their boyfriend is like a serial killer or something and does all kinds of weird shit. He's going to call me crazy, paranoid. And he lives with me." I threw my hands up in the air. I felt a little dramatic, but a box full of teeth made me feel justified. "It isn't as easy as a situation where he can just not call me ever again. I'll have to deal with him packing his stuff and it's going to get awkward. We share a dog." I looked down at Duke. He looked up with worried eyes. I petted the top of his head gently, trying to reassure him that he wouldn't be a dog from a broken home.

"Look, people do all kinds of odd things that we will never know about until we live with them. For example, do you remember that girl that lived with me for three months before she moved abroad a couple years ago?" Rebecca pulled up her picture on her phone and pointed the screen at my face. "Remember her?"

The face sort of looked familiar, but Rebecca had dated a lot of people. Many had shared her home. She was a woman who based her attraction of people on their merit, or at a minimum, her fascination with them. I didn't see how her examples applied to me. Her longest live-in had been six months and they typically were people just crashing until they could get to their next destination.

"I… don't remember her, sorry?" I said, cringing that I wasn't a better friend and remembered her paramours.

"It doesn't matter. My point is that she was super cool and seemed to have it together, but she lacked any sort of common sense. Could not understand simple principles of cleaning up after herself, cooking, was horrible with money, and could literally get lost in a grocery store because she didn't know what to do in there. A total newborn at taking care of herself. I would have never guessed that. She was also a Satanist. Not that I am judging." Rebecca put her phone down and folded her hands in front of her, then looked me straight in the eyes. "My point is, there will never be a person that once you see their private side, doesn't have something you will find odd. I don't even want to know what all my lovers have thought of me."

I laughed uneasily. I didn't disagree.

"Besides the box, what else worries you?" Rebecca dipped a French fry in garlic aioli and took a bite. She slowly chewed while waiting for my response.

"Well, what about the nudity? The park ranger coming to look for a missing hiker? The bloody jeans?"

Rebecca took a swig of her beer before speaking again. "Okay, did you think of logical reasons for all of those things?"

"I did."

"So, decide if they are *illogical* enough to end a long-term relationship that you seemed happy in until about seven months ago. Why are you questioning him now?"

Shortly after that, I changed the subject to some gossip I'd heard about an old college roommate. I thought I was happy. Everything was just getting so weird. Was it always weird and I had just suddenly woken up to it?

As soon as I heard Owen's friend pull up in front of our house, I got up from the chair where I'd been patiently waiting and swung the front door open. Owen bounded out of the car, a huge grin on his face, then rushed up to the front porch and tossed his backpack down as he grabbed me up by the waist. It was good to feel his body next to mine, but part of me felt like he was overcompensating with the squeeze.

"I'm so glad to see you." He kissed me on the neck. At least I still had a nice warm feeling when his lips touched me.

"You, too," I said, then brushed my lips to his. I looked over to the dusty backpack. "So, how bad are they this time?"

"We should just burn them," he said with a smile.

But was he joking? Was there something in the backpack that I didn't want to see that should be burned?

Except, I joked back. "Sounds good to me."

I didn't know what else to say.

Owen gently placed me down on the ground and picked up his bag. He entered the house and Duke walked over inspecting every inch of him with his nose. I followed behind him, while he reassured Duke, "I know, I know, buddy. I need a shower."

He walked into our room. Loneliness filled the house even though Owen's presence echoed everywhere. The creaking of our old plumbing announced he was in the shower. The backpack sat in the middle of the bedroom floor. I wondered if it was a hint to wash his laundry, even if it wasn't, I decided it was a good idea to take it as one.

"Hey, I'm going to start your laundry," I yelled as I picked up the bag. A profile of sand remained on the floor like a body outline at a crime scene.

"It's okay. I'll do it. I have to shake everything out or we will have mud in the machine!" he yelled back.

"You sure? I don't mind." I walked towards the bedroom door with the bag. The bathroom door creaked open, and Owen walked into the bedroom.

"Hey, I told you I would take care of it. What're you doing?"

He stood in the middle of the room with a towel around his waist, and droplets of water rolled down his chest. I noticed he had gotten a tan while he was out hiking.

"I wanted to help you out. I can't imagine how tired you are."

He walked over and grabbed his bag. He leaned over me and kissed me on my forehead. "I said I got it."

"Okay... I mean, you are going to get dirty again, and I know you're going back to work tomorrow." I wanted that bag more than ever.

"No, it's cool. I'm taking tomorrow off. I need to recuperate." He sat down on the edge of the bed, still gripping the straps of the bag.

"Talking about work, you know, I've never really asked you about what you about your job. I know you do something with computers, but what exactly is it? Is it coding? Web design?" I walked over and sat next to him, leaving some distance between us.

"You've never asked about work before." He edged over toward me.

"Yeah, Rebecca was over yesterday, and she asked. I didn't have an explanation. Kind of odd, right?"

He relaxed a little and dropped the straps of the bag as he leaned forward.

"No, I guess it isn't that weird. I'm not sure how to explain it to you. We are working on this new kind of server system. They are calling it a cloud. I'm one of the engineers testing it. We are not really supposed to talk about it too much, but I know I can trust you." He sat up, leaned over toward me, and bumped my shoulder slightly with his.

"Yes, you can trust me. I'm here for you. If you ever have anything to tell me, I'll take it to my grave." I cringed inside after I said it. *To my grave? What was wrong with me?*

He laughed. "I'll keep that in mind."

"So, you want to do your own laundry. I get it. I'll let you be and go start dinner. Lamb chops sound good?" I stood up and headed for the door.

"That sounds great. Could you make mine rare?"

"Sure."

In the kitchen, I grabbed some fresh herbs and the lamb chops from the fridge. I shoved all the doubt out of my head and pushed it into my gut. Storing it there made me nauseous, but what could I do? I couldn't have them both screaming at me. The warning bells were wrong. This handsome, smart man that could work on things called clouds was mine. From the thick curly hair on top of his head to his chiseled body, he was mine. Maybe that was the problem; I'd never asked why he was mine. I was, on my best day, friendly-cute. He was hot. Why would a hot guy want a friendly, cute, slightly overweight woman? Unless he knew she'd never suspect how messed up he was or that she'd never ask questions because she was lucky to have his love.

The more I thought about it, it made me mad. What was I doing? My boyfriend was collecting freaking teeth! At a minimum, he'd done it in the past. And his hiking trips were weird. These backpacking bro-weekends happened as though they were timed. I didn't know Owen's friends. We'd occasionally gone out with them, but they never came to our house. His friends' girlfriends never seemed to be around, either. It was like he didn't want them to know me.

I'd just started chopping lettuce for a salad when Owen snuck up behind me and put his arms around my waist.

"Do you want some help?"

I gripped the knife more tightly. I don't know why. Was I going to stab him? I just felt so angry, afraid, and most of all, threatened by his presence.

"I'm good. Go relax. I'll let you know when dinner is ready."

"Are you okay? You just seem off."

I gripped the knife so tightly; I felt my hand tremble. What I said next wasn't completely a lie. "I'm fine. It has been a long, lonely week without you."

It had been a long and lonely week.

Owen let go of my waist and snagged a piece of lettuce before he went into the living room. "Well, be careful, if you hold that knife any tighter, you are going to crush the handle."

He sat down on the reclining couch and turned on the television.

An acrid tear fell down my cheek. What the hell was wrong with me?

———

"It is time to either talk to him or break it off. This is too weird," Rebecca said. I could hear her chewing something crunchy over the phone.

"I agree. We are coming up on nine months of this." I stared out the back window. The birds still wouldn't come into our yard.

"I mean, I don't know how you can explain away this last weirdness. This is more than sleepwalking."

"There's no way to explain it away. I found him in the backyard, naked, and snarling like a dog. There was a dead rabbit beside him."

"And you're sure it wasn't Duke who did it?"

I looked down at Duke. He was wearing a designer dog sweatshirt and licking his favorite dinosaur stuffed toy. This dog was more human than most humans.

"No, he doesn't have a murderous bone in his body." I reassured her.

"Well, he is a dog. It is in their nature to hunt."

"Right, but Duke was just sitting there, and there was no blood on him, only on Owen."

"Did you try to wake him up so you could ask him what the freak was going on?"

"Listen, I told you, I couldn't wake him. I just guided him into the house, wiped him off, and tucked him into bed. His eyes were open all the time, but he was clearly asleep or in a trance." My stomach burned and gurgled. It was killing me.

"Just ask him what is going on. The man could have a brain tumor. How the hell will you know? This isn't healthy. If you can't talk to him, this is never gonna work. Take your shit and go. Do I need to come over and help you?" Rebecca was getting testy. Her tough love attitude wasn't helping anything.

"No, no. I can handle this. I can ask him." But could I? I'd been so afraid of losing him for so long. I knew I had just let all the weird things go. I'd always quietly judged Rebecca, because of all the lost souls she would just welcome into her home. I'd never told her or admitted it to myself, but Owen had stayed over at my place the first night we'd met, and he'd never really left. We'd literally just moved his stuff from a storage building to my garage, and then called it official. I'd just welcomed him into my home with open arms. No questions asked, because he'd seemed to love me from first sight. He'd lived with a couple of his friends, so I'd never really gone over to his place.

I rubbed the sides of my temples. What was wrong with me? The stress was too much. I felt like I was going to black out. I'd been pacing around the living room. I plopped down on the couch.

"Hey, I gotta go. I'll talk to him tonight. We either start talking or this needs to end."

Rebecca breathed a dramatic sigh. "Okay…"

She didn't believe me.

"I will talk to him tonight as soon as he gets home from work. My head is killing me."

I hung up the phone and closed my eyes. I needed to rest before I blew up my life.

When I opened my eyes, the sky was a mixture of cornflower blue and orange with a slight edge of purple between the two colors. It was beautiful. I was still groggy from my nap. Duke had brought it upon himself to lay on my chest. He was so warm; I closed my eyes again and drifted off.

My eyes were heavy and didn't want to open. I wasn't sure of the time, but it had to be late. Owen should already be home. I had to talk to him soon. Maybe I could talk to him tomorrow. I opened my eyes. The moon cast a glow into our living room. Duke's black eyes glowed as the moonbeams crossed over him and my abdomen. My body was so heavy, but I knew I had to get up and see where Owen was. If he wasn't home, what had happened?

I sat up and grabbed my phone off the coffee table to see what time it was. It was after nine at night. Where was he?

It took me a minute to realize someone was sitting in the corner of the room. I froze.

"Owen, is that you?" It was barely a whisper, but I really hoped it was him that answered. Silence met my question and dragged on for what seemed like the longest moment of my life.

"It's me." His voice was deeper than usual.

"Can you turn the light on? It's so dark in here." Except for the moonlight and my phone, everything was off. My eyes were having trouble adjusting.

"I will in a minute. We need to talk."

I swallowed hard. Was he getting ready to break up with me? Maybe he'd felt the distance between us, too. I'd tried to be so careful with how I'd acted toward him while I struggled with my feelings.

"Um, sure, but can you turn the damn light on? It is too dark in here."

"No, I don't think that's a good idea right now. Let's talk and then I'll turn it on. I think it is better that we just don't see each other's faces right now. It'll make it easier."

Something bad was coming, I knew it, but I could also feel anger coming up inside of me. He was trying to control the situation. Wasn't that what he'd been doing all along? Controlling me with his sweet words and vague responses and hiding the dark stuff from me.

"Fine. What do you want to talk about?" He wasn't the only one with a voice that could change. Mine was low and calm. It scared the hell out of me at how calm I was becoming. Calm anger was terrifying because whatever was about to happen would be intentional and not out of passion.

"Why did you go through my stuff?"

I sat there staring at the light of the moon as it illuminated our couch. To be exact, it was my couch, it had been with me longer than him. It was mine. His question was fair, but he'd waited a long time to ask it.

"Why do you think I did?" I asked.

"Lilly, just stop. Tell me why you've been sneaking around behind my back, digging through my things."

"I wanted to know more about you." It was the truth.

A low growling sound came from Owen's direction. "Tell me the whole truth! Your half-truths and passive attitude are wearing on me."

Duke stood up and growled back at him. His little incisors were glistening. He barked sharply and then growled again. He circled then sat on my lap. The little dog held himself as though he was begging Owen to try some kind of funny business.

"I did want to know more about you—."

He cut me off. "But, why? I've told you a lot about myself. More than anyone."

He was angry. I was angry, but I had one thing he did not. I was tired of trying to be the cool girlfriend. This had gone on long enough.

"You want the truth? Something is wrong. I don't know what it is, and I don't know why I didn't see it before. The torn-up pants. Not one, but TWO times I've found you dirty and naked. The teeth in the box? Are you a…?"

My voice faltered. I couldn't bring myself to ask.

"Am I what?" Owen shifted in the chair. I saw his profile as he leaned forward on his thighs.

"Are you a serial killer?" I asked, then held my breath. There was no telling what was about to happen.

He laughed and leaned back. "Is that really what you think is going on here?"

"Why are you laughing?" I felt my cheeks getting hot.

"I could never hurt anyone. Are you afraid of me?"

I grabbed Duke and held him close. "I'm not sure. You had a dead rabbit with you the last time you had one of your naked spells. And those bloody pants? The hiker? Those disgusting teeth?"

"I talked to that park ranger. That missing hiker should have never been out there. I had nothing to do with him missing. They found his body. He died of exposure. Zion is not as safe as people think. As for my pants, they were an unfortunate mishap of hiking and mountain biking on packed red clay."

"But what about the rabbit and the teeth? I'm not a hysterical woman. Do not try to gaslight me. I know what I saw."

"I'm not going to say you didn't see those things. You did but try to understand. It's natural for an animal to want to hunt. I did kill that rabbit. I found where you threw it in the trash. I wish you hadn't done that. I would never have wasted its life." He paused. The silence was deafening. There was an elephant in the room, or in this case, a box full of teeth.

"What if you really knew me? The real me? Would you still love me?" His voice was gentle now.

For whatever reason, the softness in his voice was so vulnerable that I was surprised when a tear rolled down my face.

"What do you mean, the real you?" I asked as I wiped the tear away.

"The reason for those teeth. If I told you the real reason I carry a box of teeth around with me, would you still love me?"

I didn't answer.

"Do you love me?" he asked. "It is a yes or no question. It doesn't have to be hard. I've wondered many times if you do, but I've been too scared to ask."

"What do you mean? Why would you ask whether I loved you? Of course, I did." I stopped.

"Did?"

The tears started rolling down my face. "I mean, I don't know." I closed my eyes and shook my head. "I don't love *me* anymore. I have spent four years of my life trying to be the cool girlfriend who doesn't let anything bother me. Since you moved in full time, I don't get a break from it. Goddamn it, I am not cool. Shit bothers me. You get on my nerves sometimes, and I want to be able to ask what the hell is going on or say I don't like something. So, no, I don't love that this is what I've become, and I can't live like this. I can't be afraid to lose you, if I am losing myself."

"I see."

I kept crying. He had not made me act this way. I knew it after I had said it. I made me act this way.

"Can I come sit by you?" His voice sounded sad.

I didn't feel angry anymore, and I didn't feel afraid of losing him.

"No, tell me what the teeth are about."

He cleared his throat. "I was born with a disease that makes my teeth fall out every month."

"What?! There's no such thing." I laughed and cried a little at the same time. My nose was running now.

"No, there is, but it isn't talked about. Those are my teeth. I know it sounds crazy, but every month, I grow a new set after the full moon."

I laughed and cried more. "Cut the shit. I'd know if you lost your teeth every month."

"Would you? You've only found me twice, and it was after I transitioned back. You've never seen what I am before that. The thing that I become when I am a different me. You are right, you don't know that much about me. Some of it is because I want to be someone else when I am around you. You make me want to be different, but I am always going to have this disease. It is never going away. If you don't want to be what you call the 'cool girlfriend' anymore, then I don't want to have to be the stoic boyfriend who pretends like they don't have a fuck ton of problems to deal with. I have a lot to deal with. It tears me up inside to hide it from you. You have been the best thing that ever happened to me.

"If you want to break up after you see me, that's fine. I've worried about this for almost five years now. You're the only woman I've been with that has made me want to try to live a normal life and live outside of my group, but I'm exhausted. I constantly worry that once you know everything, you'll ask me to leave."

It was hard hearing this guy who I'd thought was too good for me say that he was afraid of losing me. My insecurities about myself were about me, and from inside of me. He was too worried he was going to lose me to think about my cellulite or that I was friendly-cute and not some bombshell.

I wiped my face on the bottom of my shirt and took a long, deep breath. "You don't have to be afraid. Show me who you are."

Owen pushed himself out of the chair, in the pale-yellow light of the moon, I saw him. Tears rained down my face again, but I couldn't help but laugh some more.

"I see."

"Can you love me? Can we start over, or do you want me to leave?" He did not move. He stood there in the light, and I saw who he really was.

I stood up and walked over to him. I brushed the side of his snout and understood why he lost his teeth every month. His fur was soft under my fingers.

"I can. I want to."

Duke barked. We both looked at him. I scooped him up, and he licked us both. I would deal with Duke keeping Owen's secret, later.

We stood there baptized in the moonlight, finally holding one another as we really were.

BE PREPARED ALL YE MERRY MAIDS

Alessia

"Oh, you can't quit. I'm giving you this one last chance. You should be thanking me for hiring you!"

Alessia's mother's words grated at her through the phone. She gritted her teeth and pressed the phone hard against her ear. The movement helped her stay present. Her mother always had a way of making her check out. At the hospital, they'd called it disassociation. When it happened, Alessia couldn't come back. Not without doing something stupid. The last time, it had been holding up a gas station. She'd kept it together enough to not use a gun, so she'd bypassed an aggravated robbery charge. Which is how she'd landed up on the sixth floor of a high-rise building working for her mother, cleaning the offices of the Bee-Prepared Apocalypse Prepping Company. The logo was a bee with a large stinger wearing a combat helmet inside a bright red circle. Their slogan made her laugh: *Take the sting out of the apocalypse.*

She stared out the window and watched executives, doctors, and other people who hadn't fucked up their lives milling in and out of the building for their lunch breaks.

"Mija, are you there? You know I love you. You are so lucky. Be grateful..." her mother said.

Alessia cut her mother off. "Be grateful that I didn't grow up like you? I don't want to hear the shit you went through!"

"Clean up the mess you made!" her mother shrilled.

Alessia banged her head against the window. This was not how she'd wanted her day to start.

"Mom, I'm sorry. I love you."

Guilt flooded her. She'd messed up by not cleaning the offices last night. It was too easy to sit in an office and stare off into space. It didn't help that she'd been caught taking a couple of MREs from the sample closet to give to the homeless. She wasn't a totally selfish monster. It felt like it sometimes, but she knew how to care for other people. The new girl at Bee-Prepared didn't understand that. No room for breaking the rules with her. What a bitch.

"I want that floor spotless. My other girls can do two floors a day. You'll get there in a couple of months. In a year, you'll be running this place when I'm not here. You can do this."

The loving, kind mother was back. *If I do what she wants*, Alessia thought.

"Mom, I gotta go. I'll make you proud."

"Love you, mi—"

The phone went dead.

Alessia watched as the office workers filed into the

building. Out of the crowd, six bright yellow shirts stood out. It was the Bee-Prepared sales team. She rolled her eyes. *Assholes.* She crammed her phone into her back pocket, grabbed the window cleaner and a cloth from her housekeeping cart, and grudgingly went back to work. The busier she looked, the less likely one of those prepper sales jerks would start asking her stupid questions.

Laurel

"What are the sales projections for next quarter?" Derek Marshall asked over his broad shoulder.

Laurel Regan trudged behind, silent and dutiful, her eyes directed toward the ground. If she looked up, a wall of blinding yellow assaulted her vision. Derek walked shoulder to shoulder with his youngest son, Sean, both were wearing Bee-Prepared signature polos. Derek wasn't interested in what she had to say. He wanted a secretary, not an executive.

"Good?" said Derek's oldest son, Alex, from behind her.

Laurel refrained from rolling her eyes. He might be the oldest, but he was also the dumbest. The entire Marshall family seemed a little slower than they appeared on commercials. She wasn't sure who was coaching them, but it sure wasn't Alex. Bee-Prepared was not what she had expected.

Her family had idolized its founder, the strong-willed and witted Abie Marshal. A legendary Vietnam vet who had survived alone in the jungle for eighteen months with nothing except for what he'd called, "the three Bs," bare hands, brains, and balls. His tell-all book was being made into a movie. The government refused to acknowledge that Abie had been out there. It had been a top-secret mission that could ruin relations between countries, even today. According to Abie, anyway.

"Daddy, it looks like we'll have an increase of roughly twenty-two percent over the next quarter. Adding the Bible to the bundle really seems to help with the rapture crowd," Fayth Michelle said, beaming. Of the three Marshall children, she was the shrewd one. If there was a way to save or make money, Fayth was on it. Laurel regretted mentioning to her that some of the MREs were missing. Of course, Fayth Michelle had taken credit for finding the discrepancy.

Laurel's stomach lurched at the thought of facing the housekeeper. That woman looked like she could kick somebody's ass. Thankfully, they hadn't fired her. An altercation with a pierced and tattooed Latina wasn't something Laurel wanted. Both appeared to need their jobs.

"Honey, can you help me up those stairs?" Abie pointed with his cane.

"Sure, Mr. Marshall." Laurel grabbed the elderly man's elbow. He felt like nothing but a sack of bones.

"Thanks, honey. How do you like it here?" The frail man looked down at Laurel and smiled. He was wrinkled from top to bottom, and he didn't say much. Most of the time, he wandered around the office, staring at nothing.

"Oh, I'm good, sir." Her voice was a little weak.

"It doesn't sound like you're good," Abie said. The old

man continued to hold Laurel's hand in the crook of his arm.

"Well, sir…" Laurel cleared her throat. It was now or never if she planned to get the position she had been promised. "I just wanted you to know that I applied for a sales executive position, which was what I was promised before I moved here. I deserve—"

Laurel and Abie stopped.

In the lobby of the building, fifteen local panhandlers milled around, clawing and snapping at tenants. Many of them were pale and sweating. Laurel made the mistake of making eye contact with a scraggly, bearded man wearing three sweaters, cargo pants, and rain boots. The clomping of his boots echoed in her ears as he charged forward. Her heart raced. Without thinking, Laurel grabbed Abie's cane and cracked him over the top of the head. He went down with a thud. She dropped the cane to the ground, shocked that she'd been able to take him down. One of the tower security guards ran towards them.

"Are you okay, Mr. Marshall?" The out-of-shape guard panted as he came over.

"We're fine," Abie said as he bent to pick up his cane. "My escort kindly protected me."

"Good thing these jerks aren't biting people."

A loud, shrill scream rang out behind them.

Laurel turned to see one of the vagrants attacking Fayth Michelle.

Alessia

"¡Puya!" Alessia screamed as a cold, wet hand grasped

her arm. She swung around with fists clenched. She relaxed her hand and pulled out an ear bud at the sight of her boss.

"Excuse me, sir," she mumbled and looked at the floor. All she needed was to get fired for stealing *and* punching the boss.

"I said we need some towels. Now!" Derek growled.

The words shocked Alessia. The man was totally an arrogant asshole, but he'd never yelled at her. She looked up at him. He was panting, his face was pale, and beads of sweat dripped down his temple.

"Okay, let me—"

A long scream silenced her. She turned to see the owner's daughter writhing in pain as her brothers carried her down the hallway. Blood gushed from the woman's neck. The bitchy secretary struggled to keep up with the men and hold pressure on the wound.

Alessia ran to the supply closet. She rummaged through the shelves for towels. There were none. She grabbed a handful of dark blue cleaning rags and ran to Derek's office. Inside the room, blood pooled on the floor. Fayth Michelle's perfectly tan skin was now a bright yellow, and her fingernails were turning gray.

"Hey, throw those towels over here!" the secretary said.

Alessia tossed them to her. The secretary pressed them against the girl's neck as the rest of the Marshall family stood in shock with Alessia. At the wilderness survival camp, Alessia had been taught first aid, but that was eight years ago. Back when she was still in the juvenile system. Most of the time, she'd spent bargaining for weed with the counselors and trying to figure out a way to escape or make weapons. Nothing else about it had seemed to stick.

"Abie, we can't put a tourniquet on this. Do you have any idea how to stop the bleeding?" The secretary looked up at the oldest member of the Marshall family.

"We need to call 911," he said calmly. The old man was leaned up against the desk, hands propped up on his cane. Alessia didn't think anything could excite the old fart.

"Right. What about from your last survival book? I could try to find something to clamp off the artery, but she needs real help." The secretary looked at the old guy like he was some all-knowing guru. As far as Alessia was concerned, he was some old guy who walked around confused most of the time. She didn't know much about these people, nor did she care.

"The phone isn't working." Sean pressed the button for the speaker phone. *"I'm sorry, your call cannot be completed as dialed."*

"Uh, how does your phone not work?" Alex asked. He genuinely appeared confused and helpless. He seemed oblivious to the blood splattered across his polo and face.

"Good question, son," Derek said. "You did dial 911, right?"

"Yeah, Dad. I dialed 911." Sean sighed.

"What happens when 911 doesn't work?" Alex asked.

"We're screwed. That's what happens," the secretary said. She removed her hand from Fayth Michelle's neck, then stood up and walked across the room to the curtains. She yanked hard, pulling down the long, thick-weave polyester drapes. She dragged them over to Fayth Michelle and covered her.

"She's dead. We need to get out of here. Something is wrong."

"She can't be dead!" Alex ran over to her body and scooped her in his arms.

Alessia had stood here with the rest of them, watching the woman die.

The telephone on Derek's desk rang. Everyone continued to hover over Fayth Michelle's body.

Alessia tiptoed around them and picked up the phone. An automated voice on the other end advised, *"Do not attempt to leave. The building is on lockdown."*

Laurel

Long worry lines stretched across the housekeeper's forehead as she held the phone to her ear. Laurel pushed herself up from the floor and walked over to the desk.

"What is it?" she asked. The housekeeper handed her the phone. A looped recording announced the building was on lockdown. It could be a good thing, depending on the situation outside. It could also mean they would be stuck inside this building indefinitely. Without mobility, they were a sitting target for terrorists, *if* that was the problem.

When it became apparent that no further information would be provided, she placed the phone on the receiver. She looked over to the cluster of yellow polos hovered around the body while Abie remained perched on the edge of the desk. Every year of his life showed on his face as he clenched his teeth. He seemed irritated.

Laurel walked over to him and placed her hand on his arm.

"Abie, did you know this place had a lockdown system?"

The old man sat silent. He studied the scene in front of him.

"Did you know there was a lockdown system? They shut the building down?"

Abie turned to Laurel. "Of course, dear. The shutters should be coming down soon. The exits are secured. We aren't going anywhere."

"Well, what is the plan to eliminate a threat?" Laurel's mind's eye flooded with visions of catastrophic scenarios. What if terrorists were systematically attacking each level of the building, or what if they released a biological threat? Who would save them? The lockdown wouldn't just keep things out, it would keep them in. It wasn't just a safe harbor, but a cage.

"You'd think a prepping company would have an emergency plan," The housekeeper said dryly.

"You think?" Laurel felt a twinge of worry in her gut. Her faith in Abie Marshall wavered slightly.

"We pay a hefty security fee monthly. Right, Derek?" Abie asked, oblivious to the fact that his son was wailing and blubbering over his only daughter's corpse.

Laurel headed to the window. She surveyed the scene below. A searing feeling of fear and disappointment flooded her. There was one fire truck and a police car parked out front. Their red lights spun while employees from the tower wandered around, looking confused. She didn't see the emergency workers; she assumed they were the ones she'd met in the lobby.

The phone rang again. Laurel didn't move. There was no need to hear the recording again. She understood. They were trapped.

The ringing seemed to go on forever. She finally turned around, ready to yell at the housekeeper. Before she could open her mouth, the housekeeper picked up the landline phone receiver with such force the phone base lifted from the desk.

"Hello?!" A high, desperate voice came out of the receiver. The housekeeper was taken aback. So was Laurel.

"Who is this?" The housekeeper held the phone out from her ear.

Laurel walked over and pushed the intercom button. She didn't trust the housekeeper to keep her shit together and make a good decision.

"This is Meghan from accounting. We just got back from lunch. The elevators won't open. Charlene says we're on lockdown and we can't come up unless somebody pushes the button under Derek's desk. There is some creepy stuff going on down here. These cops are weird and there are several injured firemen. We can't stay in this lobby."

Laurel looked to Abie for counsel, but he looked mentally checked out. She looked at the rest of the Marshall family on the floor. No one was fit to decide. Out of the corner of Laurel's eye, she could see the housekeeper shaking her head. Laurel was clearly the most competent person in this situation and knew the right thing to do.

"Sure. You said the button is under the desk?" Laurel felt around under the middle drawer. She felt smooth, cool wood under her fingers, but then a cold, tacky sensation hit her fingers. Gum. Her automatic reaction was to retch, but instead she continued groping under the drawer.

"Where else could the button be?"

A labored voice came over the intercom. "It's way under there. Right under the middle drawer."

Laurel leaned down and patted the cool mahogany wood. She felt a raised, round button.

"Got it!" She pushed the button hard.

The room filled with shrieks from the intercom. Whether those were of delight or terror, she couldn't be sure.

Then silence.

Alessia

"You're a fucking idiot, you know that, right?" Alessia was so angry that spit flew from her mouth, landing on the uptight secretary's face.

The look of pleasure at finding the authorization button for the elevator faded from the secretary's face as she wiped Alessia's spit away with her bright yellow shirt. The secretary stood up and walked over to Alessia. They were almost the same height. This girl had another thing coming if she thought Alessia would back down. She clenched her fists, ready for a fight. Instead, the girl put out her hand as if to shake.

"I'm Laurel Regan. Daughter to a fine family of folks that own a training facility for people preparing for the apocalypse located in the fine town of Minorville, Montana. I have over six hundred hours in multiple defense tactics, and I've been training my whole life for shit to get real."

Alessia stood still. She really wanted to punch Laurel Regan right in the nose. She didn't give a shit what this girl had done or what she knew. It didn't take a lot of training to know the elevator doors didn't need to open. Punching people in the face had shut people up in the past, so why stop now? Being locked up was why. Fighting on the street was one thing, but when you were locked up, you had to choose your battles wisely.

She grasped Laurel's hand tightly, smiled, and said, "I'm Alessia Rivera, daughter to two El Salvadoran immigrants who walked all the way from a dangerous shitty barrio to this miserable country. I have spent my whole life dealing with a bunch of other shit that being a prepper could never make you smart enough to handle. I've been to a survival camp as well, but it was court mandated. So, I know you shouldn't have authorized opening that god damn elevator door."

Alessia let go of Laurel's hand. She walked towards the hall, past the mourners who were still on the floor, hoping their dearly beloved Fayth Michelle would suddenly resurrect. She knew they needed weapons. There was no telling what was coming up in that elevator. If there was one thing she always remembered from her mother's stories, it was that people get crazy when shit gets real. There was little time left, but she'd been under more difficult time constraints.

"Where are you going?" Laurel yelled after her.

"Your dumb ass just invited a party of crazy people up here. We don't know how many of them are going to bite us, take our shit, or act a fool. We need some weapons!" Alessia yelled over her shoulder as she headed to the janitor's closet. She swung the door open and pushed up her sleeves. She pulled her hair up and knotted it in a bun on top of her head. The cool air on her ears and neck felt good. It helped her think. If she was going out, it would be with her tattoos blazing and all her piercings showing. Dress code be damned. She sure wasn't going to get fired from Merry Maids any time soon.

"They sounded desperate and they're part of the Bee-Prepared team. We couldn't leave them locked up in that lobby to be attacked," Laurel said. To Alessia, it sounded like the half-rate secretary was trying to convince herself.

"Yeah, yeah. You haven't ever really been around desperate people, have you?" Alessia asked. She grabbed a broom and stomped on the head of it. After two more stomps, a loud crack filled the closet. She turned around and handed the jagged-tipped broom handle to Laurel.

Laurel grabbed it. "Well, one time we played war games, and I felt pretty desperate to win."

"I think what you are about to feel is going to be a lot different."

The elevator bell tinged.

Laurel

Laurel stared at her newest acquaintance's tattoo-covered arms. Most of them had a blue-black tint. *Prison tats*, she thought. Laurel had met a couple of ex-cons in her life, and yes, she'd seen prison tattoos before. Most of the time, though, they were crosses doing a piss-poor job of covering up swastikas. These tattoos were at least of beautiful women, ornate crosses, elaborate names, and intricate embellishments.

"Pay attention to the door. I'm the least of your problems," Alessia said dryly.

This Alessia girl was probably right. How could she know what had happened in the lobby after they'd left? Plus, she'd overridden the elevator authorization to not only allow Bee-Prepared employees up, but anyone else that could shove in. She grasped the broom handle tighter.

In Laurel's mind, a million seconds passed between the ting of the elevator bell and the opening of the door. Laurel took a deep breath. Several Bee-Prepared customer service agents came squalling through the door, their faces scrunched in terror. Tears streaked their bloody faces.

"Thank you, thank you, thank you," one of the women said with arms stretched out towards them. She was a short, round, older lady that looked like she belonged in a 1950's library instead of a customer service center. Laurel assessed her as she came closer. She didn't appear to be wounded. Behind her, several other terrified men and women covered in blood came at them. As far as Laurel could tell, they all just looked frightened. She lowered her broken broom handle.

"Everybody, head to the bathrooms and wash yourselves off. We'll go get some first aid kits from the inventory room," Laurel instructed. She pointed her hands in the direction of the bathroom, performing her best flight attendant imitation.

She turned to Alessia. "Let's go check out this inventory room. You know more about what's in there than I do."

Laurel headed down the hallway with Alessia's footsteps behind her. A small smile of satisfaction crossed her face. Laurel felt redeemed for taking quick-thinking action. Plus, she *might* have enjoyed being snide.

"Uh, can you guys help me?" a male voice asked from behind her.

Laurel rolled her eyes. It didn't seem like anything was ever going to go as planned. She spun around. A balding, middle-aged man braced himself in the elevator door, attempting to keep it open.

Laurel moved toward him. Alessia grabbed her arm as she passed.

"What?" The grab gave Laurel a moment to pause and really look at the scene with clarity. Behind the guy, who she guessed worked in accounting from his appearance, was someone crumpled on the floor.

"There's a guy in here. I'm sure you can see him. I can't tell if he is dead, or what. I need someone to pull him out so I can take a look. I know CPR." The man continued to lean on the door. Alessia let go of Laurel's arm. They both started toward the elevator. As the girls drew closer, the elevator began to alarm. Laurel understood why he looked tired. The mechanics in the door were trying to shut it, even with him in the way.

"We'll pull him out. Do not let that door close," Laurel warned as she pointed her finger at him.

The two looked at the crumpled body in the corner. Alessia walked over to the back side of the elevator behind the fallen man. She rolled him over, then squatted down. Laurel squatted on the opposite side.

Alessia snorted and asked, "Was that you being a badass?"

"No, not all." Laurel was trying to be a badass, but apparently, she'd embarrassed herself. Her humiliation was cut short as her attention focused on the man's half-eaten face. The skin on the nose, bottom lip, and right jawline were jagged pieces of flesh. The eyes were swollen shut and half the front of his neck was missing, showing a white cartilage-like plate.

"Oh, my gawd." Laurel turned and vomited.

Alessia

"How the fuck did this guy even walk into the elevator?" Alessia looked up at the guy holding the door open.

The guy shrugged. "Can you please hurry up? My back is killing me."

"Look, you balding Rick Moranis looking motherfucker--" Alessia clenched her fist.

Laurel cut her off. "We'll pull him out. We don't want that door closing on us."

Alessia inspected the body. She'd seen something similar in lockup, except she'd known what had caused that mess: two melted plastic sporks and a lot of ingenuity.

"Let's just drag him out by the shoulders. No use being gentle. I'm sure he won't mind," Laurel said.

"We could just leave him here," Alessia suggested. She didn't see the point of messing with a dead body.

"This one is cold-hearted," the guy holding the door said. Alessia glared at him. She really thought he looked like Rick Moranis in *Ghostbusters*, except bald and miserable, but still an annoying pain in the ass. If you were going to have a rotting corpse on the floor, might as well make it two, Alessia supposed.

"You ready?" Laurel asked. Alessia stepped over the body and joined Laurel on the left side. Each woman pulled on the arm nearest to her. As his torso turned towards the door, Alessia grabbed his other arm. She braced her heels on the floor as she pulled backwards. She was shocked. It wasn't as difficult as she'd thought. He was at least six feet tall and two hundred and fifty pounds. Alessia and Laurel grunted as the body stopped moving abruptly. Its midsection was caught in the grooves beneath the door opening.

Alessia leaned in to see his wide, black leather belt stuck in the groove. She grabbed his belt buckle and unlatched it. A couple of quick tugs and the belt was off. Alessia grinned triumphantly and threw the belt into the hallway.

Without warning, the sound of metal scratching across metal flooded her ears.

"What the hell?" Alessia looked to her right to see the elevator door coming at her. She fell backwards, her butt landing on the corpse's face. Alessia rolled off as fast as she could, with the cold, wet feeling of a bloodied nose still freshly implanted in her crotch.

"I think I'm going to be sick." Alessia's stomach lurched as her face hit the cold floor. She gagged, but nothing came up. She was thankful she hadn't totally lost her lunch like Laurel.

"Uh, we got another problem," Laurel said. Alessia rolled over to see that the door had closed on the corpse, slicing him in half.

"At least he'll be easier to drag away," the Rick Moranis clone said as he pushed up his glasses. "It must have been some kind of safety override."

"Yeah, well, if I hadn't fallen back, I'd be joining this guy." Alessia pointed to the half-corpse. The building was beginning to feel more and more like a death trap to Alessia. She'd half-expected the elevator doors to slam on the dead body, but not slice the man in half.

"Turn around," Alessia instructed the man.

"Why?"

Alessia walked over and turned the shorter man around to examine his back.

"Oh shit," Laurel said.

"Yeah." Alessia agreed.

"What are you ladies going on about?" he demanded.

Three bloodied vertical cuts ran down the back of his yellow polo.

Laurel

Laurel inspected the clean slices of the polo and the

bloodied lines imprinted in the back of the Rick Moranis clone. It would never have occurred to her that a tower with commercial businesses would have failed safe elevator doors with pop-out razored edges. Of course, it would make sense that they'd still allow people up, but if you took too long, you were obviously up to no good and it was time to cut you out, literally.

Why not cut you in half to solve that problem? she thought.

"Does anybody want anything to eat? I know the code to the inventory room," the librarian-looking customer service rep offered as she handed Laurel some toilet paper. Laurel patted the man's wounds carefully, keeping the blood away from herself.

"Ow! That hurts." The elevator guy squealed.

Laurel felt like she should ask his name, but every time he talked it sounded like nails screeching on a chalkboard. He didn't seem to be a bad guy, but so far, the only person who had impressed her during the entire situation had been Alessia. The rest of them would be winning Darwin Awards in the apocalypse.

"Well, it looks like the extra perks I paid for were put to good use," Abie Marshall said as he walked down the hallway, assisted by his cane and an unsteady hand braced against the wall. Laurel grimaced every time she saw the man walk. His gait betrayed his bad hip, for sure. She just knew he was one of those elderly types who would shatter into a million pieces if they fell. That was all they needed, another injured person or worse, a dead one.

"Mr. Marshall, why don't you sit down? We can get you anything you need." Laurel looked over at Alessia, hoping the girl would get her drift and go help the man. Alessia's dark brown eyes shifted back and forth from her to Abie as she evidently tried to guess what Laurel wanted. Laurel tilted her head towards Abie Marshall.

"Yeah, Mr. Marshall, let me get you a chair," Alessia said as she backed away towards the nearest office. She scowled at Laurel.

"Abie, what other extras did you pay for on this floor?" Laurel casually asked the old man as she continued carefully patting the back of the elevator guy.

"Huh, dearie?"

"What other extras did you pay for? Like, if we try to open a window, will a bomb go off? Or what happens if we break a door down?" Laurel tried to think of other possible scenarios the old man would have thought about.

"Hmmm, well, I think the poison on the blades to the elevator was a really good idea. Let me think..."

Alessia rolled a desk chair underneath the old man.

"Wait, there was poison on those blades?!" the elevator guy yelled.

"Oh yeah, you got cut?" Abie asked as he half-twirled back and forth in the rolling chair like an entertained child.

"Yeah! I got cut. What's going to happen?" Elevator guy shrugged off Laurel, stomped over to the old man, and grabbed him by the collar.

Laurel didn't think he looked like an accountant anymore, more like an enraged *martial artist.*

Abie Marshall laughed. "Oh, dear boy, I'd be terrified, but your heart is starting to race already. I can see how flushed your face is getting. Sweat is trickling down your forehead."

Laurel looked at the old man in horror. His frailty was apparently only surpassed by his cruelty.

Elevator guy fell to the ground, twitching and writhing in pain. Foam spewed from his mouth as his nose began to bleed. He gasped for one last lungful of air then stopped breathing. Laurel lunged for him, readying to perform CPR.

"It's no use. You'll just poison yourself," Abie said in an almost sing-song voice.

The lights flickered. *Thump.* Abie swiveled the chair around toward the opposite end of the hallway.

"Ha! Chubby-butt tried to break into the snacks."

At the end of the hallway, the librarian-like customer service rep was slumped over on the wall across from the inventory room. Laurel could see smoke rising from her charred hands.

Laurel gulped. That could have been her.

Abie Marshall clapped his hands in delight as he cackled, "This is going to be fun!"

Alessia

Alessia gently nudged the charred body with her sneaker. Ash smudged the white rubber tip. She bit her lip, afraid to say what was on her mind. This reminded her of the stories her mother had told her about back home. You could just be minding your own business and then-- *Blam!*-- you were in a field being forced to huff cocaine while you helped chop up bodies. She'd always kind of thought her mother was full of shit. There was no way anybody was that crazy. Sure, Alessia had run with some messed up people, but none of them had been smart enough to really, truly mentally fuck with somebody.

Alessia felt someone come up behind her and wrap their cold arm around her. It was Laurel, she knew it. Only some dumbass white chick would be grabbing people she didn't know. To make it worse, she'd laid her head on Alessia's shoulder.

In a low voice Laurel whispered, "We need to tie that sick old fuck up. I think he's going to try to kill us."

"You think?" Alessia couldn't resist putting a little sarcasm in there. It was all that she had left; even she was terrified.

"How many of us are there?" Laurel asked.

Alessia had to think about it. There had been several panicked people who'd passed through the doors.

"Not counting our good friend, the elevator guy, or the charcoal brick here, I'd say there's eight, plus his family." Alessia guessed.

"I don't know if we can count on his family to help. There's no telling with them." Laurel let go of Alessia and leaned over. She gently pushed the old lady's eyelids down, but her attempt to close her gaping mouth failed. Alessia joined her and helped slide the woman flat to the floor.

"You girls are truly precious," Abie said from the end of the hallway. He rolled towards them, using his cane and hand against the wall as leverage. Slowly, they both backed away and looked toward the inventory door then the next door down. Alessia pulled a stainless-steel piercing from her ear and tossed it at the doorknob. A spark flew.

"Damn."

The wheels of Abie's chair squeaked closer. Alessia pulled out another piercing and tossed it at the next door; another spark flew.

"Where can we go?" Laurel asked.

"Oh, dammit to hell," Alessia said. She looked toward Derek Marshall's office. It was the only door slightly ajar.

"How bad can it be? The family seems harmless," Laurel said as they narrowly missed the fury of Abie's cane before slamming the door behind them.

"Whew. That cane probably has some jacked-up Peruvian dart poison in it or some shit," Alessia said as she laughed off her fear. Her relief was short-lived. In the middle of the room sat Fayth Michelle, looking as alive as ever and eating her dismembered family members' flesh as though she were at a picnic with all her favorite treats.

Alessia said the first thing that came to her mind. "Find a weapon."

Laurel

Remember your training, remember your training, Laurel silently chanted to herself as her vision telescoped in and out. She took long, deep breaths and tried to remember everything her father had taught her. One minute, she was in the mix of blood and guts, the next she was a thousand miles away in Montana. Fayth Michelle was unfazed by the two and continued devouring the flesh in front of her. Laurel scanned the room for a potential weapon to ward off the pint-sized blonde. There was a dark mahogany coat rack in the corner that looked sturdy enough to stave her off. Luckily for them, there were a couple of umbrellas in there too.

Laurel slid towards the rack. Alessia saw what she was going for and moved in sync with her. Once there, Alessia mouthed, *now what?* Laurel shrugged. She hadn't thought that far in advance. Alessia pantomimed a couple of stabbing motions, then acted as though she'd harpooned Fayth Michelle in the neck. Her imaginary catch was escorted to the door, then released out in the hallway. Laurel understood the silent suggestion would also eliminate Abie. Alessia gently tossed a trench coat on the floor and placed Derek Marshall's Bee-Prepared ball cap on her head with the bill in the back. Laurel pulled the cache of umbrellas out one by one setting them to the side. She held her breath as she pulled each one out hoping not to make a sound.

Tap, tap, tap.

"Ladies, I'm bored. Come out and play!" Abie yelled through the door.

The two stayed silent.

Taps became full out thumps on the door as Abie lost his patience.

Fayth Michelle looked up. Laurel watched, horrified, as the previously dead woman crawled to the door. Fayth Michelle growled to herself in a language only known to her. Her movements were rigid and awkward as she reached for the door. Laurel stood motionless studying the phenomenon. Alessia tapped Laurel's arm and pushed the coat rack at Laurel. Normally, Laurel would have been impressed with the craftsmanship of such a solid piece of work. It was heavy and meant to hold whatever was placed on it. It wasn't some cheap thing that would fall over with the first raincoat. She grasped the bottom, allowing Alessia to lead. Their position reminded Laurel of a battering ram.

Alessia looked back to Laurel and nodded. The two moved forward, their speed increasing with each step, as the coat rack neared the back of Fayth Michelle's head, Alessia pointed the sharp-edged hooks at the base of her skull. Laurel instinctively pushed all the weight from the base forward. A sharp, gristly crunching sound was confirmation they'd lanced their target. Alessia pulled up and Laurel complied, tilting the base back. The once-cute blonde wiggled back and forth as Laurel held the pole upright.

Alessia inspected their work. "You think we can toss this on him?"

Laurel held on tightly to the coat rack. It was solid wood and heavy, but she felt like a deep-sea fisherman trying to keep his marlin from jumping back into the ocean.

"I think we need to know what else is booby trapped on this floor."

Laurel wanted Abie Marshall dead as much as Alessia at this point, but letting the old fart die while there were still so many active dangers wasn't the best idea. The sadistic old man seemed to have been waiting for a day he could turn his business into a house of horror.

"You're right. But what do we do with this thing?" Alessia looked at Fayth Michelle with disgust. As shitty as

Fayth Michelle had been to Alessia in life, Laurel suspected that Alessia probably would have looked at her like that anyway.

"I'm not sure. Maybe toss her at the window and see--" Laurel's thought was interrupted as she felt a cold, wet hand grasp her leg. She couldn't contain herself. She screamed, releasing her hold on the coat rack as she attempted to pull off the hand with nobody attached to it.

Alessia

Fayth Michelle's tiny grabby hands and clicking teeth narrowly missed Alessia as the bloodied undead bumblebee of a blonde and the coat rack toppled to the ground.

"For fuck's sake! Why'd you let go?" Alessia yelled at Laurel.

Laurel sat on the ground and desperately pulled at something on her leg. Alessia looked to make sure Fayth Michelle was still attached to the coat rack and went over to Laurel.

"What the hell?" Attached to Laurel's leg was the well-groomed hand of a man.

"It won't come off!" Laurel panted like she was about to have an anxiety attack.

"Stay calm. Let me help you." Alessia looked on the desk for anything that would pry the fingers open. She walked around the desk and opened the top drawer. Inside she found a large pair of scissors and a letter opener. One of the two could potentially cut the fingers off. She heard a faint clicking sound. Curiosity got the best of her. Since Abie was so crazy, it could be a bomb ticking, for all she knew. She pulled out the large office chair to inspect.

It wasn't a bomb.

Underneath the desk, in the back crevice, something round was rocking back and forth. Alessia grabbed her useless cell phone from her back pocket and turned on the light. Derek Marshall stared back at her as his teeth gnashed away at some invisible thing he was determined to eat. Part of his spinal cord flopped back and forth, giving the impression of a creepy tadpole. Alessia shoved the chair back in place. Derek Marshall's head was the least of their problems right now. They could address him later.

"Let me see if I can pry it off," Alessia said as she squatted next to Laurel. Alessia inserted the letter opener beneath the index finger. She used the leverage of Laurel's leg to pry it off. It wasn't easy, and the mechanics of how the hand continued to work without a body were beyond her. As Alessia pried up each finger, she placed the closed blade of the scissors underneath. The fingers grasped at the cold steel. After the pinky finally released, the hand closed around the scissors. Alessia flung them both in the corner.

"Phew," Laurel said as she shook her leg. "That scared me to death."

"Really? That scared you?"

Alessia scanned the room. Blood and body parts were scattered everywhere. They hadn't noticed before, but the hand and Fayth Michelle were not the only moving pieces. An eyeball near Alessia's foot twitched as the pupil attempted to focus in and out. It occurred to Alessia that if Fayth Michelle was intact and Derek's head was under the desk, there were two members of the Marshall family missing.

"I don't think this is over. Where are dumb and dumber?" Alessia asked.

Laurel stared at the floor. "Maybe somewhere in all this." She waved her arms over the mess.

"I don't think so. The head of the chief dumbass is under the desk. Do you hear that chattering? It isn't just her. It's him."

"Where could they be then?"

A loud thump answered the question.

"Girls, are you going to come out and play or am I going to have to start turning things on in the room?" Abie's voice came through the door in a high-pitched screech.

Laurel

"Why does it smell like some stinky-ass almond lotion my grandma would wear in here?" Alessia said as she pinched her nose.

Laurel took a deep inhale in. She spat on the front of her shirt and covered her mouth and nose with it.

"You are so gross." Alessia's face was curled in disgust.

"Do it. Now!" Laurel yelled. Alessia complied, shaking her head in disdain.

"Ladies, what are you going to do? You've got about 5 minutes before you start getting sick to your stomachs!" Abie yelled.

Laurel scanned the room. They didn't have much in

the way of options. They couldn't seal themselves off in the closet; the undead brothers made that impossible. If they tried to break the glass on the window, it could end up electrocuting them, or worse. They had to go outside, face Abie, and deal with whatever else might be ready to attack.

Fayth Michelle rolled back and forth on the floor as she struggled to pull herself free from the coat rack. Laurel thought about it a little more. Abie was probably a psychopath from way back, but he probably hadn't caused his family to return from the dead. He had no control over that. She wasn't even sure Fayth Michelle had killed everyone. Maybe one of Abie's sick weapons had maimed them to the point it was easy for Fayth Michelle to tear them apart.

"Laurel, what the hell is this stuff? I feel like I need to crap my pants, and my head is killing me." Alessia gagged through the words.

"Hydrogen cyanide. There are far better ways to poison a person, but it gives us roughly fifteen minutes. He wants us to have time to play." Laurel pushed herself up. She walked over to Fayth Michelle and examined the coat rack to ensure it was secure.

"We're shoving her at him, right?" Laurel asked. Pantomiming was not the best form of communication when it came to war tactics. She wanted confirmation.

Alessia nodded. Her eyes widened. She darted behind Derek Marshall's desk and ducked underneath. Laurel couldn't see what Alessia was doing, but she could hear the bumping of a head and elbows as she struggled. Laurel thought she heard Alessia say, *"Come here, damnit."* But she wasn't sure.

Alessia popped back up, holding her trophy-- Derek Marshall's severed head. Laurel couldn't believe what she was seeing. Alessia held the CEO of the Bee-Prepared Apocalypse Prepping Company by the head of his hair as his eyes moved back and forth, his teeth clicked, and his spine wiggled.

"What do you propose we do with that?" Laurel asked.

"It's a bomb, of course. We'll toss it in the old fart's lap, then shove his dear sweet granddaughter at him," Alessia said with pride.

"Well, let's do this," Laurel said as enthusiastically as she could through her t-shirt. The smell of spit and cyanide were beginning to mix. It wasn't going to be long before they were both on the floor, muscles tightened, and vomiting their guts out.

Laurel yelled, "We're ready, Abie. It's time to play!"

Alessia

Derek Marshall's rubber mouse pad made an excellent grip and insulator against the charged doorknob. But Alessia's grip on Derek's hair was faltering. She worried his hair would fall out or she would drop him. Luckily, even if she dropped him, he wouldn't roll well. She dreaded having to help Laurel shove Fayth Michelle at Abie. They didn't know what else the old madman had up his sleeve or whether he knew that his granddaughter was ready, and more than willing, to be reunited, especially with his face.

Alessia coughed. Her eyes watered and burned. She didn't have time to second- guess herself. This reminded her of the time she had gone to the crack house with her friend Patty, and it had ended up getting raided. They had been told it was a house party, *some* house party. The fumes there had been a fucking nightmare, and this was ten times worse.

"Are you ready?" She looked back at Laurel. It was almost comical. Fayth Michelle's arms flapped desperately like a flag on a pole while Laurel struggled to keep her up.

"Yeah, the quicker we get this done, the better. Did you notice the Marshall brothers are ready to come out of the closet?"

Blue tinted fingernails poked out from underneath the closet door.

"Let's just do this." Alessia focused on the doorknob. With one swift turn, the knob twisted with ease. Without further thought, she immediately tossed Derek Marshall's head out. Her highest hope being that it would land in the old monster's lap.

Instead, the head smacked the other wall, leaving a trail of blood as it rolled to the floor. Its teeth chattered excitedly, and its eyes moved rapidly back and forth.

"Ah, dammit."

"What?" Laurel asked, her voice breathless as she tried to keep Fayth Michelle upright.

"He's gone. The only thing out here is the crispy-fried customer service rep," Alessia said with disgust. She'd wanted to see the old man shriek with terror as his son bit the shit out of him. Alessia poked her head further out the door. The dark gray carpet couldn't conceal the bloody mess that had happened in the hallway.

"Well, what are we going to do with her?" Impatience and struggle filled Laurel's voice.

"Let's just use her as a poop-stick," Alessia said.

"What?!" Laurel coughed out.

Alessia stepped back into the room, avoiding the reach of their newly developed weapon. She joined Laurel in holding the coat rack. Relief flooded Laurel's face. Together they slowly guided Fayth Michelle's feet to the floor. She began to put one foot in front of the other, ready to charge toward anything living.

"You grew up in the Midwest and you don't know what a poop-stick is?" Alessia cracked a smile. She couldn't believe a country girl like Laurel didn't know this.

"Uh, no."

"It's when somebody dips a stick in a large dog turd, then runs around chasing everybody with it."

"Is that what we're going to do?" Laurel asked.

"I think our poop-stick has a radar for fresh meat. We're going to use it to get that old fuck."

Alessia held the heavyweight at the base of the coat rack while Laurel guided Fayth Michelle. Maneuvering the coat rack out of the room was the worst part, but Alessia knew there was more to come. Abie wasn't going to let them get away easily. As they walked past Derek Marshall's chattering head, she wondered if everyone could come back to life, or only those who had been bitten.

"Where did the bloody half-corpse go, and what about the poisoned guy?" Laurel asked.

Laurel

Laurel felt relieved to have fresh air in her lungs. Her face still smelled of spit, but she didn't care. The rotting corpse on a stick smelled worse. At least she'd remembered to put her 24-hour deodorant on this morning. She wasn't sure if it or if she would last longer if the day kept on the way it was.

"Hey, watch where you're going," Alessia said from behind.

Laurel looked up to see Fayth Michelle's shoulder bump the wall. She steered her back towards the middle of the hall.

"Thanks," she mumbled. Relief had distracted her, but relief wasn't going to keep them alive. Alessia depended on Laurel to be as good as her, if not better. Laurel wanted to be badass. Her parents had prepped her whole life for this--from anthrax to a super volcano. She was supposed to be able to outlast them all.

Laurel stopped. The coat rack jolted in her hand as Alessia and Fayth Michelle abruptly followed her.

"What now?" Alessia asked impatiently. Fayth Michelle gave out a half-whine, half-groan in protest.

"Did you ever watch horror movies growing up?"

"What kind of dumb fucking question is that?"

Laurel closed her eyes, trying to maintain her patience. She drew out a long breath. "My point is, doesn't this remind you of a certain horror movie?"

Alessia crossed her arms. "What? Fucking *Chainsaw Massacre* or *Saw*? Big fucking deal, some psycho is trying to kill us. Don't matter which movie it is."

"No. I mean, look at Fayth Michelle." Laurel pointed to the undead girl attempting to wiggle her way off the pointed end of the coat rack.

Alessia stood silent for a moment. She looked at Fayth Michelle, then Laurel, then back to Fayth Michelle.

"It occurred to me that we have more than one problem, which is why no one is in the hallway." Laurel looked over Alessia's shoulder to the burned customer service rep. "I'm not sure why she's still on the ground."

"Well, who knows why this one is up and walking around?" Alessia shrugged.

"My best guess is biological warfare." As far as Laurel was concerned, it was the most probable cause of any apocalypse.

"It doesn't really matter though, does it? It could be space aliens for all we know. But we are locked up here on the sixth floor with the Tall Man and at least three of his mobile undead relatives. Who knows who else is going to pop off, especially if that crazy-ass old man is killing them!" Sweat trickled off Alessia's brow.

"Are you okay?" Laurel didn't want to point out the obvious, or seem like a total ass, but Alessia had seemed fine until this point.

"I… ugh." Alessia adjusted the weight of the coat rack base and wiped her forehead with the hem of her shirt. She blew a couple large breaths out of her mouth. "My family takes the dead coming back to life very seriously. Ever heard of Day of the Faithful Departed? Those traditions were in South America before they even spoke Spanish. Plus, is it just me, or is it getting hot in here?"

In her daze, Laurel hadn't noticed that the hallway's temperature had steadily increased.

"What do you think he's going to do next?" As quickly as Laurel said it, she got her answer.

Several of the customer service representatives walked out of the bathroom. They didn't look alive.

Alessia

Just when Alessia thought there was a plan, it was snatched away. It'd been like this at survival camp when the counselors had taken all their supplies, run off, and then chased them around. The cat-and-mouse game was exhausting. Luckily, it only lasted two days. This was a nightmare she was afraid wasn't going to end until they were dead and walking around like the rest of these assholes.

The customer service reps weren't walking very fast which, gave them a few moments to spare.

"What do we do?" she asked Laurel. Logic told her to run, but the intuition that had kept her alive in sticky situations said to start cracking skulls.

"I don't think we have a choice. We're going to have to put them down. I just don't know how. I mean, they're dead but walking around. What do you do with that?" Laurel looked as scared as Alessia felt.

Alessia hated the idea of the dead coming back to earth. Her mother had sworn before she left El Salvador, she'd seen her dead sister walking in a field. Alessia's aunt's face had been partially blown off, her dress torn, and when her mother had walked toward her, she'd growled a terrible noise. Her aunt had been killed during the civil war in 1984. Her mother saw her in 1993.

Alessia had thought her mother was crazy, paranoid, and riddled with trauma from her life before coming to the United States. At the least, maybe she'd seen a ghost, but it sure as hell wasn't someone walking after death and eating flesh.

"I don't think we have a choice but to either dismember them or impale them to the wall. They want to eat anything living." Alessia tugged on the coat hook as she backed up. Laurel followed her lead. They'd been in the process of making weapons when Abie had derailed them. It was time to get back to it.

"Do we really need to keep her?" Laurel nodded towards Fayth Michelle. Alessia had to admit the undead woman's body and the coat rack were a real pain in the ass to navigate.

"Nah, but what do we do with her? She's proof that ramming them doesn't really do anything." Alessia wasn't sure what the answer was.

"What if we bashed her head in?"

Alessia stared at Laurel. It wasn't a response she expected to hear from her, but Laurel didn't stop there. "Or cut her head off?"

Alessia turned to the closet, "I doubt it'll work, but we're definitely going to mess some shit up."

She set down the base of the coat rack and went into the closet to survey their arsenal. They were down one mop stick from earlier. Laurel had dropped it near the elevator. There were still two broom handles, a mop bucket, chemicals to clean the carpet and windows, a wiper blade, a toilet plunger, a snake for drains, and tons of paper towels for them to use.

"Here," Alessia said as she handed Laurel a broom. "We don't have time to modify this right now. Just beat 'em over the head."

Laurel nodded in agreement.

Alessia tossed everything she could in the mop bucket. They needed to be mobile and keep all their supplies.

Thwack!

The quick rasp sounded like it had hit bone. Alessia peeked out into the hallway. Laurel stood sheepishly in front of Fayth Michelle.

"I wanted to see if I could hit someone in the head with the broom."

"Well, apparently you can."

The customer service reps edged closer.

"Are you ready to fight the rest of them?"

"Ready as I'll ever be."

Alessia hoped they were ready. It seemed like every time they had a plan, something else got in their way.

Laurel

"How many hits did it take to bring that one down?" Alessia asked. Laurel thought about it for a minute. She couldn't remember for sure; she'd just kept throwing whacks until they stopped moving.

"I'm going to go with thirty-seven." Laurel looked down at the bloody mess at her feet. She'd only met this guy twice. His unruly brownish-blond hair had fascinated her. He'd kept it off the collar, which was the only requirement for the dress code, but it was still at least a good three to four inches long. Now the hair was speckled with blood and white gooey bits of his brains. Laurel frowned. He shouldn't be dead or even dead again. It was obvious that Abie had had something to do with his first death: his eyes bulged out and though his teeth had chattered like the rest of them, he and the other customer service reps all had swollen tongues. They'd probably been gassed while they were in the bathroom cleaning up.

Laurel felt Alessia behind her.

"At least we got them," Alessia said.

Laurel shrugged. "Yeah, I guess we did. But where's Abie?"

"And how many more of these dead walking are there?" Alessia finished Laurel's thought.

Laurel turned toward Fayth Michelle. Her body was limp on the coat rack. The hit Laurel had given her to the center of the head had pushed the hook up through her skull. She'd stopped moving then. It was a relief and a shock that damage to the brain would stop them. It hadn't stopped the creepy body parts when the head was active. Laurel suspected if they'd crushed Derek Marshall's skull, his hand would have let go of her.

"I can't remember how many people came off that elevator, honestly," she admitted. Laurel felt like a fool for overriding the lockdown protocol. Those people may have had better luck in the lobby than they'd had up here.

It might have been easier to take Abie down, or at least she thought it would.

"Well, where do you think they went?"

Laurel looked around the office. She didn't know. It was so hot now she couldn't really think. Her arms ached from the repetitive motion of swinging the broom.

"Can we go to the break room?"

She walked off, not waiting for Alessia. All Laurel wanted was to turn on the air conditioning and to drink some cold water. Her clothes stuck to her skin. If she found Abie, she'd beat him with his own cane for making them suffer like this. Who knew if he'd randomly placed poisoned bottles of water in the vending machine, but she was willing to chance it.

The break room was dark. There were no windows to let in natural light. She slid her hand against the wall, fishing for the light switch. She'd be crazy to walk in blind. If she could see, she had a good chance of smacking something square in the head or at least keeping it off her.

"Doesn't this room have those sensor lights?" Alessia walked past Laurel into the room.

"Uh, yeah, but don't you think Abie could have disabled them?"

"Maybe, I don't know. I'm so thirsty I could drink a thousand gallons of water. So, I'm willing to take a—" Alessia stopped mid-sentence as the lights popped on. Laurel watched as Alessia did a little wiggle dance in celebration of the illumination.

"Oh gawd," Laurel said without thinking.

"What?" Alessia stopped dancing. "There's a fucking dead walker behind me, right?"

Laurel nodded. She couldn't bring herself to tell Alessia there were four.

Alessia

Alessia took a moment to say a prayer. She'd done it in the past, and it had worked. Hopefully, today was no different. Why it was in her nature to be so damn cocky and then need to pray herself out of trouble later was beyond her. She accepted that a higher power probably had it sorted out for her. They had to. Her experience had always been that she'd be doing all right, and then she'd go do something stupid.

"Where is it?" Alessia asked. Laurel's expression told her it wasn't good.

"I'm trying to decide what I should tell you."

"I like the idea of running." Alessia moved slightly toward Laurel and heard a shuffle behind her. She assumed it would go straight at her.

"Walk towards me." Laurel beckoned Alessia like a mother would a small child.

Alessia started towards Laurel, but stopped in confusion when Laurel strode toward her.

"What? Why are you coming to me? Stay over there."

"No, turn around and look. They aren't moving."

Alessia turned around. Four of the dead stood motionless. Their teeth didn't chatter, and they rocked back and forth.

"They're asleep!" Laurel whispered.

"Why are you whispering?" Alessia returned with a hiss.

Alessia watched, horrified, as Laurel poked one of them with her broomstick. The undead didn't flinch.

"What do you think wakes them up?"

"Dude, how the hell am I supposed to know?" Alessia said. Laurel kept poking at them. Alessia didn't want to go over and take her weapon from her, but it was like she was asking for a fight with the flesh eaters.

"It's probably the dark. Maybe their bodies need sunlight to work?" Laurel said.

Alessia winced as Laurel stood on her tiptoes, peering into the face of a taller man she'd never seen before. Since he wasn't wearing a shitty yellow Bee-Prepared shirt, she assumed he wasn't one of the regular team.

"Well, do you think we should take them out and put them in the sunlight to see if they'll start trying to eat our faces off?"

Laurel pinched the arm of a guy with unnaturally black hair and thick plastic eyeglasses, who Alessia suspected hated his job more than she did. The few times they'd interacted he seemed to either be pissed or stoned.

"Maybe we could put some kind of leash on them? Guide them around like we did with Fayth Michelle? We could study what happens to them."

"No way. We don't know how long we are going to be stuck here. Plus, these assholes aren't coming back. Given the chance, they will eat us. You can bet on it." Alessia looked at the broken mop handle she'd fashioned as a weapon. She knew if the four stayed still, she and Laurel could probably disable them. Her biggest concern was they'd wake up all at once and they wouldn't be able to fight them off. All she really wanted was a tall, cool glass of water.

"Ah what the hell," Alessia said. She stood behind the tall stranger and with one swift thrust, she shoved the mop handle into the base of his skull. The crunching sound made her stomach lurch, but she held it together as she pulled out the stick. He fell forward to the floor taking two of the others with him.

"What'd you do that for?" Laurel asked.

"Because leaving them up and walking is like leaving a bunch of time bombs lying around. Who the fuck knows when they're going to go off?" Alessia systematically shoved her mop handle into the skulls of the other two on the ground. She felt a pang of guilt at the unfair fight. But it really was kill or be killed. A couple of her old crew had said that many times, but she'd never felt threatened enough to do more than whip somebody's ass.

Laurel sighed. Alessia watched as her new crew member bludgeoned the guy with the thick eyeglasses until he finally toppled to the ground.

"Do you feel better now?" Laurel asked, throwing her broom to the ground.

"No."

Alessia sat down at the lunch table and laid her head down.

Laurel

Laurel kept a careful eye on Alessia as she searched the break room for food and water. Focusing on survival basics made her feel in charge instead of completely useless. It had only been fifteen minutes since Alessia had shut down, but time wasn't on the same schedule, as usual. The day kept speeding up and slowing down. Laurel didn't think she had any more adrenaline left in her body to crank out. She opened the cabinets above the sink. The contents were sparse: concentrated dehydrated coffee creamer, a small container of sugar, some cheap coffee, and stir sticks. Laurel arranged the contents of the cabinet on the nearest table trying not to disturb Alessia.

She looked over at the pile of bodies and clenched her teeth. There was a part of her that admired Abie for the stories from Vietnam. He'd killed people to survive, or at least the way he'd told the story he had. After finding out about his twisted side, she suspected he may have run off at the time to kill for pleasure.

Abie was a threat that needed to be stopped sooner, not later. Laurel squatted down. The bottom cabinets didn't hold anything special: a couple of storage bowls, and some plastic spoons and forks. She pulled open the drawers, but there was nothing much there, either. Someone in the office had been kind enough to start a take-out drawer. She shuffled through the papers, checking to make sure there wasn't anything else hiding in the drawer. The tips of her fingers felt the blade of the knife before she saw it. Laurel pulled out her hand. Drops of blood blotted the paper menus. She stood up and grabbed a paper towel, putting pressure on the wounds.

The blade of the knife showed no evidence of slicing her. Her fingers didn't sting, but it did bother her to have open wounds while blood and guts were flying. She picked up the knife by the handle and placed it with her newly found supplies. There were fourteen bottles of water, three bags of potato chips, four candy bars, an apple, a half-eaten sandwich from the mini fridge, and a large portion of stale birthday cake. Of course, there was the coffee creamer, sugar, and coffee that she knew they would get some use out of. If they could get into the stock room, they would be set for a long time. There were multiple options for MREs, flashlights, water purification, and even a Bible if they needed it.

She grabbed a plastic fork and dug into the birthday cake. The icing was crusty, and the cake dry. It wasn't even a good cake, but the sugar high would feel good for a little while. The apple would have been a better choice, and it would last longer than the cake. Bite after bite, she shoved the cake into her mouth. She opened a bottle of water and guzzled it. Violence was not easy for her. Even when she had been learning self-defense back at the ranch, it had always occurred to her that things could possibly be talked out.

It wasn't going to happen today. Laurel grabbed the knife. She knew what she had to do, but for it to work, she'd need Alessia to stand beside her. It would take both to stop Abie.

Alessia

"You'd think it would be easy to find an old man rolling around in an office chair," Alessia grumbled as she tapped on a doorknob with the window wiper blade. Metal sparks flew. She wished that she'd kept track of the stupid mousepad with the rubber backing.

"Well, we're not going in that one anytime soon." She moved on to the next door.

"Think of it this way, even if he is behind one of these doors we can't open, he needs us alive. He needs help. Sure, he wants to kill everybody, but he doesn't have a death wish," Laurel said as she stood beside Alessia. Laurel held her broomstick up to her shoulder, ready for an epic battle at any moment, or as Alessia considered it further, an epic game of stickball.

Another spark flew from the next door.

"Well, why did he act like he was ready to take us out, then disappear?" Alessia's frustration was coming back; they knew for sure there was a psychopath on the loose, a re-animated torso, and a poisoned undead guy walking around here somewhere. The tension of the unknown made her feel unhinged. Plus, every doorknob seemed to be charged. The old man could play cat and mouse for a couple of days at this rate. He might have even locked the two undead in one of the rooms as a trap for them.

She tapped the last doorknob with no success.

"Where else could he be?" Alessia's question was as much for herself as it was for Laurel.

"Well, we didn't look in the call center. I guess we could go over there."

Alessia leaned against the wall, then slid down. She stared at the long, dark hallway to the call center. The place wasn't set up to make people happy. Tiny cubicles were packed together, creating a feeling of being caged like an animal. It was bad enough when you weren't expecting someone to jump out and bite you or do some sadistic shit to you.

Laurel sat down facing the doors to the elevator. Alessia watched as she stared at the bloody mess from earlier. Laurel giggled.

"What?" Alessia asked.

"You have to admit that dead guy getting cut in half was seriously fucked up." Laurel continued to laugh until she fell back on the floor.

This is what Alessia had seen people do in juvie when they were broken. Who was she to judge, though? She'd checked out for a good two hours earlier, after she'd taken out three of the undead. Laurel continued to roll on the floor as though she were a child at a slumber party.

Alessia looked down the hall again. She noticed something she'd not seen before. A tiny green light flickered in the corner of the hallway. She stood up and walked toward it. She tried not to think about what else could be lurking in the shadows.

Laurel stopped laughing, pushed herself up, and followed behind. Alessia wanted to reach out for her hand but held back. She was a grown woman, not some scared little girl who was afraid of the dark. As she reached the light, she bent down to pick up the object.

"What is it?"

"A cane."

The long, brown wooden cane Abie had carried wasn't wood at all. It was smooth, heavy, and reminded Alessia of super-hardened pottery. The green light was some sort of power switch. Several other buttons lined the curvature of the handle. This had been how he'd continued to change things on them. He was down the hallway if he'd left his cane. It made sense. Abie probably wouldn't go down the hallway willingly, but if he'd had an undead Rick Moranis look-alike and a torso chasing him, then he might have.

Alessia handed the cane to Laurel for inspection. She'd expected her to say something, but she stood silently, surveying the design of the cane.

"We're already down here. Might as well check the damn call center." Alessia continued down the dark hallway. The call center was deliberately located far away from the senior staff. They could have easily put an entrance near the elevators for people to walk through, but that would have given the impression they were equal and had the same access as the administrative staff.

The call center was vacant. Rows and rows of empty cubicles filled the room. The gray carpet gave the place a dark and gloomy feeling even with the natural light streaming in.

"Look." Laurel pointed to a photo on a desk as they passed.

Alessia recognized the woman as the 1950's librarian. In the photo, the woman smiled from ear to ear as she hugged two young women. She looked proud to be with them. Alessia guessed they were her daughters. It triggered thoughts of her own mother, although she figured her mom was fine wherever she was. She'd always made it through everything else. A couple of people rising from the dead wouldn't be a problem. Not for that tough old lady.

The late afternoon sun shone through the windows and magnified the shadows. Alessia noticed a trail of what she assumed was blood darkening the carpet where the light hit the ground between the cubicles.

She followed the trail.

Laurel

Laurel held back laughter as she watched the torso of a man desperately shove his fingers under the closet door. It reminded her of Georgia, her cat back home, she always stuck her paws under the bathroom door when Laurel was peeing.

Alessia shot her a dirty look. This made Laurel want to break out even more. She snorted instead. The Rick Moranis look-alike turned towards them.

"Ah, man." Alessia groaned. Laurel watched as Alessia impaled the undead guy in the shoulder, then guided him to a cubicle where she stuck the mop handle through the cork board wall. His hands reached for Alessia. She stepped away.

" We might need him," Alessia explained.

Laurel nodded. Alessia grabbed the cane from Laurel. She walked over to the door, avoiding the oblivious torso, which kept clawing underneath. She rapped twice.

"*Oh Abie*, are you in there?" Alessia asked in a teasing sing-song voice.

Silence.

Laurel didn't want to play around. The sooner they ended this, the sooner she could close her eyes and rest for a couple of minutes. It would stop her giggles, and maybe they could take a breath to develop a plan to get out of the building.

"Can we just open the door and drag him out?"

"Come on, that's no fun. Think of how he's tortured us." Alessia looked disappointed in her. Revenge would be sweet, thought Laurel, but the old guy had some important information they needed.

"Well, we could just get him out and tie him up. I'm sure he'll come around eventually." Laurel thought about it for a minute. "Maybe."

Alessia rapped on the door with the cane again.

"Abie, we know you're in there. Do you want us to get you out, or do you want to die in there?" Alessia was all business.

A muffled voice replied, "Do you ladies have my cane?"

"What cane?" Alessia said.

"Go get my cane and get me out of here. We can work something out," Abie said. His voice was less maniacal now, and more like that of a tired old man.

"Oh, I bet you want to work something out. You crazy fuck," Alessia grumbled under her breath.

Laurel knew just as well as Alessia they weren't going to be able to let him go. It made her heart sink a little. It was like when you found out too late that your dog had rabies. He needed to be put out of his misery before he could hurt anyone else.

"Abie, I know you're a good person at heart. You just need some help. We'll help you. We'll take care of you."

Silence.

Alessia gave her a thumbs-up. Laurel signaled to Alessia to pull the torso away from the door. The duo dragged him by the arms, being careful to not let him roll onto his back. Laurel stood on him while Alessia grabbed a desk chair. The two positioned the legs in a way that pinned him. Alessia straddled the chair and grounded her feet solidly on the floor. Laurel walked over to the door and without thinking went for the doorknob. She recoiled at the last moment. It was so easy to forget that anything could be booby trapped in this place.

Laurel took out her silver earring and tossed it at the doorknob. No spark. She took a deep breath and carefully pulled the door open.

"Abie?"

Laurel was smart enough to keep her head back. There was no telling what else the old guy had up his sleeve.

The edge of the door appeared to spontaneously combust. Ringing filled Laurel's ears.

Behind her, Laurel heard a muted Alessia say, "What the fuck?"

The door exploded again, this time right in front of her; the side of Laurel's face felt wet. She backed away from the door, leaving it open. She didn't feel like laughing now. Her stomach felt ice cold. She walked over to the wall and braced herself against it. The room spun around her.

Laurel watched through a daze as Alessia jumped out of the chair, letting the torso free. It reminded Laurel of an action movie where the hero does everything elegantly in slow motion, with a contorted look of vengeance and anger. Alessia pulled the mop handle with the undead walker out of the wall. She swung him around and shoved him into the closet, slamming the door behind him.

Single pops went off one by one.

Alessia grabbed Laurel by the arm and pulled her up.

"Help me shove this set of cubicles in front of the door. Even if they don't kill him, that motherfucker can starve to death in there."

Laurel looked at her friend. She knew it was blood running down her face, but the bullet wasn't in her skull, she was pretty sure about that.

"You fucking little bitches! You'll never get out of here alive!" Abie screamed.

"Well, neither will he." Alessia grunted as they shoved the square desk against the door.

Laurel let out a laugh so hard she could feel it in her belly.

Alessia

"We've got seventy-two days' worth of meals," Laurel said as she handed Alessia a chicken Alfredo MRE.

Alessia turned back from the window. She couldn't meet Laurel's eye. Instead, she gave a weak smile.

"Are you thinking about your mom?"

"Yeah," Alessia mumbled. She wished she could have a different conversation with her mother than the last one they'd had. In her heart, she wanted to believe her mother was still alive.

"I think about my family, too."

"Yeah, but your family has bunkers and shit out in the middle of nowhere." Alessia knew Laurel was probably as worried about her family as she was about her mom. It was different seeing the city your family was in crumble around you.

"Well, these assholes owned a prepper manufacturing company. Where did it get them?" Laurel chuckled.

Alessia looked back out the window. Smoke billowed from another building. They were in a fortress amidst a concrete jungle of a forest fire.

"Are we going to try to get out of here today?" Alessia asked.

"Yeah, why not?" Laurel dug her spoon into the brown foil package. "Isn't that the same thing we've been doing for the last two months?"

Alessia desperately wanted out of the building. They'd gotten used to the smell of rotten flesh. They'd dragged the bodies into Sean Marshall's old office and stuffed the vents with clothes. The door was sealed with duct tape, but the smell continued to creep through the hallways to remind them of their violent transgressions.

Modern technology didn't help, either. For all the MREs, tents, sleeping bags, and warm packs they'd found there wasn't a single transistor radio, a television that could pick up an antenna signal, or any way to communicate with the outside world. A couple of weeks ago, there had been someone in a skyscraper across the street putting up signs. The building had later caught fire and crumpled to the ground. There was no way to tell if the guy was still alive. The streets were choked with random shuffling walkers. She and Laurel had cheered when building debris had fallen on the oblivious undead.

Alessia looked out the window.

"What time is it?" Alessia asked.

"Is it out there?" Laurel scooted over to Alessia.

"Yeah, it's still far out, but it's coming."

In the distance, a helicopter flew towards the building. They sat and watched as it came closer and closer. Alessia held back her desire to jump up and scream. The two had stopped doing that after two weeks. The people in the helicopter weren't interested in survivors.

Alessia scooped up the last of her MRE, then folded over the bag. She pushed herself up and tossed it in the trash.

"You ready to start?" she asked Laurel.

"Let's do what we do every day," Laurel said as she got up.

Alessia knew they were in their tomb, but she'd wait until their seventy-two days were up to decide what to do next. Today, they would just try to get out.

AN IMPURE GARDEN

An erratic, massive wall of green assaulted Zazo's eyes as she stood at the overpowering sliding glass door to her covered courtyard. Dread filled her as she remembered the wisdom from the other garden club wives. They'd droned on and on about how the garden connected the foreign soil to the settlers of the planet, and without that connection, there would be disharmony. She'd attended the meeting while counting the days until she could get off this dreaded rock. And yet, she was still here almost a year later. Alone. She looked up at the red, rolling sky. A hexagonal dome protected the garden, but she felt like it would suffocate her if she stepped out the door. She wanted to be back on Earth. She'd gladly trade the impure air there for the stale, dry manufactured air here.

She touched the glass and smoothly dragged her finger to the left. The glass shifted open. Blue and brown engulfed the yard. Her mind knew the plants were green, but the always-present reddened schema tricked her eyes. She slipped on her color-adjusting glasses. The sky revealed a beautiful blue, and plants became various shades of green. Relief surged through her. She could appreciate the different colors of the flowers. She pulled her gardening gloves from her apron pocket and slipped them on. They tightened automatically around her wrist, promising to keep the soil and all undesirable things from her hands.

The plants had not stilled in her hiatus. There were large patches of grass in areas where before there'd only been mulch and tulips. The honeysuckle swirled and twirled, wild and overgrown. The rose bushes were taller than her. She stood beside one of the behemoths and felt the top thorns scratch at the top of her head. Some of them were the size of her thumb. She didn't remember them being that big at home.

When she'd moved to planet R-062109, she'd followed her husband, Captain Nhong, as a naïve galactic air bride. Now, she sat at home while he traveled the galaxy. He'd laughed at her when she'd asked to go with him. He had told her she should be thankful to live in such a great colony. There were other women for company, activities to do, and when he came home next time, he'd give her a baby, so she didn't feel so lonely. It wasn't that she felt lonely; it was that she felt unfulfilled. Nothing could fix that except her. Her purpose was not to tend a garden. Her purpose was not to throw lavish parties where everyone was so drunk, she wasn't sure they'd have the sensibility to switch on their breathing apparatuses as they walked home across the complex. She'd been someone before she'd met him. She'd been a real person. Now she was just a memory on a red planet, standing beside a rosebush that could shred her if she wasn't careful.

She'd always hated roses.

She moved away from the bush and walked along the stone-paved path. The squares were loose; there was no wonder grass had grown underneath them. She kicked one of the stones with her toe. It moved easily. Her toe seared a little from the impact. The pain surprised her. She'd thought there was no feeling left in her. The captain had seen to that. She shook her head, thinking about their last words before he'd flown out. Sure, at the beginning of her time here, he'd promised a baby, a trip to Earth, and the hope that she wouldn't ever come back here. But before he'd left the last time, he'd promised she would never leave this planet. No one would have the guts to help another's wife escape. Marriage counseling was not part of their business. Moving cargo and people without asking questions or worrying about the happiness of wives was.

She opened her small shed and looked at her wide array of tools, trying to decide which one would help to recreate the environment that she'd seen the first time she'd walked into the unit. She'd walked to the back wall of glass and had been breathless at the beauty that had lain before her. She hadn't realized then when she took the glasses off how red and harsh everything would look. She'd kept the glasses off for so long now. The red made her feel exhausted and hopeless. She wanted her old perception back. She grabbed a machete and steadied it in her hand. She grinned.

As she approached the honeysuckle bush, she

crouched down and looked under the large rambling mess. As the rose bush had grown upwards, the honeysuckle had wrapped around the base, trying to choke it out. The rose bush had kept growing upwards, but the roots were dying. She hacked the tentacles of the honeysuckle away from the bush with her machete. Pulling the vines that dangled from the roses' stems, she yanked them away. That's when she noticed the attached tendrils were dry and brittle near the base of the honeysuckle. She lifted the green of the honeysuckle to reveal a gray, dried base. The rose bush was imploding upon itself. It couldn't sustain the weight of the green. She hacked at the dead bits underneath. That's when she saw it. She gasped.

In the center of the honeysuckle bush, a native plant had embedded itself. Its deep brown stems were snaking through the bush, trying to reach out to the rest of the garden. She'd been warned to check the gardens every day. These plants were parasitic, and their spores could get into the air filtration system and kill everyone in the compound. A tear ran down her cheek. Feelings of anger, frustration, and shame coursed through her. Shame was the worst of all. Shame kept her from admitting she'd let such a vile plant be tracked into her sanctuary. It was her job to keep this from happening. She was tired of living like this but didn't want to hurt anyone else. It was her part to help create air for the artificial ecosystem. Now everything was in jeopardy because of her selfishness, her hatred of gardening, and her resentment of Nhong leaving her all alone on a planet she hated. She'd sacrificed her friends, family, and career to be his wife. She sat down and cried as she watched the interloper pulsate.

How had the plant gone undetected for so long? She touched her dry, brittle hair, and looked at her cracked skin. She'd been told to moisturize every day, but the bathhouse seemed pointless. The bathhouse was for women who wanted to feel alive, who wanted to keep up appearances, and cared about themselves. None of that applied to her. The garden was destroyed, the ecosystem was potentially in danger, and there was nothing left of her. She pushed herself up and wiped her eyes with the back of her arm. Getting the deadly plant out of her garden was now her priority. Though she needed to seal off the vent to the garden, she'd have enough oxygen to complete her task and resolve the issue.

She stared through the back glass panel to the courtyard with satisfaction. Black soot covered everything, the dome panels, the walls, the floor. Everyone had thought she was insane. She ran her singed fingertips over her scalded bald head.

"Mrs. Nhong, are you ready to leave?" The military police officer asked.

"I absolutely am." She turned to the officer and smiled.

Her garden was pure, and now she could leave.

MANEATER

November 1, 1982

Rich Girl

"So, you think he'll do it?" Julie asked, arching one of her perfectly coiffed Brooke Shields' eyebrows as her pouty lips spread into her wicked trademark smile. She turned back to the mirror and teased her frosted bangs.

Sarah stared at her friend, afraid to say what she felt. She wasn't allowed to say no to Julie. Well, she could say no, but it would be social suicide. She shifted her weight from one Ked to the other, leaning her hip on the cracked porcelain of the bathroom sink. She looked around the dark room. Toilet paper littered the floor. She swore there was a needle in the corner of one stall. Her stomach lurched with fear. This place was a dive, and she knew Julie was desperate if they were slumming here.

"Um, sure. I bet he'll do it for you." Sarah couldn't be sure that Chad would write the paper. He was one of the best writers she knew, could research anything, and fool anyone into believing he was an expert. He had shown Sarah around the card catalog a few times in high school. She'd pulled away when he'd touched her fingers as they'd flashed through the stiff manila cards. She regretted it now. How was she supposed to know that the guy who wore enormous glasses and polyester pull-overs would turn into such a babe?

Chad had metamorphosed from the class dork to the guy wearing a trench coat, smoking cigarettes in the bar, and experimenting with film. He was her dream guy, though it sure didn't look like it since she'd been running around with Julie. Her own frosted hair, pink polo, and knock-off Tiffany pearls would clash next to his dark brooding self.

Now, *she* felt like a loser. In moments, she would hand over her dream guy to someone who would devour him for his brains and then kick him to the curb when he was no longer useful. What kind of person trades a chance of love for popularity? Her, that's who. She'd changed everything about herself to fit in with the Alpha Kappa Alphas, and she was the servant to their president, or as some liked to call it, her best friend.

If Julie wasn't so rich, she'd tell her to go to hell, and hit a rehab center on her way there. Julie's cocaine habit was killing her. It was the reason the girl stayed so skinny and peppy but also why she couldn't finish a paper to save her life.

It was about that time. Julie ran her finger over her eyebrows, ensuring they were in place, teased her hair one more time, slathered fuchsia pink lipstick on her lips, and popped her collar. It was time for her "fairy dust", as Julie liked to call it. Sara sighed. Tinkerbell from hell was about to come out.

You Make My Dreams Come True

Julie thought the white powder sparkled like diamonds, and according to her dealer, this batch was supposed to be exceptional. She lined the powder up on her compact with her platinum credit card. The card had many uses. Thankfully, her dad was a sucker for keeping her happy. It was one of Julie's many skills, making people feel like their only job was to keep her pleased. Of course, she would let them feel the consequences if they decided her happiness, wasn't their priority.

Just take her dealer, such a nice guy. She'd met him in Chemistry 101 freshman year. It had taken little to convince him that his aspirations and skill could cure cancer and synthesize coke. All she'd had to do was give him a little confidence, some money, and the promise of a kiss. That was it. He was hers.

She giggled. The thought of getting high made her high.

The little voice in her head that encouraged her worst habits nudged her. Julie placed the edge of the straw on the mirror and leaned over. The night was going to be a blast. She'd charm the hell out of Sarah's crush, get her paper written, and move on to the next thrill.

"You should try this. You'd lose those ten pounds you're struggling with." She turned to Sarah. Her frumpy friend leaned against the corner with arms crossed, looking uncomfortable. Julie frowned a little. After tonight, she'd have to talk to Sarah about her looks. She needed to lose her freshman weight, and what was she doing wearing black jeans with white Keds?

"I'm good, Julie. Let's just get going before I lose my nerve."

Julie leaned over and snorted the three lines. It only took about fifteen seconds before she felt the rush. A huge smile crossed her face. Her heart raced as adrenaline surged through her. She could do anything! She was going to graduate on time! She would get a great job! She would be everything she needed to be and rule the world!

She stood up, snapped her compact together, tossed it in her handbag, and threw her handbag over her shoulder.

"Let's go, bitch!" Julie yelled at Sarah as she yanked open the bathroom door. She walked out into the darkness of the club. Strobing lights moved around her, and synth music engulfed her.

Her heart slowed and the feeling she was going to rule the world faded to a sinking feeling that made her panic. The glowing strobe lights were darkening, the sound of the music was lowering, and a sinking feeling pulled inward from the pit of her stomach. The pull strengthened with every beat of her heart. She couldn't stop herself as her head tipped backward and her legs gave out.

Bad Habits and Infections

Chad shifted the sleeves of his long black mariner trench coat. The cuffs were a little short for him, but he'd stolen it from his stepfather's closet over the summer, anyway. The old man did not know what day it was half the time. He would not miss a musty old coat he'd worn in the late sixties, training new recruits for war. Chad liked the symbolism of wearing it to college and for something other than its intended purpose.

He scanned the room, searching for Sarah. She'd caught him off guard when she'd asked him to hang out tonight. They hadn't spoken since their senior year of high school in Cortland, a place best known for apples than anything else. He'd seen her on campus a few times over the past two years. He hadn't had the nerve to talk to her. She was always with her sorority sisters, and he couldn't deal with them, especially Julie.

Julie was a blonde viper, as far as he was concerned. One of his friends in the dorm obsessed over her and always stared at his pager, waiting for her to call for him. He felt bad for the guy. But he wasn't a victim, he always bragged he could create anything in his homemade lab inside his dormitory. Chad was not into drugs. His only drug was creating, and destroying his brain would not help him create, even though some of his classmates swore by it.

A beacon of light popped into the back of the club. Chad squinted. The black lights accented the white in Julie's hair and the bright pink of the shirt she wore. She looked wild-eyed as she came through the bathroom door. He shifted his head back and forth to see around her. Julie's arms flailed upward, her mouth flew open, and he couldn't tell if she was about to have a seizure or that is what she called dancing. She rocked backward as though she was about to limbo. Without thinking, he rushed toward her. She was going to fall straight into Sarah.

By the time he pushed through the bodies on the dance floor, they were both on the ground. Sarah had already pushed herself to a seated position and held Julie's head in her lap. She patted Julie's cheek, trying to wake her up. Chad knelt beside her.

"You, okay?" He held out his hand to Sarah.

"I'm fine." Sarah didn't take his hand, and instead she gestured toward Julie. "Can you help me with her? I'm afraid we are going to get stomped on."

"Yeah, let me grab her." Chad slipped his arms underneath Julie's armpits and scooped her up toward him. Sarah stood up and motioned for him to share the weight. They placed Julie's arms over their shoulders, walked her to the wall of the bar, and plopped her on a barstool out of the way.

"Can you get her a soda and some water? Maybe a little sugar and water will help her?" Sarah asked.

Chad was doubtful.

"She's going to be okay. This has happened before. She snorted a little too much cocaine a couple of minutes ago. It isn't the end of the world." It wasn't hard for Chad to believe her.

All American Girl

Saying Julie had snorted a little too much cocaine a couple of times was an understatement. Sarah didn't want to mention the multiple times the nursing students in the sorority had either started CPR on Julie or called 911. The way the night was going, Sarah decided she'd rather roll the dice than get the cops involved. Julie's wrath would be worse.

"Here," Chad handed her a fizzling cup of clear soda, "I figured she didn't need the caffeine."

Sarah looked up and smiled at him. She remembered how thoughtful he was.

"Can you help me with her?" Sarah shifted Julie's weight onto Chad.

Sarah tilted her friend's head back and poured a small amount of liquid into the side of her mouth, careful to make sure Julie didn't choke. She placed an ice cube on the back of Julie's neck, trying to stimulate her senses. At least she appeared to be breathing, and her body wasn't any limper than Sarah had seen before.

"Do you guys do this often?" Chad shouted over the music.

Sarah didn't know how to answer. Did she clean up Julie's messes often? Yes. Did she go along with bad ideas? Yes. Did they go to dive bars that needed to be shut down by the health department? No. Did they go to fraternity and sorority houses that needed to shut down for their horrible antics. Yes, they did that.

"Not really. I wanted to see you and heard this was a cool place to hang out." Sarah took a deep breath, trying to keep herself calm. It was only a half-lie.

She looked out over the bar. Yeah, it was okay, she guessed. The light blue and white lights strobed to the sound of heavy synth music. Everyone in the place was wearing black, and Mohawks bopped up and down throughout the dance floor.

"Yeah, I guess. Not a great place to talk, though."

Chad made an excellent suggestion.

"Let's get her out of here. At least at my dorm, we can get one of the pre-med guys to look at her, and we have a guy who deals in biochemistry that might have something to kick her back to life."

"Sure." Sarah tried to shake an uneasy feeling coming over her. Julie wasn't waking up and there would not be much more they could do for her.

Sarah tried to ignore the shouts from the patrons in the bar as they pushed through the crowd.

"I think your friend needs a hospital."

"Hey, that prep is wasted!"

"Dude, that girl is fucked up!"

"Watch where you're going!"

Sarah just nodded and smiled as they dragged Julie to the door. When they reached the exit, a fine mist of rain flew through the night air. It magnified the orange from the streetlights to make them appear on fire.

Once out on the street, the rain came down in sheets.

Julie groaned.

"Julie?" Sarah asked, hoping for a response.

No Brain No Pain

Julie wondered if this was what they talked about by having an out-of-body experience. Magnified sounds overwhelmed her–heartbeats, breathing, even stomach growling flooded her senses. Yet, for every sound and feeling of those around her that magnified, her body felt numb. She was paralyzed. Nothing wanted to work. Sarah was prattling on about something. There were words, she was sure of that, and now the loser guy was nearby. Oh man, the smells were everywhere. Drakkar Noir filled her nostrils to the point she wanted to puke.

They'd heaved her over somewhere. She couldn't tell because her eyes wouldn't open. After what seemed like forever, they were on the move again. It didn't hurt physically, but it hurt her soul to know that her feet were dragging her favorite Gucci loafers across a dingy ass bar floor. She'd *almost* had to beg her daddy to let her go to Italy and get these. You couldn't just pick them up in upper Manhattan.

After what seemed like an endless parade of human bodily functions tormenting her ears, the environment changed. It was quieter, though they were still on the move. Large drops of wetness hit the top of her head and assaulted her face. One of her senses was coming back to her. A sound of happiness came out of her throat. Something was changing! Her skin tingled. She didn't even care if the water ruined her hair, her makeup; it didn't matter. She was coming back to life. After this, she'd never do coke again. Hearing and smelling everything, she detested and nothing else made her realize that her body needed a break.

Her mouth opened on its own again. She let the rain trickle in.

"Aaaaahhhh."

Sarah and the loser's voices were still garbled. She didn't care what they had to say, anyway. Thankfully, her body was shaking off the paralysis. Her arms twitched, and then one of her legs came back to life. She lunged forward but felt the tug of her escorts keeping her in line.

If everything kept up at this pace, she'd be back to dancing and getting what she wanted in no time.

Adult Education

Chad's resident assistant, Jack, popped out of his room, leaned on his doorframe, crossed his arms, and frowned. "You know you can't have girls in your room after midnight."

"It's 10:45. What's the big deal?" Chad scoffed as he pushed by. He knew Jack would pound on the door at ten till midnight, ready to kick the girls out.

Jack squinted with suspicion. "Is she okay?"

"She's fine. We're just going to sober her up." Sarah spoke up before Chad could make something up.

"Huh, well, let me know if you need a hand. I'm trained in this." Jack started walking with them.

"We're good, man. Don't sweat it. I'll come get you if we need you. We just need some water and time." Chad waved his hand toward Jack's room, hoping the nosey bastard would get a clue.

"Oh, okay." Jack backed away and went back to his room. Chad noted he kept the door open. That wasn't too out of the ordinary. The guy took his job way too seriously.

At Chad's door, he struggled to find his keys. Julie's arms and legs twitched and trembled. He wasn't sure if she was attempting meaningful movement or what.

Sarah grunted. "Who knew a hundred- and ten-pound

person could weigh this much? The more she moves, the heavier she feels."

"I can't find my keys." Chad patted every pocket of his coat. This was the worst time to lose his keys.

"Aaaaaaargh." Julie complained.

"Yeah, yeah, yeah. I hear you."

Down the hall, a door opened. Chad knew it was the biochemist himself, Paul.

"Hey, whatcha doing?" Paul asked as he came upon the group. He towered over them all but was thin as a pencil. It didn't help his look that he wore large wire-framed glasses and attempted to bleach his jet-black hair, leaving it more orange than blonde.

"We've got a friend who's having problems sobering up. Do you got anything that can help her?"

Paul eyed Julie. "Sure. Let me go see what I have already made up."

"Thanks." Chad patted his last pocket and found his keys, "Excuse the mess." He opened the door to a room filled with pizza boxes, storyboards, and video equipment.

"It's fine, let's get her on the bed. Put her on her side," Sarah instructed. Julie continued to make guttural sounds and flail her arms and legs as they placed her on the bed.

"What is wrong with her? A stroke?" Sarah asked. Chad had no idea. His grandpa had experienced a stroke, it looked a little like this, but Julie was so young. She reminded him more of a zombie than anything else.

"Yeah, I don't know," he said, running his fingers through his hair. "I just hope Paul has something that can help her."

"Me, too," Sarah mumbled. She'd propped herself on his desk. She kept rubbing the sides of her arms as though she needed to warm herself. Her brow furrowed in worry.

"Do you need a jacket? You look cold."

"No, no, I'm okay. Don't worry about me. Let's just get her better. If this Paul guy can't help her, I'm going to just call an ambulance. If she wakes up pissed, I'll deal with it later. Her father will get their lawyer to fix up anything I can't clean up." Sarah pushed herself up on the desk to sit back. She leaned her head on the wall and closed her eyes. "Do you have anything to drink?"

"What do you want?" Chad asked, going over to his fridge. He didn't keep alcohol in his room; it was too risky.

"Anything." Sarah smiled.

"Let me grab a glass." Chad prayed he had a clean one somewhere. He found one that met the minimum criteria of not having water stains in it. As he walked past Sarah, she leaned forward and grabbed his arm. She pulled him near, then kissed him on the cheek.

"Thanks. You've made my night a lot easier."

"You're welcome? This seems like a nightmare. You go through this all the time?" Chad didn't want to think about that kiss. If he let his mind go there, he'd analyze it to death, and they didn't have time for that.

"I'm tired, and you made it a lot easier."

"Maybe you need to get a new class of friends," Chad suggested with a half serious smile.

"Maybe?" Sarah let go of his arm.

Julie groaned in the background.

"I'll be back. I just need to grab some water down the hall."

"Cool." Sarah leaned back again and closed her eyes.

Say It Isn't So

Sarah's eyes popped open at the sound of a thud. Julie was flopping around on the floor and foaming at the mouth.

"Shit!" Sarah jumped down from her perch and crouched by Julie's side. She slapped her friend's cheek. "Damn it, wake up. What is wrong with you?" She attempted to roll Julie onto her side. Julie's mouth went for Sarah's arm, teeth gnashing.

Sarah pulled back. "Julie, what the hell?!"

A knock at the door pulled Sarah out of her shock. She pushed herself up and went to see who it was. She prayed it wasn't the nosey resident assistant. Before she could reach the door, Paul opened it and peeped his head in.

"Everything going, okay? I've got something for your friend." Paul's smile and friendliness put Sarah on edge, but she felt like she didn't have any options.

"Come on in. She's started getting worse." Sarah moved out of Paul's way. The room was long and narrow. She wasn't sure how they'd all fit when Chad returned.

Paul squatted beside Julie. Sarah's stomach soured as she watched Paul lick his lips, before caressing Julie's face with his hands. What an odd way to assess someone. Before Sarah could say something about his behavior, he pulled a stethoscope out of his pants pocket and placed the ends in his ears. Then he leaned over Julie and placed the bell on her chest. He grinned a little.

"I can fix this. Easy, peasy." Paul pulled out a syringe from his back pocket.

Sarah was shocked at the color of the solution in the syringe. It was neon green with ultraviolet specks swirling through it.

"What is that?" Sarah asked. This night seemed to be getting worse.

"Don't worry. It just looks intimidating. Give me a sec. I'm going to give her a low dose and see what happens."

"See what happens? What is that stuff? Have you tested this on anyone?"

"Nah, sometimes you've just got to wing it. You got anything I can tie her arm with? I need her veins to pop out."

Sarah scanned the room, looking for anything that could help. She paused. What was she doing? A strange guy was asking her to find a tourniquet to tie her best friend's arm off so he could shoot her up with a weird solution.

"You know, I think I'll just call for an ambulance. I don't know what I've been doing. This is nuts…"

Paul stood up. "Are you sure that is a good idea? I mean, you have been letting her use drugs in front of you for years. What if she is brain dead? Her rich daddy isn't going to appreciate a vegetable being shipped home at Thanksgiving."

"How do you know anything about either of us?" *Who was this guy?*

"Seriously, don't worry about your friend. I've got this

all under control." Paul walked toward Sarah and despite his words, his motion seemed threatening. Sarah backed up against the door, blocking herself in. She grabbed for the doorknob and stepped back to pull the door open. Paul's lanky arm shot out around her waist and pulled her close. She felt a sharp sting in her neck. The room spun, then went black.

Falling

A familiar scent entered the room, but Julie couldn't figure out what it was. At least the Drakkar Noir had dialed down a bit. If she could just get control of her arms and legs, everything would be fine. A muffled voice spoke close to her ear. She groaned as gravity pulled her head backward while her body went forward in the air. Someone was picking her up. From deep in her throat, she pulled out a louder groan in protest. This night was not going at all how she'd planned. The fact that she couldn't see made everything even scarier.

More muffled words reached her ears. Was someone trying to reassure her? It sure wasn't helping anything if they were. Blood rushed to her brain. Was she upside down now? Her pelvis bumped up and down. They were moving. A warm sensation overwhelmed the side of her head. Had something hit her? She tried to swing her arm.

Where was Sarah? Didn't she basically employ that hanger-on?

The bumping stopped. Julie's head flung backward again, and she fell onto a soft surface.

Pressure leaned on her abdomen and a familiar smell

assaulted her nose. Someone was in her personal space, way too far in her personal space. She didn't like it at all. She groaned as loud as she could in protest. If she ever got out of this situation, she would make everyone pay. This was turning into the worst night of her life.

The pressure lifted off her. Shuffling and shifting sounded in the background, and then music began. She couldn't understand the words, but she knew it was music by the beat and vibration.

I Don't Wanna Lose You

"So, how's your intoxicated friend doing?"

Chad looked up into the mirror. Jack stood behind him with his arms crossed.

"She's getting there." Chad lifted his cup. "Water always seems to do the trick."

"Yeah, so how did you come to know two AKAs? Aren't you a film guy? Those two do not look like film-o-philes." Jack leaned on the sink and inspected Chad.

"What're you getting at?" Chad turned to leave the bathroom.

"I'm just saying, there are ways to compel chicks out of your league to take a vacation to a slum town." Jack grabbed Chad's arm. "You better not be drugging girls on my floor."

Chad shrugged his hand off. "Dude, not cool. I would ne—"

A door slammed so hard it shook the floor.

"What the fuck?" Jack jumped to attention and ran out

of the bathroom with Chad close on his heels. The hallway was clear.

"I need to check on my guests." Chad started toward his room.

"I'm coming with you," Jack insisted.

"Fine." Chad sighed. It wouldn't hurt to have witnesses.

The doorknob to his room turned with ease, but something prevented Chad from pushing open the door.

"That's odd." Chad pushed harder. "Sarah? You, okay?" A million scenarios raced through Chad's head. Were they both acting like Julie? Had Sarah used a bunch of coke, too?

"Here, let me help you." Jack pushed Chad out of the way and banged on the door. "Open up, it is the RA. You are required to open the door."

Chad rolled his eyes. "You think yelling at the door and saying you are the RA is going to help?"

"It's worked before." Jack shrugged his shoulders.

"Just help me push the door open. Just be gentle. We do not know what, or who, is blocking it." Chad's only thought was of Sarah.

After a couple of heaves, the door opened wide enough for Chad to squeeze through. His foot hit an old pizza box, and he slid into the room and fell to the wall.

"I gotta get this place cleaned up," he mumbled. He turned around and saw Sarah crumpled behind the door. "Sarah!" He leaned toward her, but Jack pushed the door further open, knocking Chad to the floor.

"Could you have waited a minute?" Chad said, pushing himself up. "Be careful! Sarah's behind the door."

Jack peeked around the door. "Well, you could've said something."

Jack pushed himself through the door and closed it behind him. He stared down at Sarah, then stated the obvious. "Somebody knocked her out."

"No shit, genius."

Some Men

"Can you hear me?"

The voice sounded to Sarah like it was coming from the end of a long tunnel.

"Hmm?" Sarah's lips felt stuck together and her mouth felt like it had cotton in it. Her head moved back and forth as someone jostled her.

"Sarah, you gotta wake up. Where's Julie?"

Julie? What about Julie? Sarah tried to recall what had happened, but before she could open her eyes, or even her mouth, a cold cascade of liquid poured down over her face. Her eyes flew open in shock. The room was dark, with only a tint of a pale blue light glowing in the distance. Her eyes focused on Chad. Sarah squinted and noticed a sheepish guy holding an empty glass behind him.

"What happened?" she asked in a whisper that she could barely hear herself.

"We found you passed out. Where's Julie?"

"I don't know. The last thing I remember is your friend coming over —"

The guys said the name in unison. "Paul."

"Stay here. We need to go find him." Chad grabbed a pillow and placed it under her head.

"No, no. I need to go with you. Julie will never forgive me." Sarah pushed herself to a sitting position. The room spun. "What did that guy give me?"

Chad held her up. "There's no telling at this point. He's a natural born chemist."

"Or sociopath," Jack added. He headed toward the door. "I've had my suspicions about that guy for some time. He's always alone, his room stinks, and he plays Dungeons and Dragons. You know what that means, right?"

"What?" Sarah wasn't sure what the RA was getting at.

"He's a Satanist. That's what. He's going to sacrifice Julie." Jack's eyes widened at his own realization.

"Calm down," Chad warned, "we don't know what he is up to. It could be anything. Paul's harmless." He paused. "Okay, he seems harmless. The worst he might do is fondle Julie while she is …"

Sarah couldn't help herself; she smacked Chad in the chest and frowned. "You need to go find him, that's enough."

"He's in room 408," Jack said as he headed out the door.

"Help me up." Sarah held out her hand for Chad. "Do you have a baseball bat or anything we could stop this guy with? He carries instruments that can put us out of commission."

Chad pulled Sarah up. The momentum placed their bodies next to one another, and even in her dulled state, the sparks flew between them.

"Let me look." His voice was quiet. He placed his hands on the sides of her arms, testing her stability.

"I'm fine. Just get me a weapon. This guy is gonna pay."

Possession Obsession

For the first time in what seemed like a million hours, Julie's eyes were open. Nothing else was working right, but it was very clear to her she was lying flat on her back in her drug dealer's dorm room. The large, thick-lensed glasses, horrible hair, and goofy smile were recognizable to her anywhere. The only difference tonight was that he made direct eye contact with her. She'd never noticed that his eyes changed color depending on the light in the room; they transitioned back and forth between blue, gray, and purple. It was fascinating, since they were the only thing in her view when he got too close.

She tried not to panic when he talked so close to her lips. It was as though he was trying to convince them to pucker up and kiss him in gratitude for saving her. She wasn't convinced he had saved her from anything. The last memory she had of being herself was right before she'd snorted the cocaine that he'd made. She blinked a couple times, hoping he'd see she was conscious. Maybe he already knew? She couldn't be sure.

She tried to pull her mouth apart and make her vocal cords move. It came out as a loud groan. If she could talk, she'd demand and persuade; both were things she was good at. Right now, she was a captive, and it was not a feeling she wanted to last any longer than necessary.

"Listen, I am going to bring you back to life. It is necessary that I do this, or all your neurons are going to be scrambled and you'll never work right." Paul stroked her forehead and then played with her hair.

The description of her not working right did, in fact, aggravate Julie's nerves. She was not a machine or a toy to be played with! Plans started running through her head of what she would do to Paul when she got out of this situation. The bizarre thought that streamed through her consciousness all the way from her gut was that she was going to tear his damn face off with her bare teeth. She'd eat every morsel of him while he screamed in agony. She hadn't been this hungry since she'd eaten a tray of pot brownies.

"Since your eyes are working, let's try your toes. I'm going to give you a little more medicine and let's see what happens. Shall we?" Paul pulled away from her face. A warm sensation went into her arm. She was going to kill him when she got out of this. He'd better hope he released her mouth last, because after she got done screaming at him, she was going to devour every piece of him.

Within minutes, Julie felt her toes wiggle. She was horrified when a warm, wet sensation enveloped them. Her stomach lurched in disgust. She realized what was making her toes wet. It was Paul's mouth.

Murderous rage was a gentle term for what was brewing inside of Julie.

Alone Too Long

Sweat beaded Chad's brow and his shoulder ached.

Paul wasn't answering and the steel door wasn't relenting. They'd been pleading with him for over an hour. Nobody wanted to escalate this. The longer this went on the more trouble all of them would be in. He regretted not insisting they call the ambulance at the bar. His desire to spend more time with Sarah had won over his common sense to save her deplorable friend.

"Paul, open the damn door!" Jack pounded. "Do you want me to call the chief resident? Because I will. You're going to get kicked the hell out of this dorm. Good luck finding cheap housing."

"Should we just call the cops?" Sarah asked in a haze. It surprised Chad she was standing. A large purple bruise was growing on the side of her neck.

"Yeah, what choice do we have?" Chad leaned on the wall and slid to the floor. What the hell were they supposed to do? His trench coat was suffocating him. Aggravated, he shrugged the coat down his arms and slipped it off. He ran his fingers through his hair. He never sweated like this. Of course, he never got himself into crazy shit like this either.

"Let me call the chief resident first. I'll just say one of you guys locked yourself out. Maybe he'll give me the keys and let it go. I'm sure he won't want to come up here for something so trivial."

Chad looked up at Jack. It was apparent that this craziness was sucking them all in and no one had any common sense anymore. They were all screwed.

Chad just shrugged his shoulders. "Sure."

"Let me run down to his apartment. Do nothing until I get back," Jack warned as he walked toward the exit.

"Don't worry, we're not going anywhere or doing anything." Chad reassured Jack and looked over to Sarah. She'd sat down on the floor across from him and was leaning on the bat. "Do you want to go back to my room? You can lie down. I'm sure Julie won't mind as long as we get her back."

"Nah, I'm okay. I'm just ready for this crazy night to be over. I don't know how I never met Paul. Maybe I had just ignored him? I don't know. Julie has so many guys hanging around, they all just blur together. She has them all on a string. They are like her servants. I wouldn't have imagined any of them would want to harm her." Sarah pulled her knees to her chest and curled into a ball. "Just like her drug use. It was just such a part of her, it didn't faze me. I accepted it."

"Were you guys meeting me at the bar to recruit me to the servitude of Julie?" Chad wasn't sure he wanted to know the answer. It would just make all of this more ridiculous.

Sarah took a long breath. "The truth? Yeah, I was going to ask you for a favor for Julie."

"I see."

"But it wasn't like I didn't want to see you. I wanted to know how you were doing." Sarah's face held fear and sadness. He believed her, but he also believed Sarah hadn't done Julie any favors by enabling her behavior.

"So, what did princess Julie want from me?" Chad had an idea what the answer would be.

"A semester of papers. She's running out of writers who can mimic her voice, but still get her the grades she needs. Professors are catching on to her. I knew you'd tutored in high school and won many awards." Sarah scooted across the hallway and sat beside him.

He could sense the energy of her now that she was closer. It was a feeling he was getting used to and wouldn't mind having around. "What about you? Why didn't she ask you? If I recall, you were one of my biggest competitors."

"You can't be a full-time student, babysitter to a socialite, and do all her homework. It is just too much." Sarah half-joked with a slight smile. Her face straightened and a slight frown came across her face. "I was the first. Freshman year. After that, it seemed easier to just help her enchant guys to do the work. I'm sorry. Trust me. If I could take tonight back, I would."

Sarah's eyes filled with sadness and vulnerability. Chad felt an overwhelming need to kiss her. Her honesty was real, and he couldn't blame her. Columbia was tough, and it was lonely. It was a far cry from their hometown and they both knew it.

"It's fine. I think we both just want this over with. We'll get Julie back, you guys can get back to the sorority house, and I'll see you around. We'll pretend like none of this ever happened. Agreed?" He put on the most confident, charming, good guy face he could muster.

"I don't want to agree to that." Sarah looked frustrated. "I don't want to pretend like we never reconnected. I like you."

Chad felt himself blush. For a moment, he wasn't sure what to do, but he remembered what any good screenwriter and director would do at this exact moment, and it was like a whisper in his ear, *kiss her*. He leaned in toward

Sarah. If he hesitated, he would screw it up. To his surprise, she leaned in hungrily, ready to kiss him. Her soft wet lips met his, and he was gone. Desire completely erased any fear that he wouldn't know what he was doing, and he let Sarah take the lead. He grabbed her waist and pulled her to him.

One on One

Waves of desire and relief engulfed Sarah. She'd never felt so honest and raw. She'd been lying to people for the last three years. Whether large or small, each lie had eroded a piece of her. It was exhausting. To tell the truth about what she'd been doing, and how she felt, exhilarated her and it made her want to kiss him more than she'd ever had. The petty part of her that cared about decorum screamed how inappropriate this was. The part of her that could not cope any longer told that voice to shut right the hell up.

A crash shook the wall. Their magnetism became a repelling force as they pushed one another away as the situation behind them reminded them of why they were sitting in a hallway.

Chad stood up and rushed to the door. He started banging with both fists.

"Paul, open the door! Julie needs medical attention. Dude, we're going to call the cops. You aren't giving us a choice."

Sarah sat for another moment, trying to listen for any clue as to what was happening in the room.

Between Chad's screaming and banging, Sarah swore

she heard moaning or groaning. She couldn't tell if it was Julie or Paul. She pushed herself up from the floor and grabbed her bat.

"Here, let me help you. You're going to need your hands," Sarah said as she pushed him out of the way and swatted the bat at the door. The high-pitched ding of metal on metal made her grit her teeth. She'd had enough of all the craziness for one night. "Open the door, you freaking psycho! Give me my friend back."

As much as she'd had many dreams of making Julie as miserable as she made her, she would not let this guy have his way with her friend.

"Open the door!" she screamed at the top of her lungs.

Chad started kicking, and she kept banging with the bat. At least they would draw everyone out of their dorm rooms, and that would put the pressure on Paul.

Just when she thought she couldn't take any more of the sound, Jack swung open the door at the end of the hallway. He walked through triumphantly, holding up a large key ring.

"Got 'em."

"Oh, thank god." Sarah dropped the bat. Her ears rang and her throat raged on fire. This was all going to be over in a couple of minutes and they could go back to normal.

Method of Modern Love

It was becoming clear to Julie that Paul was going to turn on every section of her body one at a time and molest it as he went along. In a different situation, she could get into this, being tied down and kissed everywhere until she couldn't stand it sounded like fun. In this situation, it was a hell no. The longer it went on, and the more her senses came back, every touch, lick, and kiss felt like razors on her skin.

Plus, if he talked about how he was a genius one more time, she'd go for his vocal cords first. She knew she could be a rip-roaring, raging bitch, but she'd never harmed anyone in her life. Julie had hurt some feelings and broken some hearts, but the closest she'd ever come to hurting a living thing is when she'd thrown a shoe at the cat for shredding a pair of her leather pants, and she still hadn't hit the cat or gotten rid of him.

This time, she was going to make an exception.

"How do you like that?" Paul's voice got creepier every time he talked. His breath was short and ragged. It made Julie sick to her stomach.

Her left index finger twitched. Now, she did like that. She groaned with happiness. She was one finger closer to choking this fool. Then her other index finger twitched, then another finger, and then another. They were moving. He had no clue what he was getting himself into. She groaned again.

"Oh, you like that, huh? I'll give you a little more."

Suddenly, she had full control of her hands. Sensation was returning. She ran her finger along Paul's thigh, the texture of his rough jeans made her squeal inside. She was getting back to normal.

A high-pitched metal clanging rang through the room. Paul winced.

"Ow, can't they just leave us alone?" He turned toward the door then looked up at the wall clock. "We're going to run out of time if these idiots don't leave us alone." He stood up and walked over to his desk where he had some kind of glass contraption set up. Julie could only assume it was some kind of chemistry thing. She'd seen it in the one class she'd attended in Chemistry 101. After that, she paid a super smart girl to go to class for her.

Paul pulled up a neon green liquid into two syringes, and then walked back over to the bed.

"I'm going to trust you to control yourself." He patted her leg. "I wanted to be as gentle as possible, but your nitwit of a friend woke up way sooner than I'd hoped. So fascinating how people metabolize everything differently. I hope I can study that more. Anyway, let's see what happens."

The sharp prick of the needle woke up Julie's senses so fast that her head started spinning. Smells rushed in; Paul's breath wreaked of garlic and not flossing from over a yard away, dirty socks with a hint of dry human fluids emanated through the space, a moldy pizza was somewhere in the room, and the dreaded Drakkar Noir was back, though she suspected it was out in the hallway. Her hearing was magnified and the metal pinging from the door felt like ice picks being jammed into her ears. Then she heard her voice. The best friend she'd ever had. Sarah's screaming sounded like salvation. Her friend was still trying to help her. Julie noted that she needed to be a better friend.

"You'll be upright, and we will be out of here before they know it." Paul pricked her with the needle again.

Julie could only hope she'd be upright and on Paul before he knew it.

Out of Touch

The keys jingled as Jack shifted through them, looking for the one that would open Paul's door.

"Just another minute… I think we're getting close." Jack tried another key.

Paul was getting anxious. Things had gone silent inside of the room. There'd been another burst of movement and then nothing.

"Do you need me to help? Are you sure they don't have the room number engraved on the key?" Paul didn't want to state the obvious, but Jack appeared nervous as he attempted to be heroic.

"Nah, I'm good, I'm good. Do either of you have a flashlight? I just can't seem to get the light right to look at the letters and numbers. They aren't making sense."

"Let me look." Chad reached for the key ring. Jack gave it up easier than he'd expected. Each key had a code on it. He understood Jack's careful review of each key. "What does the code mean? Do you know?"

"Uh, I'm not sure. I think it is floor, wing, room, or one of the combinations of those three."

"So, we are on the fourth floor, wing B, and this is room 408?" Paul looked for keys starting with four; there were none.

"Yeah, that is what I was thinking, but as you can see, there are no keys starting with four." Jack grabbed one key from the ring for emphasis.

Paul pulled the key ring back. "Did you get the correct key ring?"

"It is the only one." Jack sighed. He looked around the

hallway. "Do you think an ax would do anything to that door? I know there is one downstairs for fires, but once we smash the glass to get it, we're done for. EMS, fire department, everybody will be here."

"What do the keys start with?" Sarah asked. She'd waited for Chad and Jack to finish fumbling around.

Chad looked at the keys. There were several letters, then numbers, followed by more letters. It was an odd numbering system. "The groups start with EAM, TWL, LEX, GIL, AKC."

"Does that mean anything to you, Jack?"

Sarah had a valid point. They weren't thinking.

"I don't know. Acronyms for the buildings the chief manages? I mean there are a lot of keys." Jack clutched his chin in thought.

Sarah took a deep breath then said, "Just go pull the fire alarm and get the ax. The fire department will flush them out. We're already in over our heads. We'll keep looking for the key."

"Uh, is that even a good idea? Like, what if he killed her and now, we are accomplices?" Jack's voice was riddled with stress and fear.

The ridiculousness of this night was only getting worse, Chad snapped, "Just go. If she's dead, she's dead. We're only to blame if we keep going like this. We're just a dumb bunch of kids."

Chad had never felt dumber in his life, and there had been plenty of times he'd felt damn stupid.

Looking for a Good Sign

"Okay, what the hell is the name of this building?" Sarah had paid little attention to the dorms. She'd moved into the sorority's brownstone her second semester freshman year and had never looked back.

"Schapiro."

"Well, unless we know what these acronyms mean, there's no point. The best we can do is just start trying keys." Sarah felt defeated.

Before she could think about it much more, the fire alarms screamed, and a bright blue light flickered in the hallway. There was no way she could think straight now.

She put her hands over her ears and looked up at Chad. He was placing a key in the lock. It didn't turn. He went to the next. At least he was doing something, since there wasn't anything else to be done until the police department arrived. All she could was hope that Paul wasn't doing anything that he couldn't return from.

Going Thru the Motions

Julie was on her feet, which was better than where she'd started with Paul over an hour ago. This was what Paul called dancing, him towering over her, body to body, his face rubbing in her hair. She'd heard him sniffing it. Her body was still limp and having trouble moving, but sensation was returning. She tried to control her head and lift her face upward. She moaned. If she could only get him to give her enough of that juice to open her mouth, she would rip his throat out. Her only recourse currently was to feign interest toward him, Julie tried to nuzzle his neck. He shivered. Her point came across loud and clear.

"Hold on there, little lady, we will get to that. I just want to enjoy you some more."

She groaned louder. This was really frustrating her. She rubbed her mouth on his neck some more.

"Okay, okay, fine. I'm glad to see that you're coming around." He guided her back to the bed and sat her down. He leaned her against the wall. Julie smiled inside. In a sitting position, she had more leverage for pushing upwards and onto him once she had her strength back.

Paul walked over to his chemistry set and pulled up more of the liquid into the syringe. There was a lot of liquid. How much was he going to need to use on her?

Before she could ponder it further, blue lights and a loud screeching sound flooded her already amplified senses. She fell over and groaned in agony.

Mano A Mano

One key at a time. Chad chanted it over and over in his head. He couldn't think straight anymore. There was only one thing left to do, and that was act. That was it, simple, put a key in the lock and keep turning. The siren was making it hard to even do that.

On the hundredth key, the exit door at the end of the hallway burst open. Chad turned to see three of the largest, broadest firemen in the city walk down the hallway. They were suited up, including masks and oxygen.

"Get away from the door!" the one in the lead yelled at them.

Chad looked to Sarah. Her eyes were wide; it obviously wasn't the reception she'd been expecting, either.

"Go to the other wall and put your hands up."

Chad and Sarah complied. These guys were acting more like the police than fire and rescue. He should know. There'd been plenty of fire drills, an occasional small fire from a lit trash can, or an illegal hot plate meltdown, that had caused a bigger ruckus than this, and none of those guys had talked to them like this.

"Are they in there?" the lead firemen asked.

Chad nodded.

The other men stepped in front with what appeared to be some kind of ram.

The lead tapped at the door. "Open the door, kid! If we bust this down, you're done for."

A muffled voice came from inside.

"We can't hear you. Open the door! I'll give you 'til the count of five. One, two, three—"

The two with the battering ram went for the door. Chad could only guess they were willing to take the chance of mowing down Paul. They could ram Paul straight out the window of his room for all Chad cared.

The door was as cooperative as Paul. A large dent stated the obvious. The door, and Paul, were not giving up easily.

Head Above Water

Sarah stared down the hallway at three men wearing white suits with masks and oxygen tanks. They'd come in shortly after she and Paul had been instructed to stand with their hands on the wall. She assumed they were also firemen. She couldn't be sure; they didn't act like it. It filled her with relief to see the medical bags they rolled in on a gurney. Julie was going to be safe.

Do What You Want, Be What You Are

The sounds of the sirens were driving Julie mad, but it was working to her advantage. Between the shrill of the alarms and her moaning, Paul couldn't handle the commotion. He drew up a larger dose of liquid than he had noticed or planned, Julie knew this because when he leaned over and shot the solution into her arm, she was on fire. Every cell in her body worked, even her brain, which had a hard time sorting things out on a clear and sober day, let alone on a night when she'd had too much coke, but she could probably do an equation or two right now. The worst part was that she was so hungry. Aching, ready to take a cow down in the middle of Texas on a drought ridden dust-be-damned day in July kind of hungry.

She was done with Paul and this foolishness. She'd whimpered and simpered to get this dummy to this point, and she was d-o-n-e. She flexed her fingers, testing their strength. She was going to claw his eyes out and rip out his throat with her teeth. He leaned in with his hot, smelly breath. When she leaned forward to meet him, his eyes widened, and his pupils dilated; there was fear and pleasure in there. She's seen that look a thousand times in even the most attractive of men when she'd met them toe-to-toe with her appetite.

This one was about to see how voracious her appetite was. She grabbed the collar of his shirt and jerked his neck toward her and planted her mouth on top of his. If he wanted wet, sloppy, suffocating kisses, she'd be more than happy to give them to him. The taste of metal and fear filled her mouth and every one of her tastebuds loved it.

A loud bang disrupted her as male voices boomed through the door. Paul tried to scream, but she had already taken most of his tongue. Julie would not let him get away from this. It didn't matter who was coming through the door. They weren't taking Paul alive.

Intuition

A loud boom rang throughout the hallway as the firemen bum-rushed the door with their battering ram. Chad twisted his neck as far as he could without removing his hands from the wall. As the door swung open, he swore he saw blood spray on the wall. The firemen grabbed both Julie and Paul. The guys in white rushed into the room, blocking it off with their gurney. Chad turned to check on Sarah. She had laid her head against the wall with her eyes closed. Past her head, Chad noticed new people at the end of the hallway. They weren't uniformed cops. He found that odd, since firemen and uniformed policemen always seemed to go hand in hand.

One of them noticed him staring and waved for him to come toward them. He pointed at his chest. The guy who waved at him nodded his head this time. Chad walked to the end of the hallway. The man had a large bushy mustache, wire-rimmed glasses, a receding hairline, and an expanding stomach. He was a desk jockey if Chad had ever seen one.

"Hey kid, what happened here tonight?" the man asked.

Chad's instinct was to keep his mouth closed. He had done some stupid shit tonight, and he really didn't want to admit to any of it. He wasn't going to tell a cop or whoever that he'd pretty much pissed his whole life away for a kiss from a girl he'd fallen in love within high school. Screw that.

"I'm not sure what happened, sir. I'm not involved in any of this. I just live on this floor."

"Yeah, sure, kid. And I'm the pope because I go to Mass. What about your little girlfriend down there? She going to be a pain in the ass, too?" The man looked over to his partner. "Call this in. We need to get this contained." He looked back to Chad. "Go tell your girlfriend we need to talk to her. And I don't want to hear anymore bullshit from you. Don't try to run."

All Chad could do was nod. He had a bad feeling about all of this.

Sara Smiles

Sarah stood up on her tiptoes, scanning Paul's room for Julie. She just needed to see if her friend was okay. She doubted Julie was, in fact, okay. How could she recover from a creepy dude abducting her? Especially since Sarah had led Julie to him. Chad placed his arm around Sarah's shoulders, interrupting her thoughts.

"Those guys at the end of the hall want to talk to us."

He tilted his head toward the exit door at the end of the hall.

"What do they want?" Sarah couldn't imagine she could say anything that might clear up this crazy night. The only thing she knew was that she looked like a shitty friend and an enabling accomplice.

"From the clothes they're wearing, I'm guessing they are detectives or the FBI. Not sure how they are getting away with not identifying themselves. They just smiled when I asked for a badge."

Sarah knew little about the law in real life. The only thing she could recall is what she'd seen on television. "Aren't they supposed to tell us who they are? Read us our rights or something?"

"I doubt these guys are doing anything they don't want to," Chad mumbled under his breath as a middle-aged man with large wire-framed glasses and a bushy mustache walked over.

"Can we talk to you two?"

Sarah smiled weakly.

Lady Rain

Julie knew she was in danger as soon as the door burst open. The tall, broad men slammed her to the bed. Paul's screams filled her with disappointment. He was still alive.

"Sedate him!" one of them yelled through their gas mask. He turned and pointed at Julie. "She's next. Don't let either of them bite or scratch you."

Another fireman sat on top of Julie and held her arms down. Through his mask, Julie guessed he wasn't too much older than her. She'd have loved to have met him in a bar one night and gone home with him. Now, all she wanted to do was rip his lips and nose off his face. Destroying faces seemed to be one of her biggest desires now.

Julie turned to the fireman working on Paul, who was crumpled on the ground. Two other people in white suits walked in the door.

"Get me an ET tube, stat!" one of them said as they ran over to Paul. A tear rolled down the side of Julie's face in frustration. Putting a tube in Paul's throat meant he would survive even longer.

"Don't worry, hon, we are going to save your boyfriend. We'll take care of you, too."

Julie let out as loud of a scream as she could expel before everything went dark.

Your Imagination

"All I know is Paul was, I mean, *is* a chemistry student."

Chad wasn't giving anything to these guys. They'd politely but firmly escorted him and Sarah to a nondescript building in downtown Manhattan. Once they'd separated him from Sarah, he'd stopped cooperating.

"I need to see my friend. We haven't done anything wrong." He ran his fingers through his hair.

"You don't think living down the hall from a drug dealer and predator doesn't make you an accomplice?" The one with oversized wire-rimmed glasses and a bushy mustache was doing all the talking. He'd told Chad to call him Ted.

"No, I knew nothing about that. I didn't know he was a creep." Chad was telling the truth. Paul was weird, but Chad hadn't thought he was *that* weird.

Ted stroked his mustache, then leaned over, "What if I told you that Paul has been messing with girls on campus for a couple of years now? Your friend is the first one that we've found alive."

"Are you bullshitting me? Paul is barely capable of selling coke." Chad winced at the slip.

"So, he is a drug dealer?" Ted asked as he scribbled on a piece of paper.

"You already know everything! You don't need me." Chad took a deep breath and let it out. He sat for a minute staring at the galvanized stainless-steel table. If they knew everything, why were they asking him questions? He thought about Sarah. She was somewhere in this building, and he did not know where. Julie and Paul were fucked. He already knew that. There wasn't anything he could do about them. When they'd rolled Paul out of the room, they'd been helping him breathe with a tube. Julie had been not only strapped to a gurney but also handcuffed. She was the one they were afraid of.

"Paul's a drug dealer. Yes. He makes all kinds of stuff in his room. From what I can put together, he was Julie's dealer. Sarah didn't know. I didn't know. I've seen a lot of people go into his room, but they all come out alive and walking." Chad slammed his hands on the table. "Are you happy? I want to see Sarah."

Cold Dark and Yesterday

A woman with a slicked back bun and bright red lipstick stared at Sarah. This was the kind of lady that the AKAs would have mocked as they passed on the street. She couldn't be over thirty, but she looked way older and more serious than her age. They'd sat in the room for over an hour and Sarah was the only one attempting to break the silence.

"Are you a cop?" Sarah asked for the sixth time. She was pretty sure that if you asked a cop, if they were a cop, they had to tell you.

The woman continued to stare. Her face unflinching. Sarah stared back with her eyes wide and bottom lip puffed out. She crossed her eyes. This was ridiculous, and she knew she was being the worst. It didn't matter. Julie was counting on her.

"Where's Julie?"

The woman crossed her arms. Sarah wasn't sure how the woman could move anything in the snug, starched tweed suit she wore.

Before Sarah could react with another absurd face, the doorknob turned. The woman straightened and then stood up.

"Good evening, sir." The woman greeted the man with a bushy mustache that had escorted her and Chad to the facility.

Once the man came in the door, Chad followed. He ran to Sarah and embraced her. He whispered in her ear. "Follow my lead."

"Thank you, Officer Gooding, I'll take it from here."

The woman nodded and walked out of the door. The man with the bushy mustache stuck his hand out to Sarah.

"Good evening, Sarah. Call me Ted. Let's have a seat. I need to ask you some questions."

She's Gone

"What'd they say to do with her? It's not like she can die anymore." The male voice spoke close to Julie.

Julie didn't want to believe what she'd heard, but she'd suspected something was wrong ever since she'd awakened the first time. She'd never wanted to rip the flesh from someone's face and eat it before tonight.

"I'm guessing we'll keep her sedated and put her in the cooler with the rest of them?" another voice said from farther off.

"Yeah, I wish she hadn't taken the sociopath's tongue out. At least he could tell us what the hell is in the concoction he brewed up," the voice closer to her said.

She heard a door open, and a cool draft of air ran over her.

"Seems inhumane to lock her in there. The first successful reanimation of an entire person placed on ice."

Julie swore she heard a *tsk* in the last voice. What the hell were they going to do with her? She was the victim in all this. If it weren't for Paul, she would be at the sorority house nursing a hangover or slipping out of some guy's apartment she'd met the night before.

She wished she could talk. If she could, she would talk her way out of this like she'd done so many times before.

Her mouth was gagged, but she tried to groan and shake her head.

Where was Sarah? Funny how she'd taken her on and Sarah had stuck by her side as long as it got her somewhere. Julie was screwed, and Sarah wasn't there. Typical. Sarah was a user. It made Julie a little sad, but she'd used everyone she could, as well. At least Sarah had been taught by the best.

Julie felt pressure in her arm then fluid coursed through her. She felt weak and sleepy. They were sedating her.

An alarm went off in the background.

"He's coding!" the voice in the distance yelled.

"I'm coming. Let me slow this drip," the voice near Julie said.

Julie felt more tired by the moment. They were going to put her to sleep, and she didn't know when, or if, she'd ever be awake again.

In the distance, she heard the two voices talking about what she could only assume was Paul.

"He'll go in the cooler next to her." It was the last thing Julie heard. She would be damn sure if she woke up again, she'd finish tearing Paul limb-to-limb even though he was just as undead as her.

Private Eyes

"So, we can't go back?" Chad asked as he accepted the forged identification papers, checkbook, and a large wad of cash.

"No, we'll know. We're watching you from now on," Ted said.

It had been seventy-two hours since they'd been held against their will. People were dropping all over the city from Paul's killer coke, and teams rolled in more and more people restrained on gurneys. Ted and the other men in the suits reassured Chad that there would be only so many incidents before it would be contained. After Chad figured out that Julie was dead and reanimated, he'd had no problem with taking their offer for him and Sarah to disappear out west. He'd seen Night of the Living Dead more than once and believed George Romero knew something that the rest of them didn't. George created new mythos, but those always came from some kind of truth.

"We can't say goodbye to our families?" Sarah asked.

"No, like I explained before, you'll be one casualty from the bar fire in Soho." Ted's eyes were bloodshot, and his mustache hairs stuck out haphazardly. He'd slept even less than Chad and Sarah.

Chad squeezed Sarah's hand from under the table. She squeezed back.

Ted slid Sarah's documents across the table. He noticed she didn't get any cash or a checkbook. He looked at Ted.

"Just in case you all get the idea to split up. You need one another, and besides, a woman shouldn't be walking around with that much cash."

"She needs her own money. What if something happens to me? It's not coming out of your personal pocket, is it?" Chad hated to speak for Sarah, but they didn't seem to think much of women around here.

Ted looked up at the ceiling. Within a minute, the woman with the tight bun walked in with an envelope. She handed it to Ted. He slid it across the table to Sarah. She placed her hand over it but didn't open it. Chad didn't want to seem bossy, but he wanted to make sure they got the money.

"Can we see Julie before we go?" Sarah asked. Tears welled up in her eyes.

"Why would you want to see her? She isn't who you knew anymore. She's..." Ted paused. "She's something else."

Chad would explain everything to Sarah on their way out west. He was antsy to get the hell out of New York as fast as he could. No dream of making films was worth his life.

"Sarah let's go. We need to get on the road."

Some Things Are Better Left Unsaid

It was somewhere in the southwest corner of Indiana that Sarah lost it. Her shoulders trembled first, then her entire torso quaked. All at once, she couldn't breathe. The sobs became uncontrollable, and tears and snot ran down her face.

"What the fuck just happened?" she screamed.

Chad pulled the car over. It was a nondescript, average car that two people in their twenties would appropriately drive as they moved across the country.

Sarah kicked the dashboard. She punched at the air

and screamed some more.

She was mourning her friend, her family, and her life. For all that mattered from this day forward, Sarah was just like Julie, undead and reanimated in her own way, just under the name of Laura. She was married without ever having had a ceremony. Chad was now her husband. She still didn't believe what Chad had told her he'd pieced together. It was much easier to think that they'd been caught up in a drug ring scandal, they were in witness protection, and that Julie had died from a drug overdose. Maybe it was true. Julie couldn't stay suspended in animation for eternity, right? What about Paul? Fucking Paul, that creep had ruined all their lives. Sarah kicked the dashboard one more time.

"Laura, you gotta get it together," Chad said. He looked ridiculous in a brown and yellow striped polo shirt.

Sarah laughed.

"Keep it together, huh? How are you going to keep it together wearing polos and working for an oil company?"

"I think some things are better left unsaid," Chad said as he pulled her close. They both laughed and cried on each other's shoulders.

Chad pulled away first. Sarah felt a little better. Not much, but enough to compose herself so they could get back on the road. They had to report at certain times, in certain places, or they'd really disappear. Chad turned on the radio and pulled out back onto the road.

In other news, Columbia University and the surrounding area have been shut down. An unusual batch of cocaine has rendered hundreds of students and locals paralyzed. We'll keep you updated on the latest with the War on Drugs.

HELL WILL HAVE TO WAIT

Hey, hey, watch it, why don't you?

Deeva de Satanica growled as the powerful hands of a stout, older human scooped her into a cat carrier before she could protest with her claws. The handlers at the animal shelter were experts at manipulating the animals from points A to B with little fanfare. They always whiffed of sunshine, urine, and death. Deeva's senses went from one assault to another as the overwhelming smell of multiple cats invaded her nose. She shifted herself around in the cat carrier, eyeing the scratches and dings. This carrier had seen better days.

It was a quick jostle from the shelter to the back seat of a car, where a young human female wedged herself between Deeva and a fat, tan and black dog who smelled of heaven and the oily, dirty musk of the canine persuasion. The smell engulfed the car. A dull, sinking feeling hit her stomach. If the dog was an angel, there was likely an enormous problem, and it probably involved the humans who'd adopted her.

Why couldn't Satan have dropped me about thirty minutes earlier? Deeva thought to herself. A groan from across the car caught her attention.

Can you hear me? Are you an angel?

"Ruff, ruff," the dog replied audibly. Deeva's ears rang.

"It's okay Mama. We'll be home soon," the girl soothed.

So, what are you protecting them from? Because maybe I could make your job easier by moving the issue out of your life. Deeva edged to the front of the cat carrier, trying to get a look at the dog.

No, you can't. I've been told everyone needs to stay alive. Justice must be served.

At the sound of the word *justice*, it was apparent Deeva was in the right place. That word was typically a sign of evil humans or people scorned by them. She was on the correct path, even though having an angel in her way would make it more difficult to do her job.

Hey dog, I mean, angel, how long have you been with these two?

Mama Dog laid with her eyes closed, her head and paws on the little girl's lap. She pried one eye open.

Well, this dog, Mama Dog, has been with Heather and her mom, Justine, for about seven years. I've been in Mama's body for about six weeks.

So, dog, what's your real name? I'm Deeva de Satanica, Special Assistant to the Dark Lord in the Division of Revenge and Rage, the DRR for short. I don't think we've met before. You know, we're the ones that do all the work your type can't stomach. Deeva wasn't above making small talk. That was when you could get some of the juiciest information on your enemies, and gossip was just fun.

I know what you are, but just call me Mama Dog. I'm kind of a motherly type, anyway. Unlike your sort, we don't kick the soul of the animal out, we just sort of gently put it to sleep for a while. Hearing the little girl's voice will keep her anxiety down while she is in her long sleep.

Deeva wondered if Mama Dog was serious. Animals had souls? That couldn't be right. She'd felt nothing in these bodies except the pumping of blood through the veins, heart racing, and euphoria when she instinctively killed a mouse or a bird. Cats didn't have moral compasses, did they? All the cats she'd mingled with, like the real non-demon inhabited cats, didn't really seem to care about anything or anyone but themselves. It was why cats made such great bodies for demon-inhabiting, though she suspected there were a couple of demons inhabiting the smaller breed dogs. Before Deeva could opine on her existential crisis any further, the car stopped.

"We're here!" The little girl squealed with excitement and shook the carrier. Deeva decided maybe she could call her Heather. It might make things go easier with the angel.

As the car door swung open, a whiff of rotten flesh hit Deeva's nose like nothing she'd ever smelt before. Decay didn't smell the same on earth as it did down under. Maybe it was the heat down there or the moisture up here, but there was a distinction.

Do you smell that? Aren't you supposed to have superpowers at smelling or something?

A yawn and flapping of jaws from across the car were Mama Dog's only acknowledgement. Deeva rolled her eyes. She really hoped this angel wasn't here to protect these humans, because there would not be much it could do.

Did you hear me? The smell was overpowering to Deeva. Humans weren't meant to be around this much death. What monsters were these two?

Yeah, I heard you. I'm not deaf. But unfortunately, I can't smell. It's the reason Justine could afford this fine specimen of a hound. Mama Dog is nose blind.

Great, between the smell of a hundred cats in this carrier and now rotting flesh, I'm thinking that God and Satan have terrible senses of humor.

Justine grabbed the carrier out of the back seat, upending Deeva. Her small cat body couldn't handle the change in gravity, and Deeva slammed to the side of the carrier.

I don't know if God has a sense of humor. I mean, they usually put me right where they want me on these assignments. Everything is intentional, as far as I can tell.

Deeva felt like she was going to vomit from the tossing and swaying of the carrier as they headed toward a large, white Victorian farmhouse with a massive wraparound porch.

Staging things with intention can be the most amusing of all to those who are twisted.

Deeva's head smacked against the top of the carrier as Justine placed it on the porch with a ceremonious thump.

"We're home!!" Heather screamed at no one in particular.

From atop a tall and almost equally wide china hutch, Deeva watched as Justine and Heather sat at the table, eating. The dining room was decorated in what reminded Deeva of something she'd seen probably 50 souls ago. A lace tablecloth, yellowed with age, draped over the dining room table, aged photos peppered the walls, and there was actual china being used, the delicate type with dainty swirls and flowers adorning it. This didn't look like it was their house. Though Deeva rarely spent the time to truly examine the people assigned to her, these two humans did not match up with the big white house packed with old stuff, on a farm with the smell of dead bodies everywhere.

She tried to read Justine's aura a little better. Nothing suggested she had performed an act so vile that a little of her soul was gone, although she looked tired and anxious. There wasn't even a sign that she was beckoning revenge, which brought Deeva to the little one, Heather. The child got a bit too excited about animals, but that was no reason for all the odd smells. The aromas annoyed Deeva. As far as Deeva had experienced, a keen sense of smell was not a cat's greatest strength. In the past, she'd used the cat's body to make mayhem occur, whether it was jumping from high places, swirling around legs, clawing out eyes, or sitting on a chest and sucking a soul out. This nose business had to go. Heather looked up and smiled at Deeva as though she knew she was thinking about her.

"I hope Uncle Bobby likes Dee-Dee," Heather said as she scooped up a small red potato and shoved it in her mouth. As she chomped down, her smile widened, making it possible for her perfect little teeth to crush the vegetable.

Mama Dog crawled out from under the table. Of course, her dog instincts to keep the floor clean were still there, as far as Deeva could tell. She'd been licking every breadcrumb she could find.

Did she just say what I think she said?

"Honey, the kitty's name is Fluffins, remember?" Justine looked up from her phone with concern.

It was just a guess. There is no way she can hear us. Deeva wondered, though. It wouldn't be the first time a child could hear them, and probably wouldn't be the last.

"She said her name was Deeva."

Justine looked back and forth between Deeva and Heather while Deeva tried not to stare at either of them. She needed to look like the nonchalant, didn't-care-about-anyone-but-themselves cat she was supposed to be. What Justine said next would determine her move. It had been fun while it lasted, but she wasn't in the mood to be kicked out on the street. Being a homeless cat in the country was no fun; she'd done it before, and Satan could be a real jerk about making her stay until she finished the job. Killing field mice for sport was one thing, but depending on them for your meals was another. Plus, the cold wet mornings made it take all day for her fur to dry out.

"Baby, we talked about this. You can't pretend you talk to animals, see dead people, or can make things happen with your words."

"Mom, great Nana told me I could do it and I can. She

said you used to do it. She summoned us here to help Uncle Bobby. Remember? I told you."

"Heather, we are here because great Nana left us half of this house. We're going to help Uncle Bobby clean and stage it, and then we are going to sell it. We're moving back to Boston with the money we make from the house. I let you get a new cat to help keep mice out of the house." Justine stood up and walked over to Deeva. She gently placed her hand on top of Deeva's head and slowly stroked her fur. Deeva couldn't keep it in.

"Prrrrrrrr." It was a natural mechanism that came with the cat's body. There wasn't much to be done about it.

"See? She's just a regular old cat. Right, Fluffins?"

"Meowr," Deeva responded.

Justine placed one hand underneath Deeva's stomach and the other over her back. She gently pulled her from the hutch and placed her on the floor.

"Why don't you and Mama Dog show her around the house? She'll need to know where she's going to sleep. Plus, it'll give her time to figure out where all the mice are located. She's gotta earn her keep."

Heather was obviously smarter than Deeva had given her credit for. Initially, the kid had played off as though she were a couple of watts short in her light bulb, a facade that her mother was encouraging from the looks of it.

"Come on, DEE-DEE, let me show you our room." Heather stood up from the table and pushed her chair in ceremoniously, startling Mama Dog. Heather stomped to the hallway, then beckoned the two.

"Rawr?" Mama Dog stood up and wagged her tail.

Did you really fall back asleep that quickly? Deeva laughed at the dog.

Humph, I've been here long enough to know this place is pretty low key. You know, we also get the qualities of whatever dog we inhabit, and this type of dog likes short walks, long naps, and big scraps. Did I miss anything important? Mama Dog waddled over to Deeva.

You missed nothing important except we're in a house of WITCHES. Did you miss that important detail of your assignment? Because who knows what witches these are, and what they're doing with animals. Oh, and by the way, the little one is telepathic. If Deeva had been in one of her more humanlike forms, she'd probably have smacked her forehead at the realization that came to her next. *She can probably hear everything I'm saying right now.*

Oh. Mama Dog flopped to the floor. It occurred to Deeva that either angels couldn't control their ethereal forms very well, or this angel was a sloppy, dopey mess.

"Are you two coming or what?" Heather glared at them, her hands on her hips. She was obviously losing her patience with the two of them.

"Heather, be nice. Don't take your irritation with me out on the animals. Remember our deal, the animals do not go outside. Understand?" Justine looked back at her phone.

Let's just play it cool and see what happens next. I mean, what could go wrong? She's only a little girl, right? Deeva had been lucky enough to steer clear of witches on earth as far back as she could remember. The problem with witches was they sometimes didn't believe in heaven or hell. They did their own thing, which was a problem for the two entities that were fighting for supremacy over the Earth. Sometimes they worshiped Satan, but they still really weren't around a lot in the part of hell that Deeva hung out in. Deeva strutted down the hallway. Before she got too far, she felt a tug on her tail. She turned to scowl when she saw a forewarning look on Mama Dog's face.

Never underestimate a witch. They have all the cunning of demons from hell, the passion of any angelic creature, and their own earthly will that makes them a challenge for those above and below.

Deeva couldn't help herself. She chuckled at Mama Dog.

Sure.

Heather, when do we get to go outside? Deeva curled up beside the little girl's head on her pillow. She was reading a book.

"Mom said if I wanted to keep you, I had to make sure you didn't go outside. You might disappear." Heather continued to stare at the pages, her concentration unbroken.

I'll be fine. I promise.

Deeva revved up the little motor in the cat that relaxed humans. She'd started communicating with the little girl out of fear. It didn't seem like people came around much, but it would only take one savvy human who knew of the underworld to figure out she was a demon. Then it might be lights out for her and the mission.

Are you sure? I'm a tough cat.

"I know you think that, and I also know you and Mama Dog are looking for something, but I'm not even allowed in certain places here. I promised Mom that I'd stay right here. We don't want to make Uncle Bobby mad. He doesn't like cats."

Deeva peeked over at Mama Dog to see if she was listening. One eye was slightly open, but that was also how the dog slept.

Do you think the other cats were special like me? I doubt it. I'm smart, quick, and I'm not afraid of anything. Those other cats were not me; I can assure you. Did the others talk?

"Dee-Dee, it doesn't work like that. Great Nana said that each animal speaks its own way. You use words, but others use images and feelings, and some even use physical sensation. Like Mama Dog, I can't hear her, but I can see things through her eyes. She likes you, but she shouldn't. She knows that."

Mama Dog lifted her head and looked at Deeva. *I did not say that. You're a demon.*

"See, she's upset now. I can't hear the words, but I feel the protest." Heather put her book down, rolled over, and looked at Mama Dog. She grinned at the dog. "You thought you were going to hide from me?"

"Humph." Mama Dog laid back down, her head on her front paws.

Deeva flipped on her back and wiggled beside Heather. She cackled softly. *Heather, you're funny. Now, what can we do to get out of this house?*

"Ugh, I'm not helping you until I know why you want to go outside so badly."

That's the thing, I am looking for something. There's usually a bright red mark on what I'm here to retrieve. I haven't seen it yet, so I need to get out of the house and find it. Could you give me a rub on the belly? I'd like that.

Deeva couldn't help herself. Three strokes on the belly made something in the cat brain have pure happiness, but one too many strokes and it turned on this weird mode that made her want to grasp something with her claws until she couldn't let go.

Heather cautiously placed her fingers lightly on Deeva's stomach. She stroked gently with each finger, drumming down the cat's chest. After exactly three rounds of belly rubs, Deeva swatted at Heather's arm as the feel-good chemicals in her cat brain went into overdrive. Deeva rolled over on her back; she didn't need to get on Heather's bad side by leaving a scratch on her vulnerable skin.

Well, let's go outside and look around. Once I find the mark, I can retrieve the item and be on my way.

"You can't leave me. I'm really lonely here. I didn't have any friends in Boston, either."

Deeva realized she'd mis-stepped. Heather was enjoying their companionship. Not that Deeva was opposed to the idea of being a cat for long periods of time, it was just that she'd never done it before. Her longest missions typically lasted for two or three weeks. Then again, who knew if the little witch was even telling the truth? Maybe she knew Deeva was a demon and was trying to trick her.

I don't think it's that easy for me. See, I'm sent to earth for certain reasons and then when I complete those tasks, my owner asks me to bring back what I've retrieved. Some cats sort of live in other worlds. I'd have to make some kind of deal with my owner to stay here longer. They might say no. But, if I don't do the task, something bad might happen to me.

"Like what?"

Honestly, I'm not sure. I've never failed before. My other owner can be a little demanding and not nice. I haven't tried to cause problems. Anyway, never mind that. Tell me about Uncle Bobby. Where is he? What does he do?

Deeva hoped that curiosity wouldn't kill the cat.

———

Do you really think it's necessary for you to stand on my back to open the door? I mean, I hear other cats just keep jumping at the doorknob or running at the door to get it open. Mama Dog whined.

Shhhh, do you want to wake up Heather? Or worse, Justine? Just gimme a second and we'll be in the room. Deeva's hind claws dug into Mama's back. It wasn't intentional, but the limits of cat balance only went so far. It would be worth it if they could find out more about Uncle Bobby. He hadn't been home since Deeva had arrived, which didn't seem odd to Justine or Heather, as he was a truck driver. Deeva's gut told her he was the mark. But why? She hoped getting into his room would give them a clue.

The doorknob creaked, and the door swung open, causing Deeva to fall forward. Luckily, she rolled with the fall and landed on her feet. She turned to check on Mama Dog. Horror filled the hound's face.

Look in the corner, Mama Dog said. The thick, black

hair on the back of her neck stood up. Deeva wasn't sure if she wanted to turn. ***Look! Look at the corner.***

Fine, fine, I'll look. It can't be that bad. Deeva had seen some crazy, bloody horrible things in hell; it really couldn't be that bad. She whirled around, anticipating some weird art. Or maybe the guy worshiped some old god and had an extravagant altar. What she saw instead didn't really surprise her with the intel she'd received from Heather. *Well, at least we know where all the cats went.*

In the corner were probably, if Deeva understood anything about bones, twenty to thirty cat skeletons arranged into a weird tentacle-like statue. Tufts of cat fur were still attached to tails that adorned the waistband of the bone creature.

Is this some witchcraft stuff? Mama sounded more unsure of herself by the moment. Deeva had never seen this type of human depravity before, but it made her even more certain that Uncle Bobby would wear the mark.

This isn't about worship; this is about being a little messed up in the head. There is no telling what we'll find once we get out on the farm.

A quick scan around the room brought up nothing other than the bone creature. There were a bunch of items under the bed that smelled like women: wallets, earrings, a handkerchief. Deeva could only hope that Uncle Bobby had kept mementos of his girlfriends since he was always on the road, but Deeva had seen this type of behavior before. Killing animals and keeping mementos, but she couldn't place the image of the reason when she retrieved the person. There were so many questions to be asked. Did Justine know about the bone creature, and if so, why hadn't she taken Heather away from here? A mother should know this probably wasn't a good idea for a short one to be around.

We've gotta get out on the farm. I'm worried about Heather. This isn't a safe place for her.

Mama Dog nodded her head in agreement. The duo backed out of the room and Deeva curled her paw up under the door frame while Mama tugged at her tail to assist Deeva in pulling the door shut.

"Reowr!" Deeva growled as sharp canine teeth pinched her delicate tail.

Sorry, I can't always control myself.

It's fine. Let's get back in Heather's room before she figures out we're gone.

Once Deeva was curled up in bed with Heather, she listened to the rise and fall of the little one's chest. This entire trip was confusing and frustrating. She'd been hanging around with an angel and a witch for over a month, with no sign of the soul she needed to retrieve. Her feelings for the little girl were growing every day. The human was smart and sassy. She wasn't typical of her age. She was also cunning, because she could appear as a simpleton and act younger when needed, as she'd done the day they'd met. If trained right, she'd be an amazing servant to Satan someday. Well, if she wanted to be one. It wasn't for everyone, that was for sure. That whole free will thing, and all.

Which brought Deeva to thinking about Mama Dog. She'd shared some fun times with Mama Dog. The angel was funny, kind, and probably not as insane as some of the other heavenly forces she'd had to deal with over the years. She'd taught Deeva how to enjoy being in an animal form a little more, activating parts of the cat's brain that Deeva hadn't known existed.

Why was an angel even here? Justice? It didn't seem like that was needed here at all. Uncle Bobby needed to go to hell, and as quickly as possible. He wasn't a nice guy, just based on the fact he'd apparently killed cats to make art. This was a simple case where Deeva could sentence him with no problem.

The sun peeked through the curtains of Heather's window. As Deeva looked around, she wondered if this was Heather's room. The porcelain dolls, the ruffles, the lace, and the various shades of pink didn't seem to fit who Heather was. This had to have been Justine's room since childhood. It didn't really matter. The quicker they could get Uncle Bobby out of here; the better Deeva would feel about the safety of Heather. She snuggled closer to her, feeling the warmth of the little girl's body and soul.

A loud thump awakened Deeva with a start. She stretched out and lifted her ears to listen for what had caused the commotion. Heather's eyes were still closed, so for a moment Deeva thought it had been a dream. She scanned the room for Mama Dog. Though Mama Dog's nose was broken, her big floppy ears apparently still worked. The old dog was sitting next to the door.

What's going on? Deeva walked to the edge of the bed, not daring to jump in case it would wake Heather.

Well, Uncle Bobby is home, and he is not happy. Looks

like Justine has hired someone to clean out the barn, and he is yelling at her to stay out of there. He's trying to negotiate buying Justine's portion of the house so the two will leave him in peace. Justine is insisting that it must be sold as directed by great Nana. She seems a little scared of the deceased.

How long have you been listening? This is like a two-hour conversation you're recanting to me.

You asked me what was going on. I'm telling you. But you're right. We gotta get out of this house and see if we can figure out what's on this property. Mama Dog leaned her ear closer to the door.

A large thump of the front screen door startled them both. Heather sat up in bed.

"What're you two doing?"

Deeva strutted to the top of the bed nonchalantly. *Oh, nothing. Sounds like Uncle Bobby is home.* She really hated to manipulate Heather, but they had to get out of the house and figure out what was going on. Justine and Heather's lives might depend on it.

"Oh, he wasn't supposed to be back for a couple more weeks. He must've talked to Mom about the barn."

You knew about the barn being cleaned?

"Yes, Mom said that she was going to do it when Uncle Bobby wasn't here, so he couldn't be mad when the men who were coming to clean it threw all his old stuff away."

I'm curious. Has your mom been out in the barn before?

"I don't know. I just know I was told not to go in there. It's ancient. I think Mom wanted it torn down but didn't think that would go over well with Uncle Bobby. Great Nana said this place had to be sold. Uncle Bobby can't have it, we can't have it, and she also said that you would come to help us."

Well, if I'm here to help you, then why aren't we going outside? Mama Dog and I need to check it out before the house gets sold. I bet that is why great Nana asked me here. Let's go look at this barn.

"If you really think Nana would want it, let's go look. It can't hurt anything, I guess. But if either of you gets hurt, I'm not to blame, okay?" Heather threw back her covers and slipped out of her pajamas. She threw on a t-shirt and shorts.

Agreed, I think Mama Dog and I will be perfectly capable of accepting the consequences of any actions we might take. Also, what can you tell me about Nana? Was she a good witch, a bad witch, or somewhere in between?

"Great Nana wasn't a witch. What makes you think that?" Heather frowned, then slid her feet into a pair of bright green flip-flops.

Oh, just a wild guess. Did great Nana have any special herbs or sayings she'd chant around the house?

"Yes, but I think all old ladies do that stuff."

Heather opened the door to her bedroom and walked out into the hallway. "You two better not run off. It is lonely enough around here. I don't want to lose another cat."

We won't leave you; I promise. Deeva purred as she followed.

From behind her, Mama Dog tramped along. **Deeva, you're such a liar.**

No, I'm a revenge demon and it is time to get down to business.

Well, this was a bust. Mama Dog flopped on a bale of hay, out of breath. Dust rose around her and made all three of them sneeze.

"I don't know what the big deal is about this barn. There's nothing here. Dirt and old stuff, plus this straw that is super scratchy." Heather walked around the large open space.

This must be the place. I can smell the rotting flesh, and the energy in here emits feelings of horror like you only feel in hell. I know we're in the right place. Damnit, Mama Dog, I wish your nose worked. Deeva jumped from one hay bale to the other and peered around. *Maybe if I get up on the second floor, I'll see something. There's a force, or pressure, in here. I know it.* Deeva jumped onto the second tier. She found nothing but more old hay. She sniffed and sniffed, but the smell wasn't any worse, or better, up here. It frustrated her that no one else could smell it. Deeva doubted Heather's sense of smell was much better than Mama Dog's. The child hadn't protested a single night of Mama's farts and had only laughed at the old dog's feelings of embarrassment. Deeva wasn't leaving the barn until she'd seen every inch. At the end of the barn, the hay went all the way to the rafters. Deeva made a run for it and, though she hated heights, she ran as fast as she could and jumped up onto the rafter.

"Deeva, get down! I can hear Uncle Bobby's truck. We gotta get out of here."

You two go without me. I'm going to stay out here a little longer. Uncle Bobby won't even know I'm in here. I promise.

Deeva scrunched herself as tight as she could on the rafter, hoping that she'd concealed herself.

Good luck. I do not know what you're doing, but I'll keep Heather preoccupied while you stake this place out. Mama Dog pulled at Heather's shorts. The two slipped out the side door of the barn and left Deeva on her own.

Deeva didn't mind. She'd always worked on her own. Being around an angel and a human child wasn't the worst thing that had happened to her, but her job was to retrieve a soul and that was what she planned to do. Her only issue was that for it to be a fair trade, she had to figure out who had called for the revenge, and make sure there was a darn good reason for the retrieval that related to it. The scales of justice weren't always balanced, but they weren't completely skewed, either.

The large barn doors opened wide. An old Ford pickup truck backed in and a man that Deeva could only assume was Uncle Bobby jumped out of the driver's side. He wasn't the nicest looking man, but he was older than Deeva had expected. He had a good ten years on Justine. Deeva looked for the mark. It wasn't there. He walked over to an area of the barn that looked empty and stood with one hand on his hip, staring at the dusty, open space. He put on work gloves and started picking up the air. Deeva blinked her eyes. What was he picking up? A shimmer of light reflected off the barn ceiling and caught Deeva's eye.

She zeroed in on the shining object dangling from the rafter beams by a single nail. The object was high enough that unless you were looking for something, the small reflection of light wouldn't catch your attention. It was a pendant! It cloaked the barn in a spell! Deeva needed to grab it and move it out of the barn. If she could see what Uncle Bobby could see, an inconvenient accident might occur, leaving the farm to Justine and Heather. She just didn't know how she was going to get to it. It was high in the barn's framing. She would have to jump for it and wish for the best, hoping that she'd somehow make the twelve-foot leap from the floor to the rafter beam. If she missed, it was game over. It would leave Heather alone with Mama Dog to fend for themselves against Uncle Bobby's wrath. Unless… Heather seemed talented. Maybe she could use her magic to levitate Deeva. Before she could consider the problem further, a rock zoomed past her head.

"You piece of crap, cat. Get out of here!" Uncle Bobby yelled. Spit flew out of his mouth with each word.

Deeva would not waste any time becoming part of Uncle Bobby's bone collection. She didn't have to be told twice. She scrambled down the side of the barn furthest from Uncle Bobby and ran out the door before he could get to her. The thud of a pitchfork fell short behind her. Luckily, Heather and Mama Dog waited on the porch.

Deeva ran past Heather into the house.

"Keep your cat out of my barn! Do you hear me? This is still my home! I don't want anyone or anything in there! Especially some vile cat!"

"Yes, sir. I hear you." Heather looked down at the ground. Her bottom lip stuck out.

Uncle Bobby pointed at Heather. "The next time I see that cat, it'll be dead."

Heather stood on the porch for a moment as Uncle

Bobby walked away. He angrily grabbed the pitchfork from the ground and headed toward the barn. Deeva watched as a glowing, bright blue aura surrounded Heather. The girl was tapping into her energy, whether or not she meant to. The wind blew and with a great smack, the large door to the barn slammed shut before Uncle Bobby reached it. His cursing could be heard from the house.

Heather laughed.

Did you find anything? Mama Dog asked as she walked into the house.

Deeva smiled.

Of course, I did. I'm not only a revenge demon, but a pretty darn good detective. Someone cloaked that barn. There's bad stuff in there and we just need to get the right people to see it. I've got a plan.

Good, it is time to get justice served.

Deeva ignored Mama Dog's comment. She was ready to make a move to get her mark. If they found out Uncle Bobby had hurt someone, Deeva would make him pay in hell.

Heather, did you make the wind happen? Do you think you could move other stuff? I've found the object I'm here to get, but it's out of reach.

———

Heather wasn't ready as quickly as Deeva had thought she would be. They'd spent the past two days moving chess pieces, doll hands, twigs, and making the wind blow over things. Uncle Bobby had continued to play around in the barn and refused to leave it for the slightest moment from sunup to dark.

The cleaning crew was coming today, under protest from Uncle Bobby. Deeva had heard Justine telling him they were just coming to pull out the old hay, wash out the interior, and paint the outside of the barn. Nothing fancy. They wouldn't be taking his old tools or anything like that. He'd grumbled about a man having a private space but had agreed to take the truck out of the barn so the guys could do their work. The delay had given Deeva plenty of time to construct her plan. It just relied on the cleaners being slow and Heather being good at moving things.

As Heather worked on moving the chess pieces across the board with her thoughts, Deeva thought she'd be just unguarded enough to tap into why great Nana had called for her and put a cloaking spell over the barn.

Tell me about great Nana. Did you get to meet her? It sounds like you did.

"Not really. I mean, she came to me when I was about four. She sat at the end of my bed at night and talked to me."

What did she tell you?

"That I was special, like her and Mom. She would sing me songs. We talked a lot about how I would always have to balance things, and that power can be good and bad. She told me she'd had to do a bad thing once, which is why when you were to arrive, she would leave me."

Oh, what did she do? Deeva picked up a chess piece in her mouth and walked it across the room to place it on top of a high dresser. *Do you think you can move it from here?*

"She said she'd taken too good a care of Uncle Bobby. That he was naughty, and she'd allowed him to do things he wasn't supposed to."

I see. Okay, now lift it up and knock it over.

The chess piece lifted, and then promptly fell to the ground next to Mama Dog.

Sheesh, can't a dog get a nap around here? Mama Dog sat up, startled.

You needed to wake up, anyway. It's showtime.

Deeva had watched at the window for hours. The cleaners had arrived around ten in the morning. This seemed to have irritated Justine, as she'd expected them to be done by three. Instead, the entire house had been subjected to Uncle Bobby slamming things in his room and walking back and forth from the barn. In between his walks, he'd stood in the doorway of Heather's room, staring at Deeva. She'd played the stupid cat and rolled over on her belly to play with a toy. Inside, she'd seethed at him. His aura was so ugly that it hurt her eyes to look at it.

Once the two cleaners were in the barn, Uncle Bobby had switched to Mr. Charming mode. He'd gone and smiled at the two men and asked them if they needed help with anything. He'd thrown bales of hay into the back of their truck. His behavior was making it hard for Deeva to raise enough suspicion for Justine to come out to the barn. It took her a while to concoct a solution to catapult the plan into action.

Listen, you two. When you hear a scream, call for your mom and head out to the barn. We're going to need the paramedics when I'm through. Open this window; I've gotta get to work.

Heather opened the window. "Good luck, Dee-Dee. We'll be waiting."

Just remember, heaven wants justice, Mama Dog warned.

Yeah, yeah, let's wait and see what's behind the facade before we make up our minds, okay? Deeva shot back.

As she landed on the ground and headed to the barn, Deeva wasn't sure what to expect once she pulled the facade down. She almost felt bad for whomever would be her most convenient victim for getting emergency services to the barn. Hopefully, it would be Uncle Bobby and this whole thing would be over.

She slipped into the side door of the barn and looked for the first person she could trip and cause to fall. The older guy would be the easiest, and the least likely to kick her. Deeva slipped behind a bale of hay and got ready to weave through his feet as he fiddled around with a broom that stirred up the dust more than it cleaned anything. She was deciding on which way to go—weave through his legs and twist up his feet, or just plain outright trip him—when she felt a sharp, searing pain on the back of her neck.

"Grrrrrr." Her claws came out, and she readied to rip the face off the first human she could reach.

"I told you to stay outta here. Why can't cats listen?" Uncle Bobby shook Deeva so hard she saw stars.

"Uncle Bobby, stop! Don't hurt Dee-Dee. She's my friend."

Deeva looked up to see Heather standing in the barn doorway.

"I told you cats are no good. They're evil."

If Deeva had been in a better position, she might have laughed. Instead, she tried to grab at Uncle Bobby with her claws and swatted mostly at thin air.

Look up to the beams! There's a pretty necklace I need you to pull down. Once you get the necklace, run and find your mom.

"Hey man, you're not going to kill that cat, are you? We don't want to see that crap." The younger cleaner came over and grabbed Uncle Bobby's hand. It was then that Deeva saw the metallic shine of a meat cleaver.

Mama Dog, can I get a little help over here? Deeva yelled.

"Aaaaaaawwwwwooooohrrrr!" Mama Dog bayed as she ran towards Uncle Bobby. Deeva had never seen the dog move so fast, nor seen all its teeth flash. Mama Dog latched on to Uncle Bobby's leg with all she had. He dropped Deeva, but he tore his other hand away from the cleaner and, with one fell swoop, hit Mama Dog with the cleaver. Deeva ran towards the second floor of the barn, trying not to look at her friend. Heather had to knock the amulet down.

Up there, look at that shiny spot! Make it move. Deeva watched as the amulet swung back and forth from the high beam. *You can do it. Get it down!*

The amulet finally fell from the nail someone had tacked it to on the rafter's beam. Deeva watched as the amulet hit the bottom of the barn floor. Luckily, the cleaner was struggling with Uncle Bobby. Deeva was grateful the man appeared to be an animal lover. Next to the two struggling men, Mama Dog lay still, a pool of blood under her. Rage filled Deeva. Mama Dog was probably the best angel she'd ever met. The dog didn't deserve to die at the hands of Uncle Bobby!

Deeva shook off her overwhelming feelings. *Grab the amulet and run!*

Heather ran past the two men and scooped up the amulet. She ran out the side door.

Slowly, the barn walls became darker. There were auburn splashes on the walls, some brighter than others, as if whatever had painted the walls had been going on for a long time. Various hooks and chains hung from the rafters. It did not surprise Deeva to see the debris of hair on some hooks. She ran to the window on the second floor and looked out at the truck. Dark plastic trash bags were piled high in the back of the old pickup. Deeva knew what was in there; she just didn't want to think about it right now. Those souls were probably lost somewhere in between, neither in heaven nor hell.

In the distance, a siren roared. Heather had done as Deeva had asked. Now, she needed to retrieve Uncle Bobby and get out of here.

Deeva jumped down from the second tier, landing on one of the remaining bales of hay. The hay was really there. It was just way more disgusting than the mirage had been. She stalked over to where Uncle Bobby now lay, where the two cleaners held him down. He was seething with rage and foaming at the mouth. If she jumped on him just right, she could bite his jugular and he would bleed to death most horribly. She imagined pulling what was left of his rotten soul down to hell with her.

Let him live.

Deeva heard the quiet voice of Mama Dog. She looked over and to her surprise, the fat old dog was alive but breathing heavily. She walked over to the creature she now considered her friend.

It would be too easy to let him die. He needs to rot on this earth before his eternal damnation. If the families know what happened to their loved ones, they can leave the in-between and rest in peace. Give them justice.

Deeva was so sick of the word. *What am I supposed to do if I can't retrieve a soul? Sit around here and help raise a child? I can't do that. I like the kid, but my job is revenge demon-ing.*

"Yes, but the debt for revenge was for me."

Deeva looked up to see an apparition of an older woman. She was cloaked in the chains of hell. Fire singed the edges of her hair and clothes.

"I'll pay for him until he's ready. I have already agreed upon it with *him*." The old woman looked downward.

Of course, I don't get a say in what I do with myself, do I? Deeva asked no one in particular.

Mama Dog wheezed out a laugh. ***We're not even middle management.***

"You two will take care of my great granddaughter and ensure she doesn't shut off her powers like her mother. She needs the balance of both of you."

I'm not so sure Mama's going to make it, Deeva pointed out.

"Don't worry, she will. Heather needs you both. Besides, you'll have eternities to go back to claiming souls. Heather will only be on earth for ninety years, at the most."

Great, so we'll be reincarnating? That sounds like a wonderful life, doesn't it, Mama?

There was silence from Mama Dog.

"She'll be back." The elderly woman looked over at Uncle Bobby. "I wish I hadn't covered for you for so long. That is my biggest regret. I'll make it up to all those you hurt, and I'll pay for my part."

The police entered the barn.

"Nobody move!" the officer yelled as he pointed his gun at all three men.

Another cop came up behind him. "Who owns the old pickup truck out here?"

The two cleaners pointed at Uncle Bobby and let go of him. He continued to lie flat on his back with the cleaver in his hand.

"Sir, drop the knife and roll over. You're under arrest."

Deeva sat beside Mama Dog and watched as the police escorted Uncle Bobby from the barn.

As soon as it was clear, Heather rushed in and scooped up Deeva.

"I'm so happy you are okay."

Deeva rubbed her head on Heather's chin.

Mama Dog didn't make it.

"I know. I felt her light go out. Will you stay with me for a while? Mom is really upset."

Deeva looked around the barn. She suspected that a

glamour had always surrounded Uncle Bobby, and Justine had never seen him for who he really was.

Sure, I'll stay with you.

"What do you think of our new house, Dee-Dee?" Heather twirled around on the dark hardwood floors in the expansive living room. Deeva sat in the bay window and looked out over the waterfront; it was almost time for the snow. They hadn't made it to Boston as Justine had planned. Instead, they'd ventured to upstate Maine and found a house on a nice lake. Who knew so many people would want to buy a farm that a serial killer had murdered a bunch of people on?

I like it. Deeva couldn't help but miss Mama Dog. She felt like the balance was off. During their time together, the three of them had created a trinity, of sorts.

Justine opened the front door. "Hi, guys, guess what, or should I say, *who* has arrived?"

A small golden ball of fur waddled into the room with its tail between its legs.

"A puppy?!" Heather ran over to the golden ball of fur. Large brown eyes looked at her with excitement.

Dear Satan, who are you? Deeva held her breath as she waited to see if it would talk. The young golden ball of fur stuck its tongue out.

Hi, I'm ---. Uh, I'm not sure. I feel like I know you, though.

Deeva squinted at it and smiled. *Your name is Minnie.*

Like a mini-Mama. I'll help you remember who you are. It'll take time. You can call me Dee-Dee.

Oh good. I just know I'm here to help a little girl. I'm from heaven. Where are you from?

It was an enthusiastic little thing, Deeva observed. It looked like she was going to be the old lazy one now.

Yeah, we're all here to help a little girl.

"Dee-Dee, she likes you!" Heather squealed as Minnie curled up next to Deeva.

People and puppies seem to love me. What can I say? Hell will have to wait.

AFTERWORD

Thank you for purchasing Bizarre Stories for Proper Ladies. This collection of short stories is bizarre, but definitely not for proper ladies. It is for the reader that loves horror, sci-fi, has a sense of humor, and is not easily offended. I wanted to take a moment to say thank you to every person who is ever said, "Hey, when are you putting something new out?" Or, another favorite, "I love the way you write, why aren't you writing more?!"

Without those comments, I don't know if I would have had the willpower to put another collection out. This one is six years overdue. If this is your first encounter with my writing, and you liked it, check out my short story collection, *He Left Her At the Altar, She Left Him to the Zombies*, and zombie young adult novel, *Maxine*.

ABOUT THE AUTHOR

Katie Cord loves writing sci-fi, horror, and speculative fiction with an emphasis on the female perspective. When she isn't writing, she is either creating ridiculously cute and funny art or spending time with her husband, two stepchildren, and their menagerie of fur babies. She is married to fellow author, Timothy W. Long, whom she met at a zombie convention.

Made in the USA
Middletown, DE
17 August 2024